CONGLOMERATE

CONGLOMERATE

RITA JENRETTE

RICHARDSON & STEIRMAN
NEW YORK
1985

Dedicated to my parents,
C.H. and Reba Carpenter.

Acknowledgements

I am grateful to the late Professor Herbert Woodbury of the English Department of Monticello College in Godfrey, Illinois, for believing in me. And to Dr. Claudio Segre of the University of Texas in Austin, for turning me into a history buff.

Thanks also to the following friends for their confidence in me: Gladys Brown, Gayle Eaton, Harriet Rawlings, Katie Gallagher, Ted Del Borrel, Reverend Jerry Everley, Stacey Brown, Ginger Brown, Brad Brown, Bob Rose, John G. Sullivan, and Milton Stanson.

I would also like to thank my editor, Hy Steirman, without whose encouragement this book would not have been written.

Prologue

AT 7:15 A.M., the breakfast meeting had been going on for an hour. The six men, their jackets slung across the backs of chairs, were seated around a conference table heaped with buttermilk biscuits, bagels, blueberry muffins, assorted jars of jam, and a litter of cups and saucers. A short, thin man in a white jacket, his shining bald head bobbing up and down, moved around the group pouring coffee from a mono-grammed silver coffeepot.

"Slade, no more coffee or we'll all drown before the meeting."

"Yessir, admiral," said Slade who had been the admiral's orderly for over thirty years. He was seventy-five, the same age as the admiral, but looked older. The admiral, then a lieutenant-commander, had saved his life when they had come under enemy fire while serving together on a destroyer during the Battle of Leyte Gulf in World War II. They were later reunited on an aircraft carrier in the Pacific during the Korean War. Since then he continued to serve the admiral until both retired from the navy in 1975. He joined Tompion International when the admiral had been appointed chairman of the board.

The six men around the table were as different as the letters in the alphabet. The admiral, tall and handsome with stark white hair and a tanned face, was a commanding presence. His body hadn't an ounce of fat on it, and even seated at the head of the table in shirtsleeves, he remained dignified and imposing. At his left, Tom Grosso, forty-one, the bubbly president of Unicorn Life and Casualty, was five inches shorter than the admiral but his square bearing revealed an arrogance equal to a Rhode Island rooster. On the Admiral's right, Ronald Cohen, forty-one, execu-tive vice president and general counsel. He listened silently, eating buttermilk biscuits and promising himself no more late nights before annual meetings.

Opposite the admiral sat Roscoe Tompion Granby, president of Tompion who, at fifty-one, looked fifteen years younger. He had the flush of good color with good living written all over it. He represented the Granby family interests at Tompion, but he was uninterested in big business and had no knowledge of high finance or what made a business tick. He sponsored artists, was a patron of the Metropolitan Opera, the New York City Ballet and spent much of his time writing poetry or donating money to dozens of worthy cultural causes. He was active in the Kennedy Center in Washington and was well liked but little thought of by the Wall Street power brokers. He didn't care. But his apathy toward business matters was deceptive: it didn't mean he was foolish. He was gentle as well as wealthy, therefore powerful enough to do as he pleased. It was Roscoe Tompion Granby who, ten years earlier, on his father's deathbed, suggested that the brilliant Admiral Orville Dutton, his father's cousin on the poor side of the family and a man the elder Granby always admired, might make a brilliant frontispiece for Tompion. His dying father, distraught about the future of the family empire and family affairs beyond his death, kissed his gentle-hearted son for the first time in his life. Both had tears in their eyes. Just before the tough old man's death father and son finally understood each other.

For the Granbys, the Dutton connection was a match made in financial heaven. In ten years the corporation had quadrupled in size and profits. Mismatched divisions had been reorganized and made profitable or been sold. Acquisitions had accounted for some of the growth, but it was the infusion of young blood that had brought about the change. Other than the admiral and Granby, the other men on the executive committee seated around the room were all in their early forties.

The fifth man was the enigma, but there was no denying his right to be there. Roger Evans, also forty-one, was a quiet man who said little. When he did speak, his words went to the heart of the matter. He was a half inch under six feet, but looked taller. He was slouching in his chair. He was energy at rest, a jaguar pausing before checking its prey. His head was covered with a mop of curly brown hair that never seemed to stay in place atop a face that appeared quite ordinary. He wore horn-rimmed glasses, and his fingers kept creeping back to his shirt collar, where occasionally he ran his right finger over a long scar. He was president of Tompion Financial Services, the most profitable division of the conglomerate. Because of his silence, it was widely rumored that the genius behind the growth of Financial Services was Orville Dutton. The admiral, Evans, and Cohen knew better, but they never bothered to contradict the rumor.

"I honestly don't care about the stockholders," said Grosso, "We're not obligated to tell everything we know. A quick soft shoe and a little soft soap won't hurt."

"Tom, in the Navy it's called CYA — Cover Your Ass — but we're not going to do it here. Tompion's strength is honesty and candor, and the performance of our company is going to be measured by those standards. Your division has lost a ton of money. The board agrees there are extenuating circumstances, and everyone is going along with your reorganization program. The stockholders are distressed enough by your division's performance and with the thirty point drop in our stock without any soft soap from you."

Grosso was biting into a muffin, dripping with butter and strawberry jam. He began to choke. Ron Cohen slapped him on the back, perhaps a little harder than he should have and Grosso straightened out. He was coughing and unable to answer the admiral.

"Ron, what's the status on Pigglies?"

"As of midnight last night, the FBI had no further word for us. They're still trying to track down those stories that hundreds of people are in hospital with food poisoning from Pigglies Ribs. I'm sorry to report that there are new rumors of several fatalities — which are not being reported by the media — because the media, allegedly, has been bought off." He paused momentarily to let everything sink in.

"We're bound to be interrogated sharply on this matter," added Cohen, "so be prepared for it."

"Any ideas on how to handle it?" the Admiral asked. He surveyed the committee members. There was silence for a moment, then he added, "We can't remain on the defensive. We have to devise a way to defuse these rumors." He picked up an English muffin and bit into it.

Suddenly Evans spoke in his quiet, almost passionless voice. "The way to turn it around is to make the rumors work *for* you."

"How the hell do you that?" — Grosso, had recovered his voice — "start a rumor that poisoned ribs are good for you? Or maybe Pigglies Ribs make you passionate?"

Cohen spotted a flash of anger in Roger Evans's eyes and said quickly, "Tom, you have a brilliant mind and a big mouth. Right now you're exercising the wrong one." Grosso kept silent as Evans continued.

"As I said, get the rumors to work for you because they won't go away and business will continue to drop until they do. Start an ad campaign; offer $100,000 reward for the identity of the person who started the rumors and $100,000 to any person who can prove he got ill eating Pigglies Ribs." There was quiet as his words sank in; then everyone began to smile and show their approval.

Ron Cohen applauded silently.

"Thank you, Roger, that's inspired," the Admiral said. "I like it because it's simple. Unless there is someone against the idea, we'll go with it. Ron, you handle it."

Smiling, Ron said, "It'll be in the works before the annual meeting starts." Then, with ice in his voice, added, "Tom, you don't have to apologize." Tom Grosso ignored his sarcasm because no insult in the world could deflect his ego and verbosity.

It was now 8:10 A.M. "We have to review Empire Films," the Admiral said.

The sixth man sighed. Arko Puchakis, forty-three, the wunderkind of Hollywood, was heavyset, about six feet tall with black hair. At twenty-six he had been hailed as the new Orson Welles when his $20,000 home movie, *Anger*, startled moviegoers around the world. When it grossed $90,000,000, he was also considered a financial wizard. At this point, suddenly he invested his profits in a small company, the nearly defunct Empire Films. He bought the film library and its deteriorating studios. The industry watched with smug skepticism.

In 1975 Puchakis was thirty-three and financial troubles were starting to disturb him at the time the admiral was taking the reins of Tompion. Empire continued downhill just as Tompion began to climb. Two years later, Empire was acquired by Tompion. Roger Evans had pointed out quietly to the admiral that Empire's real estate was worth more than the total value of its stock and that the library of old Empire films could become a gold mine when sold to TV. Furthermore, Puchakis was a genius filmmaker. It didn't automatically follow that he could run a studio. After the acquisition, Puchakis was made chairman and given movie projects to produce and Julie Greene was brought in the run the studio. Everyone was happy until the film *Charlemagne*

— the movie about the legendary King that would rival Camelot — got under way.

"Admiral, the stockholders will eat me up alive. I don't like facing a hostile audience." He had a lateral lisp so words like "hostile audience" sounded like "hoshtil audiensh."

"All right. It's basically my responsibility, so I'll field those questions." The admiral sounded best when he was girding for battle, which is why he regarded opposition as war. "Anyway, the news isn't completely bad. Gentlemen, things have been going too damn well these past few years. Now we have to show that we can take the bad times with the good. Let's go."

"One minute, admiral," said Ron Cohen as they all stood up. Just a reminder that you have a sense of humor, sir. Use it the way Ronald Reagan does. When you're asked a sticky question — try and joke your way out of it."

The admiral smiled and patted Cohen on the back. Grosso immediately moved to be near the admiral as Cohen and Evans nodded and left the office together.

PART I

CHAPTER

ONE

THROUGHOUT his distinguished naval career, Admiral Orville Dutton had a reputation as the unflappable man. Yet now, in the main ballroom of the Waldorf-Astoria Hotel in New York City, crowded with angry stockholders, he was standing at the podium listening to stormy questions thundering at him from the floor — and slowly losing his cool.

It was the annual meeting of Tompion International, Inc., and, as chairman of the board and chief executive officer, the admiral was attempting to explain the drastic drop in the value of the stock from a high of 92 in January to 59 1/4 in July, a little over six months. His dark gray suit, cut for the occasion, suddenly felt as tight as the collar of his shirt. His white mane, so recognizable from the *Fortune* and *Forbes* articles which had headlined him "The Strategist of the Fastest-Moving U.S. Conglomerate" and "The Darling of Wall Street," now seemed disheveled.

"Mr. Chairman. My name is Oscar Baldwin, I own 1,200 shares. I am concerned about Empire Films. Despite its profitable movies, how could you let that division blow $50 million on a stinker like *Charlemagne?*"

"Mr. Baldwin. I make no excuses for *Charlemagne,* but I have an explanation." He paused, took a deep breath and continued. "Tompion has had a streak of bad luck. Two of our divisions have had unanticipated problems. One of those divisions is Empire Films. Like any family, the sick child gets the attention.

"*Charlemagne* was budgeted at $25 million and approved by the board. The increase in the strength of the dollar created problems. The financing was being done with European currencies — from our holdings in France, Britain, and Germany. Then as the U.S. Dollar got stronger, our buying power diminished.

Then we ran into a scandal — —"

There was a ripple of laughter. Everyone knew about the two stars caught making love in a trailer by their cuckolded mates who were accompanied by free-lance photographers who had a field day. The scandal erupted like Vesuvius, and the accompanying photos outraged the world and embarrassed Empire Films and Tompion. The movie company had been denied its location by the religious mayor of the southern French town, and in the ensuing turmoil, it took two months to settle on a new location and move in personnel and equipment. The cost of firing the stars on grounds of moral turpitude, casting new stars, reshooting many scenes, and rescoring the film had been astronomical.

"The movie did not get good reviews. One British critic said it was over-long, over-dull, and over-here." The stockholders laughed despite themselves. "An Italian critic said we should have filmed the off-screeen action — it would have been more exciting." Again there was a swell of laughter. "That's the terrible news. The slightly better news is that the movie is making money in several foreign countries that prefer less hyper films and may be purchased as a miniseries by ABC for $8 million. We credit publicity for that. Now we are experimenting with cassette sales to schools around the world in different languages. We're trying to minimize our losses. Chances are we'll come out of it losing between $10 to $12 million." There was a small ripple of applause, a small sigh of relief.

As the ex-admiral lifted a glass of water to his lips, someone in the audience said, "Betcha it's vodka." The admiral heard but did not respond. To himself he thought, *I wish it were.* He adjusted his jacket and stood ramrod straight, once again looked like what he was, a retired naval hero, a former head of the CIA, and a man who was vain enough to know that he resembled Cary Grant.

"Mr. Chairman. I'm Alana Carpenter. I own 150 shares of Tompion. I like the $2-a-share dividends. I would like to see them keep coming. I would like you to tell me, how do you account for the drop in profits in Unicorn Life and Casualty?"

The admiral turned to Thomas Grosso and said, "Tom, would you answer that?"

Tom Grosso rose to his feet. He wore a light gray suit, a light blue shirt with a white collar, and a red Gucci tie. He was a man who felt that he, not Sylvester Stallone, should own the nickname of The Italian Stallion. "Miss Carpenter, the insurance industry is in a turmoil. It will probably last several years. The problem, basically, is the new tax law. The biggest bite into profitability came with the new husband-wife inheritance laws. Men used to buy insurance to take care of the inheritance taxes and leave their estates more-or-less intact for their heirs. Today, under the new law, the husband can leave everything to his wife with no inheritance taxes due the government until her death. For the present, the industry will have to look to new areas for busines opportunities as well as tighten up on current operations. But the whole industy is confident, as I am, that it *will* turn around once realistic adjustments are made." There was a round of applause.

"Mr. Chairman, I am Roscoe Girard, I own 100 shares. What is happening to Pigglies?"

"Mr. Girard, Pigglies is down 17 percent in sales for this past quarter. Until three months ago, it was the fastest-growing food chain in America—growing faster than McDonald's, Burger King, and Kentucky Fried Chicken. You are all familiar with the malicious rumors about our food that have been circulated around the country. I won't dignify them with repetition. We suspect some kind of deliberate, malicious smear campaign designed to hurt the company."

"Are you having it investigated, sir?"

"Yes we are, Mr. Girard. We also are preparing ads offering $100,000 in reward money for information leading to the arrest of the perpetrators. Despite these setbacks, Tompion Financials, Rainbow Electronics, Adirondack Commodities and Med-Pharm have each had outstanding years. All in all, our company has done a volume of $7,640,000,000. Our earnings have increased by 6 percent, despite the setbacks, producing net income of $424 million. In other words, there is no bottom-line reason for our stock to drop in value. Confidence in our company will soon return to normal, and the market forces will adjust the price of our stock accordingly."

"Mr. Chairman, my name is Leonard Morgan. I flew out here from Des Moines, Iowa. I would like to know why our company remains in the field of nuclear research when everyone knows it is a potential danger to mankind."

There was an angry buzz filtering through the audience of some 900 people. "Mr. Morgan, I agree that nuclear research may be potentially harmful. I also know that nothing good happens in this world unless men take risks; whether it's breaking the sound barrier or walking on the moon. It was Samuel Johnson who said something to the effect that nothing will be accomplished if one had to first overcome all objections. The research we are doing is strictly in the field of nuclear medicine, nuclear pharmacology, if you will. We develop radioisotopes, a medical diagnostic tool that is a definite benefit to mankind."

Applause.

Suddenly there was shouting at the left rear of the hall as three women in their late twenties stood up in unison, one brandishing a large placard:

TOMPION INTERNATIONAL
DISCRIMINATES AGAINST
AMERICAN WOMEN

"Mr. Chair-man. Mr. Chair-man." The source of the shouting was the tallest of the three, well dressed and obviously their leader. It was apparent that she had stage-managed her appearance for the newspaper photographers at that left end of the hall who were already set up to take pictures of her. The admiral pointed to her, giving her the floor.

She made a deliberate show of walking toward the aisle with her placard hoisted high. Wearing a tan blouse inhabited by a well-endowed chest, and a light beige skirt stretched tightly across her hips, she was well aware of her physical charms. Walking in the exaggerated manner of a clothes model by swaying her hips, she reached a hotel page holding a hand microphone, grabbed the mike, cleared her throat. There was a hush as she began to speak.

"Mr. Chair-man. Our company discriminates against women: do you deny that?"

"Yes, I do. Now, if you wish to address the board and the other stockholders, you'll have to abide by the rules. First tell us who you are; then tell us if you are a stockholder."

"Mr. Chair-man, my name is Adrianna Pernell, chairperson of CADOW, the Congress Against the Discrimination of Women. I own one share of Tompion, and I *demand* to know why our company discriminates against women."

"My dear young lady, Tompion does *not* discriminate against women. You will have to be more specific than that."

"Mr. Chair-man, I am not your dear young lady. I demand to know the number of women who work for Tompion and how many of them are executives earning more than $100,000 a year." There were suppressed sounds of disapproval and some laughter.

A hard-core feminist, Adrianna Pernell was playing to the audience, and she knew how to handle them. As the admiral paused, she began shaking her head slightly from side to side as though she were a teacher admonishing a young student.

"Ms. Pernell. Approximately 61 percent of our work force is made up of women. This includes all our companies including insurance, films, electronics, food, and financial services. Unless someone got a raise in the last four hours, (laughter), twelve of these ladies earn more than $100,000 a year. That number does not include actresses, producers and consultants, women we hire on a contract basis."

After a burst of applause, the three CADOW members regrouped and began to argue animatedly among themselves. Suddenly, with a triumphant shout, Adrianna Pernell returned to the microphone and pointed an accusing finger at the admiral. "Mr. Chair-man. Why isn't there a single female director on your board? Answer that — *if* you can."

The admiral was beginning to show his annoyance at this line of questioning by someone who owned one share of stock in Tompion. His voice took on the timbre of sarcasm as he spoke. "Ms. Pernell, are you familiar with our various companies?"

"Yes, sir, admiral. I read the annual report from cover to cover." She executed an exaggerated salute in an attempt to annoy him further as a counter to his sarcasm. There was a round of applause. This was the type of confrontation the audience could enjoy whether or not it agreed with her. And, clearly, Adrianna Pernell was writing tomorrow morning's headlines for the *Wall Street Journal*.

"Do you honestly feel we should have a woman on our board whether or not she is qualified?" asked the admiral, his voice losing none of its edge though he appeared somewhat agitated as he wiped his face with a handkerchief.

"Come, come, admiral. Surely you can find one li'l ole lady who is competent enough to serve on your precious board. However, seeing as how you can't — or won't — I am now prepared to place my name in nomination." A wide grin registered on her face as the *New York Post* and the *Daily News* photographers began shooting. The Admiral waited patiently until the strobes stopped flashing.

"That would be a little premature, Ms. Pernell," Again the Admiral took out a handkerchief and mopped his brow. "You see, to serve on our Board, you have to do a little more homework. It so happens we do have a woman on our board. Sidney — — "

A tall, attractive woman in her mid-thirties, seated in the front row with the other executives, rose and walked to a floor mike next to the podium. With obvious presence, accentuated by a simple but exquisitely tailored black suit, she looked around the room slowly, making eye contact with everyone who was looking at her. Then she began to smile. It was a warm smile that was charged with contagious electricity. Soon everyone was smiling. Her brown hair was cut stylishly short, her face was white and without makeup except for the slight blush of lipstick. Her eyes were a piercing emerald green.

"My name is Sidney Howe," she said in a soft, throaty voice. "I am a member of the board of directors of Tompion and have been for over five years. I am senior vice president in charge of corporate relations. Prior to that I was a vice president at Med-Pharm/Rainbow Electronics until we merged into Tompion, and before you ask the question — yes — I do earn more than $100,000 a year."

At this point everyone was laughing and applauding as Sidney left the microphone and returned to her seat. It was quickly apparent that the admiral has feigned distress in order to make his point more dramatic.

By the time Sidney reached her seat, there were several sharp whistles. She half-bowed graciously in acknowledgment, smiled to the crowd, waved, and received another round of applause. She also knew how to play the audience. Without another word, the CADOW members left the ballroom. Just then an usher approached Sidney and handed her a sealed envelope marked URGENT. She tore it open and read the note.

The admiral, who seldom missed anything, watched her read it. She looked at him, moved her eyes to indicate that she had to leave. He gave a slight nod. Such was their relationship that they did not have to speak to understand each other. His nod indicated that the meeting was now under control and she could be excused if the matter was urgent. She stood up and hurried out, not unaware of the numerous males taking admiring looks at her long legs.

The assistant manager, a tall, painfully thin young man in a dark suit and wearing a white carnation, intercepted her as she exited. He told her she could take the phone call in his office. She followed him but he waited outside and let her enter alone so she could have privacy; she yanked a pearl earring off her ear and lifted the receiver. Her face began to glisten with perspiration as she listened in horror. Her only comment was, "Oh, my God! My God!"

By the time she hung up, she was fighting to maintain her poise. For several moments she remained transfixed, not moving, barely breathing. Suddenly, moving into action, she picked up the phone and dialed her secretary. She began to wipe her face and hands with a tissue as she waited for the connection. "Amanda, I want the company Learjet ready in two hours at LaGuardia.

Steve and F.D.R. are somewhere in the building. Tell them to be in my office in twenty minutes. They should get ready to fly with me to Med-Pharm—the plant in Carlyle, Georgia. Clear an emergency radio frequency for me so I can be in touch—tell maintenance to make doubly certain the scrambler is working. I'll have somebody's head if it isn't operational."

For a moment, she paused, sobbing involuntarily. Then, shaking her head to clear it, she continued, "Alert Anne. Tell her,"—for the first time, her voice broke— "tell her Peter Wallack, president of Med-Pharm just committed suicide." She paused again, still fighting to to retain her composure, then added, "The directors are still at the meeting. They know nothing. Under no circumstances are they to find out until *after* the meeting ends so the company can't be accused of withholding information. I'll be at the office in fifteen minutes."

She took out a small notebook from her purse and wrote swiftly;

"DIRE EMERGENCY. GO TO MY OFFICE AFTER MEETING. CONTACT ME VIA AMANDA"—Sidney

Then she requested an envelope from the assistant manager, who hovered outside should Sidney need his help. She wrote the admiral's name on one envelope, underscored—*URGENT*—in large letters, and sealed the note inside. The young man, eager to please her, assured her that he would deliver it to the admiral immediately after the meeting.

Now, slightly disheveled, Sidney half-ran out of the hotel from the Lexington Avenue side, not concerned about her appearance, and flagged the admiral's limousine, a tinted-glass, black stretch Lincoln that seemed a block long. "Gates, get me back to the office quickly."

"Yes, Miss Sidney." He wheeled the car around like a race-car driver through the impossible one-way traffic on Lexington Avenue, then west for one block and finally north on Park Avenue to Tompion Tower.

Dashing into her office, Sidney motioned to her secretary. Amanda jumped up and was one step behind her clutching a pad. Sidney paced her office. Then, speaking with a firm voice, she said, "Amanda, no word is to leak from our office — that's your responsibility. Tell Anne to handle the media when the time comes. Keep everyone and everything under control until we sort this out and decide how to release the information. Most importantly, I am the first one the admiral talks to when he is free. I sent him a note at the Waldorf, but I want to double-check and hang on to him like flypaper when he gets here. Patch him through to me from my office — I'll probably be en route.

"Now, I hope I'm not caught again without my emergency overnight bag in the office."

"Not to worry. Your clothes have been cleaned and I have them hanging in the closet. I'll pack while you get ready."

Sidney nodded but didn't say anything more. She looked at the photograph of her husband in a silver frame on her desk. It was impossible to comprehend he would forever remain that young, only twenty-six. He was in his flight suit standing in front of a B-52, his navigator's wings imprinted on his chest along with his name, Howe, Harry B. The photo had been taken in Vietnam by a UPI journalist just before his last flight in 1975. The plane had been shot down by a SAM missile, and the crew was reported Missing In Action. She realized that it was ten years since the photograph was taken, three years since she received a final letter from the government stipulating that Harry's status had changed from MIA to MIA, presumed dead. She had contributed the $30,000 government insurance check to a scholarship fund at

Emory College. She fingered the string of pearls around her neck and then the gold chain bearing the letters MIA.

"Hey, Sidney, what's up?" Startled, she looked up at Steve Corcoran's broken nose and Irish grin, with F.D.R. Brown beside him. An ex-FBI agent, Steve was in charge of security and F.D.R., ex-Air Force captain, was in charge of research. Both men were corporate vice presidents, but handled other very discreet duties when necessary. Both men came under her jurisdiction. She had worked with them for five years, and she liked them and knew both men to be utterly loyal to her. They also knew her well enough to sense when they could joke with their boss and when to be dead serious. There was no question about her mood now.

"Frank, Steve, I need your help in a serious corporate situation." She outlined swiftly everything she knew of the matter. "Some strange, terrible things are happening to Tompion. We don't know their cause, but there are too many unfortunate events taking place — there seems to be a hidden design to it. That's the big picture. Yet we have to organize our priorities. I know you're busting your tail on Pigglies, Steve, but with the FBI on the case and our private investigators working around the clock, we'll leave the matter to them. I need you on this case. Right now we have to fly down to Carlyle. Frank," she said, turning to F.D.R., "this is one time I don't need research expertise. I need your investigative skills. More importantly, I need your black skin. Okay?"

Frank shrugged his shoulders and raised his hands, palms up. Sidney continued, "I spent five years at Carlyle. The town is half-black and half-white. My intuition tells me this may be part of the mysterious goings-on just as it is with Empire, Pigglies, and the rest of Tompion. If we act swiftly, maybe we can unravel it. We may get to the bottom of it more quickly in a town as small as Carlyle, where Med-Pharm is the largest employer. That's why, besides Steve, I need someone I trust to melt into the background of the black community.

"I've known Peter for ten years. I was matron-of-honor at his wedding five years ago. If there was even a hint of trouble, Jennifer would have called me. It's beyond my comprehension that Peter would commit suicide at the height of his career."

In his FBI voice, Steve asked, "Who called you?"

"The head of the local union, Tom Greeley. He doesn't think it was suicide. Neither does his brother, Lew. He's sheriff of Carlyle County. They were both on the phone. Now I have to give you two the bad news. Peter allegedly committed suicide by swallowing nuclear isotopes."

There was a pause, a pall of silence, no one daring to speak. They avoided each other's eyes. Breathing heavily, Steve's eyes locked onto the framed sign on the wall behind Sidney which read:

WHEN THE GOING GOT TOUGH
THE TOUGH GOT EVEN

He had given it to Sidney as a Christmas present three years ago, when she had helped him clear the admiral of charges that he bribed a congressman during the Abscam trial. It wasn't the first time that she'd resolved a sticky corporate matter. She was the perfect case of a steel fist in a velvet glove, a ruthless quality she revealed only to an enemy. No wonder the admiral gave her a free hand. She had a mind like a diamond and a determination made of titanium. He wondered how anyone so beautiful, so feminine, and so brilliant could be so tough. She never failed to amaze him which was why, for the first time in his life, he didn't mind working for a woman — this particular woman. He was half in love with

her. But knew beyond question that this was a lady who was way
out of his league.

CHAPTER

TWO

A STRAW-COLORED station wagon with the sheriff's insignia on the door was parked at the edge of the runway. As the Learjet touched down, there was a short wail on the siren. Sidney peeked out the side window and spotted the sheriff's Chrysler. By the time they were stepping off the plane, Sheriff Lewis Greeley was out of the car. He appeared larger than 6'4" and 240 pounds, looking like the defensive tackle he had been twenty years earlier with the Washington Redskins. Yet he was twenty pounds lighter than his playing days, a testimony to his dedicated adherence to a fitness program. He removed his Stetson and shook hands with Sidney who in turn introduced him to Steve and F.D.R. "Can I see you alone for a minute, Sidney?" he asked.

"If it has anything to do with Med-Pharm or the suspicion of murder, Lew, then you can speak freely in front of my associates. We flew down here to help and at the same time try to find out what is going on."

"There's no privacy here. Why don't we talk in the car?" When they were seated and the doors closed, he went on. "It's a sad day for Carlyle, I can tell you. Pete was very popular — a well-liked man around here. Heck, the company put up our water tower, built the golf course and playground, rebuilt the schools. Yeah, I know, maybe it was good company policy to do all of those things, but he really enjoyed doing it. He cared. He loved this town and was involved with it. Heck, the hospital — scholarships — you name it."

He paused and it was quiet, except for the sound of tires on the road. Finally the sheriff went on. "The body was discovered when an assistant entered the lab and happened to look into the radiation section. Peter was on his back, obviously dead. There is

a small personal computer in the room, and it was switched on.
The screen contained two messages.

The first one read:

TO ALL MY DEAR FRIENDS:
I AM TAKING MY OWN LIFE BY SWALLOWING
A NEW, POWERFUL FORM OF RADIOACTIVE
ISOTOPE. DON'T BOTHER WITH AN AUTOPSY.
HAVE A DRINK ON ME. LOVE.

* * *

The second one read:

TO MY DARLING JENNIFER;
I LOVE YOU MORE THAN
LIFE ITSELF. THEREFORE
IT'S BETTER THIS WAY.
PETER

* * *

"When did you get to the plant, Sheriff?" Steve asked.

"Ten-thirty this morning. The radiation section of the lab is
lead-lined with a glass enclosure, so I could see the body without
entering the 'hot' room. I checked the records and saw that the
research was sanctioned by the Nuclear Regulatory Agency.
Butterworth, Peter's executive vice president, advised me not
enter the enclosure. He also suggested that the body be transferred to a lead-lined coffin. That's been taken care of." It was the end
of his report.

"How about Jennifer—Mrs. Wallack?" Sidney asked.

"That's the toughest part. She was giving a modeling class at
Carlyle High. I drove over myself and informed the principal,
Mrs. Ellington, who called Mrs. Wallack into the office. I broke
the news to her, she took it very hard. At first she didn't beleve me.
Then, when I repeated what happened— and I didn't go into the

gruesome details — she fainted. We couldn't revive her — she was in shock, so we rushed her to the hospital. She's still there under sedation and being monitored continuously by the medical staff. I'm a cop, but this business really shook me up. Still does. I went to talk it over with my brother. We called you immediately after that."

Sidney looked at the sheriff and said, "Lew, I can't buy suicide. It doesn't feel right. I'm a psychologist. I know there are no absolutes — so I cannot make an absolute statement. But, as far as I'm concerned, Peter Wallack was not a man to take his own life. He is — was — too warm and too personal a man. He would never leave an open message — a suicide note — to his wife on a computer screen. His life was centered on his wife, and he enjoyed his work and his community. He would never bring shame to any of them.

"Regardless of what little evidence you have, I want you to proceed as though Peter died under suspicious circumstances. I think the only way it works is if Peter were murdered, and that it was made to look like suicide. I'll call the admiral. Let him decide whether the statement to the press should indicate suicide or possible murder. After that, you do what you have to do."

"I didn't want to go ahead until I spoke to you, Mrs. Howe. I'm going to handle this straight-arrow all the way. But this is a one-company town, and I'll need your input."

Steve smiled inwardly. The sheriff was respectful of Sidney and Tompion, the corporate giant. Nevertheless, he was going to follow up on his own suspicions and do his job. The husky sheriff was saying, diplomatically, that big didn't mean dumb.

"Sheriff, you'll have no interference from us. Yet the town has a big stake in this, and so does Med-Pharm. But the biggest stake is held by Tompion and its shareholders. I know you have a small staff, Lew, and we want answers, so I brought some help. Steve, here, is a former FBI agent, and F.D.R. has Air Force Intelligence background. They're here to help uncover the truth, however tough it might be. After that we can decide how to deal further with this situation.

"Incidentally, the Nuclear Regulatory Agency has to be informed, as well as the FBI. Steve can help you with that. Meanwhile, I thought F.D.R. might visit some black neighborhoods and talk to employees and ex-employees of Tompion."

The sheriff began to bristle. "I'm going to do this investigation my way, with all due respects and thanks."

"I'm just going to listen, sheriff," F.D.R. added quickly. "You know, a fresh perspective."

"I don't think it's a great idea, Brown. We've got some tough black boys down there. Sorry. Tough guys down there. Being a stranger, they may want to clean your clock. That also goes for my two redneck deputies. They walk carefully around the locals, but they can get a mite obnoxious to inquisitive strangers. They're big honkies and they ain't too bright.

"I already have two black eyes, sheriff," said F.D.R. The laughter relieved some of the tension.

"See they don't turn black-and-blue. This is *still* a southern town," the sheriff said. F.D.R.'s nostrils began to flare, so Sidney jumped into the conversation.

"Okay. Frank, why don't you grab a cab and drift into town on your own. I'll be at one of three places: Med-Pharm, Ginger's, or the hospital. Steve, as Tompion's chief of security, will lend assistance to the sheriff in conducting the official investigation. He'll be at any of those three place or the sheriff's office. If you run into anything, holler. If anything runs into you, don't hit back too hard."

F.D.R. Brown was smiling as he opened the door and began to walk toward the airport office. He was walking on the balls of his feet, as he always did when he was about to tackle a new job—just the way he felt walking towards the ring to face a new opponent. If he hadn't been drafted, he might have been the middleweight champion of the world. Or have had his brains bashed in.

His mind started ticking over an agenda of what he had to do. Get a room. See what style of clothes the black dudes wore and buy an outfit. Next, he would check the phone book and get a list of all the local bars, white and black. Then he'd rent an inconspicuous car. If there was a Rent-A-Wreck agency in town, he would get an old car there. Finally, if he could find a well-stacked young chick who had all the answers, they could have a few drinks and discuss the whole matter at her place. But it was wishful thinking. He was never that lucky. Usually her daddy had a shotgun.

Sidney's first stop had to be the plant, and the sheriff offered to drive them. Her instructions from the admiral, which were arrived at during their talk while she was in flight, was to confer with Max Butterworth and ask him to take over as acting president. If he agreed, have him call the admiral in Sidney's presence so Butterworth would understand that, for the time being, during the crisis, he would take his instructions from Sidney. Then Sidney would brief Butterworth on how to handle the staff. The second item on her agenda was to call in the top executives, outline the scenario of how everything was going to be handled by Tompion, and thus by Med-Pharm. They would be told not to talk to the press. All press relations would be handled by the public relations staff at corporate headquarters in New York. This was going to hit Wall Street like a bombshell, and the shrapnel could strike everyone.

Sidney couldn't remember a more depressing time in her

life. When her husband was reported Missing In Action, it was a bitter moment, but she didn't give up hope. Time, waiting, and hard work eased the pain. By the time Roger was presumed dead, all that remained was her emotional numbness. It were as though she had been married to a phantom — a stranger she might not remember if she bumped into him on the street.

This time Sidney knew she would have to suffer through the agony no matter how long it took. She didn't relish the job. She was worried about Jennifer even though she didn't know what she could say or do to comfort her. As the car hummed along, she looked at the familiar countryside, the trees, the barns, the gas stations, the cooperative dairy. She had spent five wonderful years at Carlyle, and her nostalgia combined with the anguish of the moment began to depress her. She opened the side window and let the wind whip against her face, not caring what it did to her hair.

CHAPTER

THREE

HE very slow, deep booming sounds of the Thomas Tompion grandfather clock reverberated throughout the house. Startled out of a catnap by the unfamiliar sounds, Sidney stared at hands of the clock standing upright. It was midnight. She kept looking at the extremely tall longcase clock made of golden-brown pearwood. She focused on the silver dial with the inscription *Tho. Tompion Londini Fecit* remembering when the Admiral had presented it to Peter after Tompion had acquired Med-Pharm/Rainbow Electronics. While there was no relationship between the world's most famous clockmaker and Tompion International, the gift was the Admiral's touch of class. The seventeenth Century clock was a museum piece.

Sidney was clad in elegant silk pajamas and wrapped up in her old, favorite woolen robe, something she picked up on impulse at Jaeger in London after falling in love with the large tartan print. She was suddenly aware of a sour taste in her mouth and realized that her tongue had the flannelly coating of stale whiskey. Spotting the half-full shotglass of Crown Royal, she picked it up and tossed off the remainder of the drink. She was not much of a drinker, but there were times when a drink or two was her only comfort.

It had been a nightmarish afternoon and evening. Jennifer had awakened and insisted on leaving the hospital. She wanted to be at home in familiar surroundings. When Sidney was reached at the plant, she left immediately in a company car, picked up Mary, the Wallack housekeeper, and then went to fetch her friend. At the sight of Sidney, Jennifer erupted into hysterics, and the portly doctor was obliged to give her a shot to quiet her. He gave Sidney a bottle of tranquilizers and his office and home phone numbers, in case he was needed. The housekeeper, who had been with Peter Wallack for over a dozen years, had welcomed Jennifer warmly to the house when they were married five years earlier. Now the motherly black woman with gray hair was weeping along with Jennifer and Sidney.

Once they were in the house, Mary coaxed Jennifer into drinking some warm milk. Then the distraught widow had gone to bed. Mary insisted on staying to comfort her. Left alone in the big colonial house, Sidney paced the familiar house and had two long telephone conversations with the admiral. He was flying down for the funeral with a number of executives. Steve and F.D.R. had called, reporting that neither they nor the sheriff had made any progress. At 10:00 P.M. Sidney checked Jennifer's room and found both Jennifer and Mary sound asleep.

Unable to concentrate on a paperback novel she had found in the study, and clammy from the sweat and strain of the past few hours, Sidney returned to her room. It was time to take a long, hot bath and reflect on the overwhelming rush of events that had enveloped the company and her friends. Undressing slowly, she examined herself in the mirror, not really seeing herself as the beautiful woman she was with the long, slender torso of a skiier, flawless, glowing white, firm breasts tipped with large aureoles. Her face look drawn. She examined her tongue and found it redder than usual. She turned on the bathtub faucets and felt aches in her shoulders. Rummaging through the bathroom closets, she found some bubble-bath beads and added them to the bath water. Finally she sank into the tub, stretched back and relaxed as the hot water began to foam and envelop her body. Soon her stiffness began to disappear.

After twenty minutes, Sidney got out of the tub, saw that her brown hair, deliberately cut short for easier care at the office, was a mess. She needed a shampoo. She reentered the tub, turned on the shower, and found that she had to force herself to concentrate on what she was doing. Her mind was in a haze. It was a signal that she was tired and hungry. She toweled off, put on her pajamas and robe. Wearing a green hand towel twisted in a knot around her head, she went to the kitchen to make bacon, eggs, and toast. She added a touch of Mary's homemade strawberry jam to her plate. Then she brewed a pot of decaffeinated coffee and drank two cups.

Finally, she drifted into the study to watch the 11:00 television news, but she promptly fell asleep. The striking clock awakened her at midnight. She walked around a room that was covered with books as well as Peter's framed graduate degrees and awards hanging on the wall. There was a Ph.D. in chemistry from MIT, a Rhodes scholarship, an Oxford degree, plus honorary degrees from half a dozen universities around the world, a Lasker Award for excellence in the field of nuclear pharmacology. On another shelf was a group of silver athletic cups, medals, and plaques from Peter's college days when he was a member of the downhill ski team.

There was a rogue's gallery of pictures: Peter with admirals Dutton and Rickover; Peter with President Nixon and Peter with President Carter. On the wall over the fireplace there was large oil painting of Jennifer, radiantly beautiful in a green and gold lame gown, but the artist could not do justice to her exquisite face and figure. Neither could he hide her large, perfectly formed breasts and tiny waist which seemed to electrify men. Peter had called her fondly, "My very own Dolly Parton."

Sidney and Jennifer had often discussed her large breasts. Jennifer didn't mind joking about them. It was the same in New York and Paris. She could not walk down the street without attracting stares, sometimes whistles. Only in Rome did the men try to pinch her rear end or her breasts. They called her "Sophia," after Sophia Loren. Both women agreed that Jennifer, no matter what the cost, must never let herself get overweight or she would look like a cow.

The sexy breasts that were so distracting tended to obscure the fact that Jennifer had graduated from the University of Texas, Phi Beta Kappa. She was an art major. At the university, on a dare, she entered and won several beauty contests and despite the fact that *Playboy* had offered her $10,000 to pose nude for a centerfold, a Hollywood agent had offered her a contract and she was dangling three proposals of marriage, she had rejected them all. She was determined to make her mark in the world of art. At the ripe age of twenty-one she had gone to seek her future in Paris.

"Sidney!"

Startled, Sidney turned around to see a disheveled Jennifer, her reddish blonde hair askew, her white dress wrinkled and ripped at the hem, her face streaked with tear-stained makeup. Sidney moved to her and they embraced one another, drawn together like magnets. Waves of emotion swept over them.

"Sidney — Sidney — I did it," she gasped. "I killed Peter."

"What are you saying?"

"I killed him. It's all my fault."

Sidney felt as though someone was pouring freezing ice water over her body. She began to tremble as she held onto Jennifer to keep her from falling. Leading her friend to a leather wingback chair, she went quickly to the bar and poured a large Jack Daniel's for Jennifer and a Crown Royal for herself. She guided Jennifer's hand as the frightened woman took a deep swallow of bourbon. The effect made her gasp. Sidney sat down on the carpet beside her and sipped her drink. It was impossible to decipher what Jennifer was saying. Fortified with another swallow of the rye, Sidney took a deep breath and said with as much control as she could muster, "Maybe you had better tell me the whole story."

Jennifer reached out with her free hand and clasped it in Sidney's. Gripping it as though her life depended on it, she said, "I'm responsible for Peter's death. It's the same as if I held a gun to his head and pulled the trigger. It wasn't that I didn't warn him. I warned him it could happen. He laughed at me. I warned him that Kaluste was the most dangerous man in the world — that he would — he would try to destroy us — if —"

"Do you mean Constantin Kaluste."

"Yes — that ruthless bastard who owns everything — emerald mines in Brazil, a fleet of ships, an airline, oil refineries, gold mines, a manipulator of world commodities like coffee, gold and wheat —"

"— a man with enough power to start a war just to sell munitions and aircraft to both sides."

"And the one man who believes that power is sex and that he is the most powerful man in Europe, therefore the essence of manhood to women — all women. He takes whatever he wants and what he cannot take he buys — or steals. He — he is the man who forced me to trick Peter to marry me."

"*What?*"

Jennifer put her head down on the arm of the chair and began to sob as Sidney, confused and startled by this revelation, began to run her hand over Jennifer's head, soothing her.

"He made me do it. *He made me.*" Jennifer began to pound her right fist into the arm of the chair, punishing herself. Then she reached out and clutched Sidney. As though a dam had broken, Jennifer began to talk — repeating herself and berating herself. Taking responsibility for her husband's death.

PART II

CHAPTER

FOUR

Paris, February 1980

"Jennifer."

No matter how often he said it, a shiver tiptoed down her spine. Jennifer Ann Black admitted secretly to herself that she was a romantic with a soft spot for any man with a deep, rich voice and an accent like Charles Boyer. Constantin Kaluste had such a voice, with a French accent, although she knew he wasn't French. No one seemed to know where he came from, and he alternately admitted or denied every rumor concerning his origins. The origin of his mellifluous voice was the product of a long period of training with a retired basso profundo of the La Scala Opera Company.

His voice, like many aspects of the man, was designed deliberately to suit the image Constantin Kaluste had created for himself. His posture, his looks, his demeanor, his rich voice were all window dressing for the world to envy along with his enormous wealth. No one ever got close enough to Kaluste to discover the real truth about where he came from or how he achieved his power.

European gossip columnists enjoyed speculating about Kaluste's birthplace. Guy Dorval of *Paris Match* said he was the bastard son of a French aristocrat and a Moroccan belly dancer, born in the Casbah. Others maintained that he was a freedom fighter who emerged from the Balkans with his sister after World War II and settled in Paris. Yet another rumor held that Kaluste was a rogue, pure Magyar from Hungary. It was the freedom-fighter rumor that seemed to be the most persistent, especially because Kaluste had a sister who had died in Paris fifteen years ago.

Even the world's most prestigious financial journals speculated about his origins, about his holdings, and even about his age. But by the end of 1979, most were in agreement that his empire was as large as the Getty or the Rockefeller fortunes. In terms of

U.S. dollars, Constantin Kaluste was one of five or six genuine multibillionaires in the world.

Kaluste was an enigma. He materialized out of nowhere, plunging onto the financial world and cutting a wide swath through it like Genghis Khan. History repeats itself. A man of mystery seems to emerge every quarter-century, like a Dr. Faustus, who possessed untold power, manipulating the world for his pleasure. Such men usually take the financial world by storm and dominate it by sheer force of personality. Kaluste's predecessors in Europe were men like Sir Basil Zaharoff and Calouste Gulbekian. It was suspected that Constantin Kaluste fashioned his lifestyle after Calouste Gulbenkian, his role model. In his day, Gulbenkian was the world's richest man, a financial genius who was successful as an oil promoter, a collector of rare art, ancient castles, and beautiful women.

Kaluste followed in Gulbenkian's footsteps, so much so that it was thought that Gulbenkian handpicked Kaluste to inherit his mantle once he passed from the scene. This theory was disputed widely, because it was well known that Gulbenkian never expected to die.

The mysterious rise of Constantin Kaluste to enormous wealth and power did not escape the notice of the world's leading intelligence agencies. His dealings were tracked minutely by the CIA, MI-6, the KGB and the Surete. Each had a thick dossier on him. The CIA suspected that he might be a Russian front in the Western world, a conduit to the USSR for high technology and other embargoed goods. Kaluste's sale of large amounts of gold on the commodities market kept alive the rumor of the Russian connection. While the Soviet connection wasn't proved, neither was it positively disproved.

"Jennifer," said Kaluste, "I think we are going to go skiing."

Jennifer looked at him with mixed emotions. For two years he had dominated her topsy-turvy world. She had learned that when Constanin made a suggestion, it was better to agree to it amiably because he never changed his mind. "That would be wonderful, Constantin," she said quietly.

"I have ordered for you new skis and new clothes in your favorite colors. Gaston will drive us to Chamonix in the Mercedes. It is a pleasant drive, and on our way, I will tell you what I desire from you. No more childish displays, eh, Jennifer?" She didn't reply. He nodded his head and said, *"Bien."*

Jennifer hated to admit that Constantin was a very attractive man, even though his temper sometimes frightened her. His volatility was disguised by his calm military bearing. Although he stood 5'10" tall, he gave the appearance of being taller. A strict regimen of food and exercise supervised by a nutritionist and a physiotherapist kept him slim. He wore exquisitely tailored lightweight suits always in navy blue or black. Beneath his magnetic personality was a vicious streak that lay just below the surface, ready to explode at anything that dared get in his way. Nevertheless, Constantin Kaluste had the reputation of great suavity and style. He rarely displayed his temper in public.

Kaluste was fifty-five. He looked ten years younger, with no gray streaks in his straight black hair and a healthy glow to his skin. No matter how often Jennifer saw him, he always looked as though he had just stepped out of a shower. He smelled of Onyx Lentheric, his favorite cologne. His moustache was trimmed carefully in a military style.

He carried nothing in his pockets to spoil the line of his clothes. Viktor, his closest business associate, dispensed cash tips, made travel arrangements, and paid hotel bills.

For a man who rarely gave interviews to reporters and never posed for the TV cameras Kaluste relished being recognized, especially when he was accompanied by a beautiful woman. This odd mixture of passion for anonymity and compulsive need for recognition of his attractiveness to beautiful women was the only paradox in Kaluste's makeup.

After two years as his permanent house guest, Jennifer wasn't exactly sure how she felt about him. She had much to be grateful for, and just as many reasons to hate him. Kaluste never told her how he felt about her.

Did Kaluste consider her his mistress or just another of his many beautiful women? Jennifer was "family" at dinners at Kaluste's home. She was his official hostess. He escorted her frequently to the opera, the ballet, the theater, and art galleries. Often he would disappear with some exciting woman on his arm and leave Jennifer to fend for herself. If she ever interested a man foolhardy enough to approach a Kaluste lady, there was always an aide to remind her that it was time to depart.

Constantin Kaluste never explained his behavior or his comings or goings. Sometimes he confided in her the details of a brilliant business conquest. He was as excited as a child. Moreover, he never failed to tell her in minute detail his sexual conquest of some movie actress, a princess, or an ambassador's wife. Yet Jennifer never experienced the great sexual pleasure with Kaluste that apparently other women seemed to; Jennifer thought that this failure was hers. She tried in every way to please him sexually, and he appeared to enjoy their lovemaking. Yet sleeping with Constantin was not like making love to Jean-Paul.

The paradoxical aspect of their affair was her puritanical attitude toward sex. She did not consider a relationship meaningful unless she was truly in love. Which made it all the more peculiar because Jennifer couldn't remember how or why Kaluste had ended up in her bed the first time. It had been the morning after a party, and she had been drinking too much champagne. He had helped her to her room. The next morning she found him in her bed making love to her. Afterwards, his visits were sporadic. He talked to her and she listened until she fell asleep. Sometimes they made love.

Outside of his servants, she was the only woman who lived in Kaluste's house, and he constantly reminded business associates and friends that the ginger-headed beauty was "family." The housekeeper remained respectfully frightened of her and went to Jennifer for her orders, so Jennifer took charge of the household, the menus, and the parties. She never had money of her own, she just ordered what she wanted. But Kaluste selected and bought her clothes. Occasionally he gave her pieces of expensive jewelry, crafted in pink gold and encrusted with emeralds. The emeralds came from his mine in Brazil.

CHAPTER

FIVE

AFTER announcing the skiing trip to the Alps, Kaluste walked out the room. Jennifer was alone now, staring out of the huge picture window watching the wet snow fall and melt on the Paris sidewalk. She knew the window was bulletproof and that the town-house palace was a fortress, but she would not let the thought interfere with the cleanliness and beauty of this winter's day.

The falling snow was pure and white, each flake different, free to float and find its place in nature's scheme of things. Unlike the snowflakes, she had no such freedom. Four years ago, she had come to Paris to study art. Only when her money was running out had she sought a job as a model.

She made the rounds of the fashion magazines and the fashion photographers. All found her beautiful, but her prominent breasts disqualified her from the world of the small-breasted mannequins who posed for *Vogue* or *Elle* magazines in Paris. But an American photojournalist suggested that she might like to pose in designer ski clothes for *Sports Illustrated*. With her upper anatomy covered, she turned out to be the model find of the year. Luckily, she was beginning at the time of the natural look.

Once committed to modeling, she was obliged to lose weight. When she finally reached 105 pounds, the last thing to shrink was her bust. Her cheekbones became pronounced, her naturally reddish blonde hair and the sprinkle of freckles on her nose gave her a healthy outdoor look. In swimsuits, lace lingerie, and ski clothes, Jennifer became the rage of Paris. She answered to "Janifer" and "Rouge," and to her American high-school nickname, "Ginger." She was swamped with more modeling contracts than she could handle. But she dated very little and stuck to her plan to complete her art education.

One ardent suitor, more persistent than others, was the famous race-car driver Jean-Paul Joubert. While she sidestepped most admirers, she could not avoid the charming Joubert, whom she saw at a gala event, the Ecole des Beaux Arts Models and Artists Ball, the annual costume event. The affair was her graduation present to herself. Jean-Paul, who had been unsuccessfully trying to date her for months, wangled an invitation from a student for 1,000 francs and came dressed as a satyr. Jennifer came masked as Miss Universe, but her distinctive figure revealed her identity. Four hours and a bottle of champagne later, Jean-Paul and Jennifer were in a hotel room at the Georges V sipping more vintage Chateau Lafite and making love. He was experienced. She wasn't. Yet, by early morning, Jennifer had discovered sexual passion for the first time. She was sure she was in love.

After a month, she still knew very little about Jean-Paul. Nevertheless, they were married quietly in a small Catholic church in Lyons. Somehow he'd managed to short circuit the posting of the banns.

The newspapers carried stories of the marriage. Only then did Jennifer discover that Jean-Paul was famous for winning the Mille Miglia twice. He was a Grand Prix driver of great fame, and a notorious womanizer. But Jennifer had found the great reservoir of love within her and enjoyed their sex too much to share him with any other woman. She promptly decided that it was her wifely duty to keep him deliriously happy and sexually exhausted.

Her life turned out to be a meaningless merry-go-round. Jean-Paul had been living in hotel rooms, so Jennifer insisted that they live in her flat on the Left Bank. It was a wild, reckless six-month marriage that ended abruptly when Jean-Paul's race car was nudged by a car into a retaining wall at Le Mans. His car

spun twice, then was struck again by another car rolling it over a
half-dozen times at a speed in excess of 100 miles an hour. Jean-
Paul's car caught fire, exploded in midair, and came to rest in the
stands injuring a dozen spectators. Jennifer had watched the
accident in horror.

Jean-Paul lay in a coma for four days. The suddenness of the
tragedy ejected her out of her champagne-and-roses euphoria.
Shocked into reality, she realized she was a stranger in a strange
country with a dying husband. She knew nothing of his family or
living relatives, or even whether she could scrape together enough
money for his hospital bills.

Jennifer's first meeting with Constantin Kaluste was startling. He simply arrived at the hospital and took charge. She
didn't know that Jean-Paul was his nephew. New teams of doctors
began to arrive and consult with the mysterious stranger who kept
staring at her, but said little. Then Jean-Paul died. Too great an
area of his body had been burned severely for him to have any
chance of recovery.

Kaluste took care of everything, including the funeral
arrangements. She watched through tear-stained eyes as the
bronze casket was placed into the Kaluste family mausoleum in a
churchyard near Rouen. She thought her life was over. With
great gentleness, Kaluste took charge of Jennifer and brought her
to his country estate.

Kaluste disappeared, but Jennifer remained alone with the
servants for a month of mourning. Since there was no one to talk
to, she began to take long walks along the country roads. Sometimes she had the grooms saddle a horse from the stable and she
would ride out onto the rolling hills, just as she did as a young girl
in Texas. Exactly one month to the day, a uniformed chauffeur in
a white stretch Mercedes intercepted her as she was walking along

a country lane. He said his master, Constantin Kaluste, would like to see her at once in Paris. Without a word, she got in the car and was taken to Kaluste's Paris town house.

Jennifer was astounded at its size. Once inside, she was petrified. As an art student she noted the Cezannes, Matisses and Lautrecs cluttered almost ostentatiously side-by-side on the wall with almost no space between them. There were five original Rodin sculptures in the hall in addition to some *animaliers:* bronze sculptures of dogs, bears, stags, and horses by artists she didn't recognize.

A butler led her to a study and departed. Then Jennifer saw Kaluste standing behind his desk, scrutinizing every curve of her body. His face never flinched. He was rock still; only his eyes informed on his mind. He was obviously undressing her. Despite being used to the stares of men, Jennifer felt strangely violated. His eyes scanned her face and settled on her cleavage.

He gestured to a chair and said, "Sit." She did. "Are you pregnant?"

"No."

"Too bad. Jean-Paul was my sister's only son, and the last male in my family. He was my sole heir. The line ended with him."

"But can't you have children?"

He look startled for a moment; then, through a forced smile said, "But of course." Then he changed the subject quickly. "We will speak English, you and I, as I want to become more proficient in your language."

Unsure what to say, Jennifer said nothing. She was looking at the sixteen-foot ceilings, the walls lined with books, fine hand-carved Chinese figurines, and the other beautiful objets d'art in the study. Yet her eyes kept returning to Kaluste. She found his deep, rich voice so compelling that she was suddenly too terrified to speak. Even if she could, she wouldn't know what to say.

"He had very little money of his own, you know. He squandered what he won while I bought his racing cars." There was a long silence. "I know you supported yourself adequately, but I cannot allow my nephew's wife to pose for magazines. It is not good for my image. There is absolutely no need for you to work. You will stay with me. After a proper period of mourning, you will resume a social life more in keeping with Kaluste standards."

Jennifer resented a stranger trying to dominate her. "And what standards are those, *m'sieu?*" Her words tinged with sarcasm.

"Ah, the beauty has fire. Perhaps even a brain. *Bon.* You will reign here as the hostess of my dinner parties and mistress of this house. You are now part of my family."

He must have rung a secret bell. Suddenly a woman — obviously the housekeeper — appeared and Kaluste motioned Jennifer to follow her. The woman led her up a winding staircase to the second floor of the mansion. At the end of the hall, she pushed open the door to a suite of rooms, curtsied, and motioned to Jennifer to enter first.

If Jennifer had been startled earlier, she was astonished now. It was a large room, perhaps forty feet square, with a fireplace, a king-sized four-poster mahogany bed with an elegant pastel green, silk brocade canopy. It looked a room for a reigning queen. It was. One had stayed here.

Jennifer was overwhelmed until she looked at the housekeeper, who appeared terrified. In an effort to put her at ease, Jennifer smiled and began to speak to her in French. The woman, obviously worried about a new mistress of the house, relaxed slightly. Madame Langois was about forty. She had a pale face and straight jet-black hair which she wore in a short, simple haircut. She spoke in rapid French through clenched teeth. Her superficial accent was Parisian, but with an inflection that was probably Alsace.

Dressed in a severe, expensive man-tailored suit, and not given to easy smiles, Madame Langois played down her attractiveness deliberately. Yet she couldn't disguise an indefinable something of the chic Frenchwoman: a casual, elegant look. Thawing a little, she showed Jennifer the suite of rooms complete with a book-lined study, a mammoth bathroom with a large Roman tub and gold fixtures, a huge closet full of women's clothes. A quick glance revealed labels by designers she had only read about in *Vogue*.

The housekeeper pressed the number-one button on a small desk-annunciator system. Seconds later, a young maid in a traditional starched black dress with white trim and a starched linen tiara appeared. "Madame Joubert," the housekeeper said. "This is your personal maid, Lisa. Please advise her if you would like breakfast in your room every morning, or with the master when he is in residence. What is your preference? At what time you would like your bath? At what temperature? It would be helpful to decide clothes you will wear the night before, so Lisa may have them pressed and ready for you."

"My clothes are in my apartment."

"*Non, madame.* The master brought them here, and they are in the attic. One dress was used as a pattern for size, and a clothes model was made. The wardrobe belongs to madame. The master himself selected the styles and the colors." She coughed politely and then added, "Let me be forward in this suggestion, madame, but the master favors emerald-green dresses to emphasize your red hair and your ivory skin. I also suggest it may be because it reminds him he owns the largest emerald mine in Brazil.

"Your seamstress will be here at four this afternoon to measure madame and adjust the dress model. M'sieu Lapin will be here at five to show Madame a selection of furs. Dinner is at eight. If you wish to rest for an hour before your bath I will schedule M'sieu Anton, the hairdresser, for seven-thirty. The box on your desk contains the jewels the master would like you to wear for dinner. Forgive me for being forward, madame, but do not be surprised by the size of the emeralds. They can never be too large for the master."

"No shoes?" said Jennifer asked wryly. The maid giggled politely behind one hand, and Madame Langois almost broke down and smiled, but she restrained herself.

"The shoes, madame, are in the closet. I selected them myself to match your new clothes. Your shoes were measured and a model made and they were handmade to your size."

Jennifer was then shown the use of the annunciator to summon any of the servants she desired. Finally she was taken to a concealed refrigerator that contained an assortment of mineral water, cheese, crackers and pate. Finally she was shown the secret bar with its large assortment of liquor. Then the housekeeper and maid left abruptly. Suddenly she was alone. She went to her purse for a handkerchief and instead picked up her wallet. All she had was 500 francs and some loose coins. She looked at the floor-to-ceiling mirror that covered a complete wall of her bedroom, studied herself dressed in an old skirt and windbreaker, and thought of Alice staring into the Looking-Glass.

CHAPTER

SIX

THE Swissair jetliner was cruising smoothly toward Geneva at slightly over 600 miles per hour. The Captain, with a charming Swiss-Deutsch accent, had just announced in English, French, and German that the jet stream was giving them a 110-miles-per-hour tailwind across the Atlantic. Except for a half dozen passengers and the stewardesses, most of the first-class section was unoccupied.

The five top executives of MedPharm/Rainbow traveling to Chamonix via Geneva planned to combine a company executive meeting with a skiing holiday. At their last board meeting, they agreed with the chairman of the board that the interests of the company would best be served by each member's flying on a separate flight.

As the founder and chief executive officer of Med-Pharm/Rainbow, Peter Wallack would never have disobeyed his own order banning executives from doubling up on one flight, but he had a great deal on his mind and resolved to break his own rule. His companion was Sidney Howe, vice president in charge of corporate relations. Unlike the other key executives, her role in the company, while important, was not crucial to the creation or manufacture of their sophisticated medical or electronic products. The two were seated in the third row. There was no one within earshot. Wallack was talking in his usual animated fashion while waving his right hand in the air for emphasis.

Peter Wallack was a tall, rangy man with a shock of thinning brown hair that gave him a perpetually disheveled look. His face was long and disjointed, which added to his charm. His wardrobe was catalog casual — pure Sears — made up of odd sports jackets and trousers. He wore only blue oxford button-down shirts and knit wool ties. In every one of his pockets were rumpled pieces of paper with scribblings on them and a curved stem pipe he never smoked but used for special emphasis when he spoke or lectured.

His musical voice rose and fell as he talked. It gave his speech a young boy's timbre, as though he were going through puberty with a changing voice. The musical quality suggested to Howe that he might be tone-deaf and not aware of it. She listened attentively as he spoke, nodding occasionally in agreement, sometimes shaking her head and from time to time sipping her gin and tonic that the stewardess had prepared heavy on the gin and light on the tonic.

"Sid, this trip is so important that I'm ready to jump out of my skin. We have a lot of tough decisions to make. The important one is which offer to accept for MedPharm/Rainbow: Tompion's or Xynatron's. Then you have to decide on that third proposal: the one to marry me. I want a decision on that before we leave France."

"Peter, you're such a darling — and so persistent. We've gone over this a hundred times. I can't marry you and you know it. Harry's been missing in action for five years —"

" — and presumed dead."

"And presumed dead." She paused for a moment to ease the pain of the situation. "Until I know for a fact that he's dead, I'm not free to marry. I'm not alone; there are thousands of women in my position. For all I know, Harry may be wasting away in a Vietcong prison camp somewhere. I just can't think about myself, I must first consider him.

"By enlisting in the Air Force, Harry was prepared to sacrifice his life for his country. When we met at a college dance, he was already in flight training, and when we decided to get married, it implied that I was prepared to sacrifice a few years of my life for him. That's when I went to work for you, Peter, when I was at graduate school at Emory. Each week Harry's pay and what's left of mine goes into a joint account for our future. This includes your generous stock options. Harry may still return — and I am hoping he does. If he does, I'm going to be here waiting for him."

"And if he doesn't?"

"If he doesn't, I'll just have to make a decision at that time."

"And when will that be?"

"When the State Department or the Defense Department or the Air Force or the president makes up its mind."

"Maybe we shouldn't have started our relationship, Sid. I didn't plan to fall in love with you. You were alone and vulnerable, and I was so steeped in my work that I was never close to anyone. We were like two lost souls in a small town, getting together for the sake of having company, to share a meal or a bottle of wine and talk about life, and Med-Pharm and the future and exchange ideas."

"Peter, we can't forget what's happened. We should look back on it as something wonderful for both of us. There have been only two men in my life: Harry and you. You're both different. He's a kind, funny type of fellow with a lot of charm. He wanted to become permanent Air Force. We were going to talk about it when he came back.

"But you, Peter, you're a special person who makes things happen. You're a genius, but at heart you're still a little boy. The hours you work and the few minuscule moments you keep for yourself — you need a woman full-time to comfort you. I've come to understand that these past few years, but I'm not that kind of woman. Except for just a little while, I — I guess I needed someone to hold on to. Maybe that's how it all began.

"Peter, darling, we're such good friends, such wonderful

friends. We can cherish it all our lives. Affairs don't have to end in sorrow. We can look back with no regrets. When we sell the company, it would be best for both of us to end our affair. I don't feel guilty every time you look at another woman. You're single and attractive. You're forty-two years old, you skiied for your college team, and you're soon going to be incredibily wealthy. I'm willing to bet that you're going to find the right lady. Very soon."

"Think so?"

"I do. I hope she'll be worthy of you."

Sidney reached out gently, put her hand in his, and squeezed it. Then she had to avert her eyes because he was crying. To avoid noticing, she continued talking "And, Peter — remember that before you and I started dating two years ago, I was faithful to Harry for three long, agonizing years. As the Bible so aptly puts it, he was the only man I had ever known. But after six months of a wonderful marriage while Harry was still stateside, I discovered what it's like to be a whole woman. I'm a woman, Peter, a completely honest woman. And I'm human, too — I wasn't cut out to be celibate. If Harry ever returns, I'll tell him about us. I'm not ashamed of us. But after three years of waiting, counting every single day, never knowing if each letter or telegram is good news or bad news, I came to a personal decision. I had a soul-searching talk with Reverend Saunders, my home-town minister, and my father. I didn't tell you that, did I, Peter? I discussed my innermost feelings with my father. I love my father. He's one of the nicest, wisest men I know, and so damned understanding. He gave me some advice — advice that I took and that I don't regret for a minute.

"He said, 'Sidney, you have a limited amount of time on earth and you have to live and enjoy it as best you can, preferably without hurting anyone, and doing the most good you can along

the way. At twenty-eight a woman is supposed to reach the height
of her sex drive, probably because it's smack in the middle of her
most fertile years. To bottle up that sexual energy will dry you up
as a woman. You'll be unhappy by the time Harry returns. You'll
be looking for a crutch no matter how smart you are or how many
graduate degrees in psychology you have. First you'll start drinking, then you'll start going downhill.

'For God's sake, and yours, and for the sake of your future
children, find a nice, kind, gentle, understanding, sensitive man
and have a fling — an affair with your body and your head rather
than with your emotions. It's the only way to satisfy your yearning
and keep your sanity.

'When Harry returns home, you may wish to tell him
everything. If you do, he'll understand. If he doesn't, then he isn't
the man you should have married in the first place. If and when he
returns — you'll have problems he will have to live with and he'll
have problems you will have to live with.

'What you are going through is nothing new. It happens in
every war. I saw a great deal of it when I was on submarine duty
during World War II. Men came home after being away three or
four years. Some women can become temporary nuns until their
husbands return, others can't, and others don't want to. You
know, Sidney, good marriages have a tendency to stay glued
together. Only the bad ones come unstuck.' "

When she finished, neither of them spoke for a while. She
was happy that at last she could confide in him, knowing he would
understand.

Finally Peter said in a more controlled voice, "Is that why
you rationed your body to one week-end a month?"

"Yes, Peter. If we had lived together or had seen each other
more frequently, I'd have gone beyond what I'd have been able to

cope with. You had no spare time anyway. You never took time off and you weren't dating anyone, so I felt that it would be the sort of affair we would be able to handle. I didn't want it to go beyond that. We discussed it all coolly and logically beforehand, remember? I hope you don't feel I used you deliberately."

"You never did that, Sidney. But I needed you, too. I get so busy at the lab, working days and nights, trying to run the company with my left hand — that I forget what day it is. For the past two years, I kept looking forward to our three-day weekends. I thank you for helping to preserve my sanity."

"My father also told me, 'Don't have an affair with a man who has less to lose than you do.'"

"Sidney, you're so damned sane about everything. Deep inside, I know you're right. We have to go our own way. I don't mean you have to leave the company — I just mean that our personal relationship is over. You're in charge of corporate relations, where does the company go from here?"

"Peter, it's decision time. The five of us will have a week of skiing at Chamonix. We agreed not to discuss business until the third evening. We bat around the offers from the two conglomerates and decide what's best for you, your executives, your employees, and the future growth of the firm. We give you all the advice we can, then, make the final decision.

"As for us, Peter, you...will be my best friend. But you're at the stage in life when you should think of getting married. I know the kind of woman you need. A woman you can put on a pedestal, can adore, protect, and cherish. And she must be able to look after you, to mother you. Your clothes are never pressed; your hair never seems to see a comb. You don't care how you look. Your pockets are stuffed with paper. You are a great big teddy bear waiting to be hugged. The right girl is one who will devote her life to you."

He looked at his glass for a moment and then tilted his head back and quaffed it. "Big drinker," Sidney smiled. "You tossed off a Coke and drowned all your sorrows."

Peter smiled and his face lit up with crinkles, a most disarming face that masked one of the most brilliant minds in chemistry. "I think, Peter, that as of this minute you are a free man. The only condition is that if I don't like the lady you find, I'll clobber you. You know something, Peter? I'll even help you look."

"Will you test her I.Q., bank account, measurements?"

"*Naturellement*. You always said you liked women with big boobs, a narrow waist and hips — as you crudely put it — love handles."

"Sidney — no matter what the future holds in store for us, can we stay in touch forever?"

"Forever, Peter."

He took her left hand in his, kissed her palm and began to cry.

CHAPTER

SEVEN

FROM the outside, Kaluste's limousine looked like a normal Mercedes 600, the extra long body giving it the appearance of yacht on wheels. However, many wealthy Europeans, terrified by the growing rash of kidnappings and terrorist attacks, became concerned about their safety. Kaluste was no exception. His Mercedes had a much more powerful engine than the stock 600 indicated because its armorplate was guaranteed to stop a .50 calibre or smaller bullet at fifty yards. The dark window glass was also bulletproof. The car's reinforced steel underbody was capable of resisting fragmentation bombs or grenades. The added weight and the need for rapid acceleration required the additional horsepower.

In the past four years, three attempts had been made on Kaluste's life. The first one occurred during a trip to West Germany to buy aircraft and armaments for an emerging African nation. A motorcycle had roared by at 70 miles an hour while a masked man in the sidecar fired a burst from an automatic rifle while Kaluste was entering his car. Only the chauffeur had been killed. The bullets were identified as having come from a Russian 7.62mm AKM Kalashnikov. The next day the discarded weapon was found and scrutinized. It was new and had a luminous scope. *Der Spiegel,* the German newsweekly, was later notified by phone that the assassination attempt was the work of the Red Brigade. The caller swore he would not miss the next time.

The second attempt on his life occurred in Beirut. After concluding a large secret oil deal with one of the shah's relatives, Kaluste was walking out of the oil minister's Beirut office to return to his hotel. One man, driving a dynamite-laden car, plowed directly into the ministry. The explosion killed eleven people and injured thirty-one more. The driver lost his life. His soul, according to the Koran, flew straight up into the arms of Allah.

The Shiite Moslems claimed responsibility for the attack. So did the PLO. The Israelis offered proof (which no one except the CIA requested) that the attack was faked in order to enhance Kaluste's position as a legitimate broker for Arab oil interests. The KGB was thought to be involved.

Long before the third attempt on his life, Kaluste acquired a new driver, Gaston Charbonneau, an ex-Foreign Legionnaire who had fought courageously in Vietnam and had retired a sergeant. Charbonneau was a Corsican, olive-skinned with the flattened face of a pugilist and a hard-muscled body latticed with scars and bulletholes. He had taken a special course in driving and evasive action conducted by a security organization highly recommended to Kaluste. A special team of Kaluste investigators checked out Charbonneau. His military service and medals were on record, but his early exploits as a smuggler and killer were not.

He enlisted one jump ahead of the gendarmes, and his background was ideal for a military career. Charbonneau was a man raised by the Corsican underworld and Charbonneau was informed that Kaluste had the full story and proof, which he locked away safely. Charbonneau understood that if he ever entertained any thoughts about betraying Kaluste, he was signing his own death warrant.

Gaston Charbonneau had been driving for Kaluste for five months when the third assassination attempt took place. Kaluste had returned from visiting his emerald mines in Brazil. His plane landed at Orly Airport outside Paris. Charbonneau had picked up his employer and was speeding toward Paris when a man in a Porsche drew alongside the Mercedes and, though he couldn't see Kaluste, opened fire at the rear seat with an Uzi machine gun. The 9mm Parabellum bullets pinged off the rear-door window.

Then the gun was aimed at the chauffeur. Charbonneau maintained his poise until the forty-shot Magazine was empty. He knew the man would have to fumble to attach a new magazine if he tried to stay even with the Mercedes. Charbonneau lowered the power window at the driver's seat calmly, pulled an ancient 9mm Luger from a door holster with his right hand, and, with a single snap shot, put a bullet through the ear of the would-be assassin.

The Mercedes didn't slow down as the Porsche swerved out of control and crashed into a building. Kaluste applauded from the rear, took a five-carat emerald from his left hand, pressed a button to lower the partition and handed it to the chauffeur in gratitude. "I will put 100,000 francs in your special Swiss account, Gaston. Good work."

Charbonneau shrugged as though he had just batted a flea off his shoulder. In his lifetime he had killed over 200 men in combat, plus an undisclosed number for his Corsican family. One more *cochon* didn't matter. A pig was a pig.

By the time the gendarmes investigated the death of the would-be assassin, Charbonneau had already reported the incident. With no clothes tags, laundry marks, or a wallet for identification, the dead man's body remained unidentified in the morgue. The car had been stolen in Marseilles. The Uzi serial number had been filed off. The crime lab of the Deuxieme Bureau could identify only the first two numbers. Mossad, the Israeli intelligence service, reported that the two prefix numbers came from guns that had been sold to Argentina.

Because of the foiled third attempt, Kaluste felt safer traveling by car than by any other way. He explained it to Jennifer differently, saying that by the time you took the car to the airport, waited for the plane, flew to Geneva, went through customs and immigration, then drove back into France through customs and immigration to get to Chamonix, it took less time to drive there directly.

Jennifer sensed that something was awry. Kaluste didn't like to waste time. Driving 300 miles by car was not his style. She also suspected his protestations that he wanted to be with her. She was certain he did not love her. Why the sudden burst of affection? Perhaps he was going to ask her to leave? The thought made her heart palpitate. What she would miss most was all the wonderful clothes she had acquired in the past two years. Kaluste's taste was impeccable.

Now she was wearing a pastel green Ellesse apres-ski outfit. Her reddish-blonde hair cascaded down to her shoulders and her ivory white skin glowed with youth and good health. She wore the merest touch of light red lipstick, and the cold had put a slight blush of color on her cheeks. "Janifer," Kaluste said, looking at her, "you look particularly beautiful this afternoon."

"Thank you, Constantin."

He leaned over to kiss her mouth, but she turned. His lips caressed her cheek. "Janifer," he purred. His voice was soft but his eyes were angry, "Is this a display of gratitude for all I have done for you?"

"I am not a girl of the evening to be mauled in front of a chauffeur."

"But of course. How uncouth. *Pardon, ma cherie.*" He touched a button, and a thin, gauzelike shutter descended on their side of the glass partition. They could not see Gaston and he could not see them. The other three sides were enclosed with dark-tinted glass. She had lost her only excuse, and now she found she had no choice but to obey his wishes. As usual, his whim was an order she could not disobey. He unzipped her jacket and helped remove it.

Then he fondled her left breast gently.

Suddenly he ripped off her gold blouse. Jennifer gasped. Then he tried to tear off her bra, but it was too well constructed to be torn. Her first reaction was to resist, but she knew it was useless. Reluctantly, she unhooked the bra and her large plump breasts popped out; two mounds of ivory ice cream topped with amber rosettes.

Jennifer was uncomfortable as Kaluste curled up on the seat and began to nibble on her left breast. Adventurous as she was, quickie sex in a car, even if it was a limousine, was not her idea of love. She was a romantic, but to Kaluste she was a toy for his amusement. Yes, a toy who got all his attention one minute and discarded the next. How long would it go on like this? Closing her eyes, she tried to think of other things as he suckled contentedly at her teats, her mind puzzled about the turn of events in her life. *What am I doing here with this man? I am only twenty-five years old. What does he want of me?*

"You ignore me, Janifer."

"Constantin — you have no respect for yourself when you have no respect for me. I am your nephew's wife."

"Ah, Janifer. Alors, Jean-Paul is dead. I fulfill an uncle's duty."

"You do not please me, Constantin. You abuse me."

He slapped her face angrily. Her eyes filled with tears and the red marks showed up vividly on her creamy skin. She scratched him and drew blood as one long fingernail gashed his cheek. He hit her again, harder this time. Jennifer pulled away from him into the corner near the jump seat. He fumed until he looked into a side mirror. "Ah, Janifer, you are no childish debutante. *Regardez*, you have given me a dueling scar. Come back here. I own you just as I owned Jean-Paul. I can do anything I wish with you. I have your passport. You have no money. I can see that you never work again in Europe. I can order terrible things done to you, like having acid thrown in your face." He paused and smiled at his own humor. "Now recline here and let me enjoy your magnificent body. Pleasure me and we shall talk about our future. If you are nice, I might let you have your own apartment and have your own bank account."

For the first time in a long time, Jennifer felt a glimmer of hope. Maybe this situation could be resolved? Reluctantly, she surrendered her body to Kaluste, then relaxed as he began fondling her breasts. Suddenly he curled up and began to suckle on her large, erect nipples like a hungry puppy. He placed her hands on his face and began to mumble. *"Maman,"* he said. *"Maman."*

To remain comfortable on the back seat of the car, Jennifer found that she had to cradle Kaluste. Though she could not prevent herself from being aroused by this most elemental expression of maternal love, it was soon apparent that this would be the extent of their lovemaking. After a while, a numbness began to set into her breast with his mouth still clamped on it. He was fast asleep. To try to separate herself from him, she began to inhale deeply, hoping to awaken him. It was no use.

Now thoroughly uncomfortable, she slowly forced two fingers into his mouth and began to pry his teeth open. Ever so slowly, she removed the painful nipple from his mouth. Now he sucked on her finger. The teeth marks left ugly welts. She took Kaluste's thumb and placed it in his mouth. Then she stretched him out along the rear seat. Resting on her knees on the floor of the moving car, she began to repair herself. Her cosmetic case open, she took out some skin cream and began to cover the lacerated parts of her breast.

By accident, she looked up at the gauze curtain and an eye peeking back at her. Earlier, Gaston must have snipped the curtain, creating a peephole for himself. If Kaluste ever found out, he would have Charbonneau killed. Then, craftily, with all the pride she could muster Jennifer put on a stage performance for Gaston, pulling on her bra as her magnificent breasts faced the peephole. She moved deliberately, as though in slow motion, pointing her breasts directly at the eye that appeared and disappeared as the car scurried along. When her bra was finally in place she waited for the eye to reappear. Then she winked at it. The eye vanished.

"That should scare you, you bastard!" she drawled in her best Texas accent.

Her gold blouse was in tatters, so she took several tiny safety pins from her model's case (known among models as the working woman's tool kit, with all its variations in meaning) and fastened the blouse together. Luckily, her down jacket was intact. She pulled out the jump seat and sat down, stretching her legs and relaxing as Kaluste lay curled on the seat sucking his thumb. The car was moving faster and swerving less. Her breast was still painful, but Jennifer knew she was a quick healer. By tomorrow the marks would be gone. The swift disappearance of men's teeth marks on women's breasts was one of God's gifts to women.

CHAPTER

EIGHT

AROUND 1:30 P.M. the car came to a sudden halt and awakened Jennifer. She had been dozing, leaning against the door with her legs stretched out. There was an ache in her back, so she rotated her shoulders to loosen the kinks. Her left breast was still sore and reminded her of Kaluste. She turned toward him and found him studying a document. The rear door opened, letting in a blast of cold air, and Gaston said, "We are at the restaurant, M'sieu Kaluste. The area is clear."

"Merci, Gaston."

Kaluste placed the papers into his attache case and he locked it. He put on his fleece-lined jacket, gloves, and Alpine hat, then stepped out of the car. Gaston proffered his hand to help Jennifer out of the car, but she gave him a withering look.

"Constantin, s'il vous plait," she said and put out her hand.

Kaluste offered his arm, smiled, and said, "We are near Dijon. We will have lunch here and stretch for a time before we proceed to Chamonix. We have much to discuss."

The restaurant displayed a sign with the painting of a dog's head and the name *Le Chien d'or.* There was a mixture of ice and snow on the ground while nearby the chilling wind blew snow devils across the fields. Kaluste held her arm as they walked gingerly up the four icy steps to the entrance. Once inside, the owner greeted them warmly, took Kaluste's jacket, but, because of her torn blouse, Jennifer refused to remove hers. They were led to a small private dining room with an eighteenth-century, walk-in fireplace. The whistling wind sang through the chimney while the hardwood crackled and gave off occasional hisses as it burned.

A heavyset women with thinning hair waddled into the room with steaming rum toddies. Obviously the order for drinks and food had been placed ahead of time. They did not speak as a basket containing fresh loaves of bread was placed on the heavy oak table along with a small tub of butter. The woman returned with a tureen of steaming pea soup, which she placed on the table, then put the matching ladle next to Jennifer. The soup dishes and tureen were obviously the landlord's best china; the wedding pattern of old Limoges, a white porcelain with a gold band around it. The woman left and Jennifer served Kaluste and herself. A marrow bone thickened and flavored the soup. Croutons and slivers of ham floated on top. Jennifer found it delicious.

Not until he had consumed his second helping did Kaluste speak. He chose his words carefully. "Janifer, we will now talk of your future." She said nothing, her heart racing as she tore off a hunk of bread and buttered it slowly. "I trust you have been happy living with me. Clothes — jewels — parties — I have treated you well, *non?*"

She didn't look, but continued eat. Knowing he expected a response, she nodded her head, barely breathing, not daring to do anything that might break the spell, make him change his mind.

"At this moment you have position, respectability — a certain standing in French society. This is something for a common American girl from Texas. Not everyone in Texas has an oil well." He laughed as though it were a private joke.

"If I so choose, I can make you wealthy. You can have an exclusive apartment in Paris, a foreign car, chic clothes, charge accounts, and the continued prestige of your association with Kaluste. You would like all this, *non?*"

Jennifer nodded rather than refute his remarks.

"But I expect something for this act of generosity. In Houston, where you were born, they say, 'There is no such thing as a free lunch.'"

Again Jennifer nodded, waiting for the other shoe to drop.

Kaluste looked directly into her eyes and said,"I wish you to seduce a man who — "

"What?" She was startled into silence until, finally, anger overcame her shock. "How dare you ask this of me, Constantin?"

"Now, now, Janifer, let us be adult — and objective. You are not an seventeen-year-old virgin. You are no stranger to men. I do not ask you to become a harlot. Let me explain before you interrupt again. One of my companies is desirous of acquiring a certain American corporation. Have no fear — it is all very legitimate. At this moment there are two contenders for this company: Xynatron, which is owned by one of my dummy corporations, and Tompion International, which is American owned.

"The company has the unique name of Med-Pharm/Rainbow and is located in the state of Georgia. It is two companies in one: the first produces nuclear chemicals to be used mostly in hospitals, research and cancer testing. The second is involved in high technology and produces sophisticated components for computer manufacturers and the United States Defense Department.

"There were two brothers named Wallack, one brilliant in chemistry, the other electronics. When one brother died in an auto accident, the second brother, keeping to the terms of his brother's will, merged the companies and placed half the combined stock in a trust for his brother's family. To convert Med-Pharm/Rainbow into dollars to please his brother's family, he is contemplating offers for the company. So, like tennis, it is the final set, and he is to decide which offer to accept. Our offer is higher, so I am certain we shall triumph in the end."

"Then why do you need me?"

Kaluste stared at her again, his jaw firm, his nostrils flaring.

"I do not want to lose this battle, Janifer. This one I *must* win — it is very important to me." He slammed a fist into his open hand. "I *must* win."

"I don't understand what you wish of me, Constantin."

He smiled at her, sensing that she would agree. "Elementary. Five company executives are en route to Chamonix for a week of business and skiing. They will arrive at a decision before returning to Georgia. The managing director is the chemist Peter Wallack, a rather naive American."

"How do you know all this, Constantin?"

"We have gathered, through our sources in America, a complete dossier on every one of these people. We have had them followed for weeks while others have traced their movements since birth. I know every important moment of their lives, including their indiscretions. Besides, we also employ someone who works inside the firm.

"*Alors,* the remainder falls into your hands. You have a reservation at the same hotel, and it is arranged for you to meet him accidentally on the ski slopes."

"If all this is so crucial to you, why are you willing to trust a common American girl to do your spying?"

Kaluste did not reply. Instead he looked at his watch. "Janifer, as of now you are moved totally out of my house. Your new address is in a briefcase, along with the keys to the apartment. All this is yours if you follow my instructions. M'sieu Wallack has a woman friend — not exactly his mistress, but an occasional lover who is a vice president of his company. Viktor does not believe this is more than a casual *cinq-a-sept* situation, a physical convenience. She is the wife of a an airman who is missing in Vietnam. She is not yet a widow. We have arranged for her to return to America.

"You will fall madly in love with Wallack. It's crucial that he seduces you. You will then persuade him to make the correct decision."

"I don't think I am capable of doing that, Constantin — I'm no actress. I am not deceitful, and I do not throw myself at men. I cannot do it, Constantin. Please don't ask me to do it."

"Janifer," he said softly as he rubbed the scratch on his face. "Remember, I know what you can do. You know what you can do. You are exchanging one or two nights of pleasure or synthetic ecstasy for one million dollars American."

Jennifer let his words sink in and she swallowed hard. "That's a lot of money, Constantin. But I still don't believe I can do it."

"Come, Janifer, now is not the time to haggle. Name your price."

For a long time there was a silence. "If I agree to do it, it will not be for money. That I cannot accept. What I desire is my freedom. I don't want you to touch me anymore, Constantin."

His hand lashed out across her face, knocking her off the chair. *"Pardon!* I must not lose control of my temper, Janifer. For a a few thousand francs, I can have a more beautiful woman than you do this minor job for me. And she would be more exciting in bed. I selected you, Janifer, from my own family — to help me with this small undertaking. Don't be ungrateful."

"All right. You may have your freedom. Keep the clothes which were made for you — and take the apartment. All this to confirm that Xynatron will acquire Med-Pharm/Rainbow."

* * *

Jennifer scrunched herself onto the corner of the rear seat as the car continued its journey to Chamonix. She could not forget her promise to go through with Kaluste's orders, and she could not stop the tears streaming down her face. To herself, she said, "I am a grown woman and I can't stop crying." Kaluste paid no attention to her as he buried his head in a document, the small reading lamp pouring a stream of light onto the pages. She realized by now that to Kaluste, everything was a matter of orders. He had a thought or a wish, and it was carried out with dispatch, no questions asked.

She opened her purse to take out a handkerchief and something fell to the floor. It was a small jeweler's box where she kept a pair of very special earrings. Opening it, she looked at the two gold Phi Beta Kappa keys attached to earring posts. She realized she hadn't worn them in two years because Kaluste had insisted that she wear emerald earrings. On impulse, she removed not only the emerald earrings, but the ten-carat emerald ring and her Victorian emerald and pearl necklace — all of which she dumped unceremoniously into her bag.

Slowly and deliberately, she put the two gold earrings into her ears and felt as if this simple act was going to change the future events of her life. One of the Phi Beta Kappa keys she had earned herself; the other had been given to her by a tall, skinny, shy boy named Ira Oppenheimer.

Her thoughts went back to her last months at college. She and Ira took some of the same classes. They chatted occasionally but were not close friends. He probably had the best brain in the school. She recalled how they had become friends. One day he had come up to her in the cafeteria and asked if he could speak to her privately. He was so nervous that she thought he would drop his sandwich and spill his coffee.

"Is it okay if we eat first?" she asked.

"Sure."

They sat down together. Ira was so bashful that Jennifer found him a refreshing change from most of the men on campus came on very strong. She knew that Ira was premed, was already accepted at five of the best medical schools in the country.

"Where will you go, Ira?"

"Probably Johns Hopkins."

"Not Harvard?"

"Well, I'm interested in cancer research. Ever since I won the Westinghouse scholarship which paid for my college, I've continued my work on genetic studies and cancer. At Hopkins I can get into an M.D.-Ph.D., program, so I will be a medical doctor and a research scientist at the same time."

"You'll never make much in research."

"That's what my mother says. But research has put me through school. You see, I can't always take, I want to give something back. Besides, I love the work."

"Can we talk here, or do you still want to see me in private?" Ira began to blush. She felt for him. This was the strangest man-woman encounter Jennifer had ever experienced. It was charming. He had no double entendres about her big boobs, no seduction line.

"Maybe we should skip it, Ginger. It was a stupid idea in the first place."

"What was?"

"It's not worth repeating."

"Ira — tell me."

"I better not."

She looked at him closely. "Look, Ira, if I scream 'rape,' the whole football team sitting in that corner will come roaring over here and turn you into raw hamburger. So you may as well tell me what you wanted to say."

"I'm too embarrassed and ashamed."

"I won't scream if you tell me."

"Honest?"

"Honest."

"Other than studying, my only interest on campus is golf. I don't date. So it's golf, reading, or study."

"No girlfriend?"

"No. I have no money."

"Do you think a girl goes out with a boy because he has money?"

"Ginger, *you* answer that."

She thought for a moment. "Well, I guess some girls go to college to get married. Okay, I take back that question, but there are lots of girls who like men just as they are. I still say money isn't everything."

"That's what I tell my mother."

Jennifer laughed. More and more she was beginning to like the young man with the unkempt dark hair and slender frame and wondered what great things the world was expecting from him. "So, will you tell me what you were going to ask me?"

"I am being given the top science award by the National Honor Society, and I'm supposed to bring a date. I thought about turning it down, but I need the money to help get me through med school. Ginger, you're the only girl I know who isn't going steady. I was wondering —"

"If I would go to the dinner with you?"

He looked at her and nodded.

"Of course I'll go with you, Ira."

The formal dinner was a huge success. Ira wore a borrowed tuxedo that was too big for him. He didn't dance well, but made up for it with his enthusiasm, so she spent most of the time rubbing her injured feet. Ira was honored with a gold medal from the honor society as well as a grant of $3,500 a year for every year he spent at graduate school. Jennifer, a celebrity in her own right as Homecoming Queen and a Phi Beta Kappa, quickly realized that there was a difference in the ways people respected you. The honor society was aching to attach itself to this penniless boy, so it could say it played a vital role in molding a young man whom it expected to win a Nobel Prize one day.

Both Jennifer and Ira had drunk more wine than they should have. They took a taxi to Jennifer's tiny apartment. She invited him in. He blushed as she grabbed his loose jacket and yanked him in. She took off her shoes and said, "You mangled my feet, O Nobel Prize winner — now figure some way to make them better. They laughed so hard that they fell down on the couch. Jennifer got up and, on impulse, removed her shoes and dress. She wore no stockings — only her bra and panties. While she felt coquettish she wasn't prudish. Besides, Ira was so painfully shy that somehow she felt the compulsion to shock him.

But Ira had fallen asleep on the floor. She shook him, but he slept on. She weaved her way to the bathroom and filled up a pitcher of water, returned, and poured the water all over him. He awoke with a start, stared at her in her underwear, and shrank away.

"What's the matter, Ira?"

Ira didn't reply. He stood on one foot and then on another, averting his eyes from her voluptuous young body, trying desperately not to stare at her overflowing breasts.

"Shame on you, Ira! Haven't you ever seen a girl in panties and bra? Are you still a virgin?"

"Jennifer, don't make fun of me — please," he begged. "I'm drunk. If I stay any longer I can't . . . can't be expected to remain a genitalman" — he gasped — "I mean, a gentleman. You're too desirable. You're too nice for what might happen. I — I would like to thank you for being so nice to me by going with me to the dinner.

"I want to give you a gift that is very precious to me." He held out his hand and gave her his Phi Beta Kappa key. "You are truly a beautiful woman. Inside and out, Ginger. I don't have anything else that I can give you that means so much to me. I want you to have it. Maybe you can have a pair of earrings made and be the only lady in the world with Phi Beta Kappa earrings."

Jennifer felt tears running down her cheeks. "Ira, *I'm* the one who was honored to go out with you, but I can't accept such a wonderful gift."

"Sure you can. You've given me confidence and self-respect, and a lot of lots of self-esteem. I would trade that for forty dollars worth of gold anytime." He reached for the doorknob.

"Ira, your clothes are wet. You can't go out that way."

She helped him remove his drenched jacket, black tie, and shirt, and saw that despite his slim body, he was well muscled. She rubbed her hand over his chest and he blushed.

"Ira, I have a present for you, too. "She undid her bra and he stood there so immobile that Jennifer thought he might faint. Instead, he said, "My God, Ginger."

They made love all night. Even with Jennifer's limited experience, to her surprise Ira turned out to be a passionate young man. The next morning Ira was a different man. He was talkative, witty, and charming. She pressed his pants and jacket so that he would be presentable. Finally she made toast and coffee before sending him on his way.

"I think I love you, Ginger."

"No, Ira, it's traditional that you love the first person you sleep with. Don't confuse sex with love. I never really expected to go to bed with you. But you are a brilliant guy, and you have a long way to go and worlds to conquer. You gave me your most precious gift — your Phi Bet key. What you gave me was a part of yourself. I wanted to give you a part of me. We will always be good friends, Ira. I expect great things of you."

Jennifer grabbed him and gave him a final kiss. She wiped a tear from his eye and thanked him again for the key.

Later that day, she thought of another way of helping Ira. It was four more months to graduation day and Ira was obviouly still broke, but there was no reason why he should be sex-starved. She thought about it carefully and selected a cheerleader who was not only famous for her conquests, but was also the biggest gossip on campus. She tracked her down the next day and girl-to-girl told her that if she promised not to repeat it to a soul, she would tell her who was the greatest lover on campus. The girl crossed her heart. Then Jennifer confessed that it was Ira Oppenheimer, the science wizard.

"Did he invent something new in the lab?"

"That's probably it," Jennifer said.

How long ago? Four, five years? Where did the years go? Ira had been only the second man in her bed. The first had been a track star.

"What did you say?" Constanin asked.

"I didn't realize I was talking aloud. I said I feel like I'm in a soap opera."

"What kind of opera is that?"

She waved her hand and smiled. He returned her smile and went back to his work. Around five in the afternoon, Gaston pulled into a gas station somewhere between Geneva and Chamonix. A Geneva taxi, whose usual run was fifty-six miles to Chamonix, was waiting. It must have been hired earlier by a Kaluste associate. Gaston and the taxi driver transferred Jennifer's three pieces of luggage and skis to the taxi. Gaston insisted on carrying her accessory case, and, as Jennifer entered the taxi, Gaston also handed her a slim leather briefcase. She glanced at Kaluste, and he nodded.

Unexpectedly, Gaston leaned into the car and whispered, "I am in your debt, madame. If I can ever be of service — " His voice trailed off, and he stepped back awkwardly and returned to the Mercedes. Jennifer knew they would continue on to Kaluste's chalet at Avoriaz, thirty-four miles from Geneva. He had never taken her to the chalet, but he had flaunted the fact that, on several occasions, he had taken world famous movie-stars there. The columnists reported that each star had come away with an exquisite piece of emerald jewelry.

Avoriaz is a glamorous ski resort started by a shrewd real estate operator and Jean Vuarnet, the French ski champion. The resort is reachable only by cable car, then one travels by sleighs drawn by horses or reindeer. It is the favorite resort of film people the world over, and Kaluste enjoyed being seen there with glamorous women. He frequently threw lavish parties for as many as fifty guests, usually directors, writers, and film stars. It was rumored more than once that he invested in films. For the film stars, this made their association with Kaluste all the more agreeable.

When the taxi pulled away from the gas station, the driver said, "Madame, my name is Gaspar. I am your driver to Chamonix. You will not *regard* Mont Blanc this night because of fog. And there is no moon. You are to stay at le Carlton-Symond. *Tres bon, madame.*"

Jennifer began to speak to him in rapid French to save him from the strain of speaking English. Then she asked if he had a lamp so she could read. He told her where it was. "Many travelers are businessmen who are not interested in beauty," he said.

Jennifer switched on the light and opened the briefcase. There were several brown envelopes. One was crammed with a variety of currencies — French, Swiss, American, and Italian — probably $1,000 in each denomination. She then recalled that the ski runs at Chamonix ran down to Switzerland, France, and Italy. There was a packet of American Express traveler's checks in another envelope, all in $100 denominations. Without counting it, she estimated that there was an additional $10,000. The third envelope contained a typewritten agenda:

1. Reservation at Carlton-Symond for two weeks, prepaid.
2. Peter Wallack, chairman of Med-Pharm/Rainbow.
3. Competitor, Tompion International.
4. Attached is phone number at Avioraz should you discover that someone from Tompion is present.
5. Viktor will be at Les Charmoz, a small hotel near the Brevant lifts. He will be nearby if you need him. It is very important that you not be seen with him. Telephone only.
6. The key to your apartment in Paris is in a separate envelope with the address and the papers of ownership.
7. All your belongings have been transported there.
8. A new BMW sedan will be waiting for you in the garage. The papers of ownership are in a separate envelope.
9. Paid receipts from Cartier for all jewelry you have received as gifts.
10. Your passport is in a separate billfold and stamped Geneva Airport this day.

11. Return flight ticket from Geneva to Paris is in separate envelope.
12. Continue to use your married name. You are a widow.
13. Viktor will advise you on which slope meeting is arranged. Viktor's name is spelled Kryszkowski.
14. If you cannot make contact with Viktor, visit Le Pele-Club. Near waterwheel ask for Alise. She will have a message.
15. *Bonne Chance.*

There it was, planned like a battle. Jennifer put everything in the briefcase and turned off the light. As the taxi sped toward Chamonix, she noticed high snowbanks on either side of the highway. Twice Gaspar stopped to stretch his legs, offering her a cup and his thermos of coffee. It was thick and black and beautiful. Later she fell asleep as the car wound its 3,500 feet up the mountain, into the ten mile Alpine valley in which Chamonix nestled. On her lap was a John D. MacDonald mystery.

CHAPTER

NINE

AFTER checking into the Carlton-Symond, Jennifer did not feel like mingling with the other guests in the hotel lobby. Instead, she ordered a steak sandwich and tea sent to her room. After settling in and eating, she read more of MacDonald's lady-in-distress asking Travis McGee for help. "Where is Travis McGee when I need him?" she asked aloud.

The room was warm, but the wailing wind outside gave her a chilly feeling. She took a hot bath. The soaking made the bite marks less painful. She was beginning to worry about her agreement with Kaluste. No matter how many ways she went over it, she could find no way out. She was trapped. Following through with the plan was her only chance of escape. He had the money and the power to do anything he pleased — and to get away with it. She had no resources other than a pretty face and intelligence. They weren't enough.

When she awoke the following morning, Jennifer discovered that she had slept for ten hours. In black Bogner ski pants and a black cashmere turtleneck, her hair tied in the back with a simple green velvet ribbon, Jennifer went to the dining room. Most skiers were already on the slopes. The dining room was populated by nonskiing wives, small children, and the victims of skiing accidents — sporting Ace bandages or plaster casts. Concerned that she was under scrutiny by a Kaluste agent, Jennifer hurried through orange juice, croissants, and *cafe au lait,* attracting appreciative stares from two men with leg casts. By the time she finished, she had not been approached by anyone, nor had she heard from Viktor. As discreetly as she could, she surveyed the room, but didn't see anyone who matched the description of Wallack.

Back in her room, she checked through her ski equipment. While she recognized that she was only an intermediate skier, she had skied Aspen and Cortina. Yet she knew she was not up to anything really difficult. She checked out her new red Raichle Molitor RX HOT boots with the flex ribs. They fit superbly. Her Rossignol skis with Salomon bindings were perfectly adjusted to her boots.

Jennifer had been supplied with long silk underwear. It would prove invaluable on a cold and blustery day. She remembered her grandfather talking about red flannels, his long underwear for cold weather. He wore them as a cowboy riding in the Texas Panhandle.

What she really needed was a new pair of ski goggles and windburn cream. Jennifer decided to browse in the ski shop. She would also check out the ski conditions, the trail ratings and the latest fashions in Chamonix. Sunday was also a good day to join some practice ski sessions offered to new arrivals by the hotel. It would help her get back her ski legs.

When she checked the hotel desk, there was a message waiting for her. She tucked it into her purse. Jennifer located the ski shop, and with the aid of a solicitous salesman with a pronounced widow's peak, a thin face, and wandering hands, she found a pair of goggles with excellent lenses. While fitting them for her, he managed to pinch her on the rear, fondle her breasts, and blow in her ear. She resented his crude behaviour but admired his skill. With her elbow extended, Jennifer turned quickly from the mirror, elbowing the salesman in the eye. *"Pardon, monsieur, un accident."* She paid for her purchases and left.

The *pistes* at Chamonix extended from 6,500 feet at Les Houches, the best place to ski on a windy day because the trails hugged the forest, to Aiguille du Midi, which started on a glacier on the Italian side of Mont Blanc. Le Brevant was the toughest run, but adjacent to it was another slope for intermediate skiers.

Back in her room Jennifer unfolded the letter. She discovered that her schedule had already been arranged. The note from Viktor was written in block letters:

RENDEZVOUS: LES HOUCHES
LUNDI — 10:00 A.M.

A map indicated the exact spot, partway down the trail. She got a bus schedule from the concierge and planned to arrive early. The tension was beginning get on her nerves, and she was restless. For a while she considered taking the first plane to the States, but she feared Kaluste. He would never let her leave alive.

That afternoon, Jennifer joined the hotel group for ski orientation on an easy slope near town. The sun shone on the grandeur of Mont Blanc, and she enjoyed herself. By the time she returned to the hotel, her cheeks were rosy.

At dinner she had to restrain a fierce appetite. Weight conscious from her modeling days, she ate no bread but savaged a bowl of hot, clear soup, rare roast beef with a baked potato, a small salad and an apple for dessert. At a nearby table, a group of Americans — one woman and four men — were involved in a deep conversation. Though Jennifer couldn't be certain, it was probably the group she had been sent to meet. The woman was chic and beautiful and looked like a very positive no-nonsense lady. Next to her a tall man in a seedy sports jacket was waving a pipe and talking.

Not wishing to attract undue attention to herself, Jennifer signed for her meal and left. From the concierge she purchased a copy of the *International Herald Tribune* to catch up on news from America, and *Paris Match*. It had been the first magazine to use her picture on the cover, and she felt an innate loyalty to it.

Jennifer knew from past experience that it was a good idea to carry one or two chocolate bars for quick nourishment, so she added two Toblerones to her purchase. The weather forecast was for a sunny day, but the temperature would stay in the low teens with a 15 m.p.h. wind. The brochure also indicated that the Les Houches trails were wind protected.

Jennifer went back to her room and into bed. Though she was exhausted, she was having difficulty falling asleep. Her conscience was gnawing away at her. She wished she had a sleeping pill and was restless until she remembered the Valium tablets prescribed for her after Jean-Paul's death. She rummaged through her tool kit and found several yellow 5 mg tablets. She swallowed one with water, then rang the switchboard operator for a 7:00 A.M. wake-up call. Fifteen minutes later, she was asleep.

* * *

At the top of the mountain the powdered snow reflected the sun into a dazzling glare. There were approximately a dozen people milling about the intermediate trail, but no Viktor. Jennifer inserted the darkest filters into her goggles and awaited her turn to set out down the trail. After double-checking her bindings and the retaining strap, Jennifer pushed off. She proceeded cautiously.

As her confidence grew, she proceeded to ski faster. About fifteen minutes down the trail she spotted a barely perceptible white figure at the rendezvous. It was Viktor. He waved his ski pole, motioning her to his side.

Close up, she recognized his white camouflage pants, jacket and hood as clothing for Alpine ski troops. At 6'2" with broad, muscular shoulders and a swarthy complexion Viktor looked formidable. He was sometimes referred to as The Baron, but Jennifer never warmed up to his detached manner and icy good looks. At dinners he seldom spoke to her or any other guest, but hovered around Kaluste. Perhaps he was, as Kaluste said, a business associate. To Jennifer he was Kaluste's alter ego and personal bodyguard.

As she stood next to him, Viktor said, "Peter Wallack is scheduled to ski down this trail in about" — he paused to look at his watch — "five minutes. His friends are practicing on easier slopes. Wallack is a first-rate skier and will move quickly, so I will go back up about 250 meters. When I give you the signal with my pole" — he raised it over his head — "it means he is coming down the trail. You ski ahead of him for a minute, then fall down."

Viktor looked down at Jennifer's boots and cursed, *"Merdre! Your left binding is not clamped properly. You will twist your ankle. Quelle stupidite! Don't you know anything?"* As Jennifer leaned over to examine her binding, Victor drew closer. *"Vite! Vite! I shall assist. Watch the trail."*

He unfastened his skis, bent down beside her, and, while pretending to adjust the binding on her left boot, loosened it. Unaware, Jennifer kept her eyes on the trail.

Without another word, Viktor clamped on his skis and hurried back up the slope. Jennifer was looking around the mountain when suddenly she heard a piercing whistle. She looked up and saw Viktor wave his pole. Then he disappeared as if by magic..

Jennifer pushed forward to gain momentum and flew down the trail. It was exhilarating. She hadn't figured out how to fall in order to attract Wallack's attention.

Jennifer was accelerating when she reached a bend in the trail. She leaned to her right. Suddenly her left boot jumped out of its binding. As though she were watching someone else in slow motion, Jennifer began to cartwheel, her loose left ski flopping against her boot, held by the retaining strap. It was only a matter of seconds, yet the fall seemed endless. She felt a wrenching in her knee as she came to rest spread-eagled in a snowbank.

Jennifer wasn't sure what happened next. There was a sharp pain in her head, but she was more worried about her knee. And she was furious with Viktor. He hadn't adjusted the binding, he had unfastened it. She began to curse Viktor and Kaluste. She forced herself to calm down. She had to concentrate on getting down the mountain. First she had to get the ski on. Her left knee was on fire, but she put the boot into the binding gingerly, adjusted it, and clamped it into place. With the aid of her poles, she brought both legs together and lifted herself upright. It was a painful ordeal.

She tried hopping forward on one ski, but was hampered by the agony in her knee. It was impossible to move on one leg. Then she made a bold attempt to stand on her injured leg. The pain was so excruciating that she screamed and collapsed on the trail. She was unconscious for several seconds, coming to just as a shower of snow sprayed her face.

In high school French, a man's voice asked, *"Est vous tombé malade?"*

Her face, contorted with pain, she gasped, "I speak English — I hurt my knee. Oh, God! It may be broken!"

"Can you stand on it?"

"No — I tried but it's too painful."

"I'll ski back up — they have toboggans up there. Or I could race downhill and have them radio for a 'copter."

"Don't leave me — I'll freeze to death."

"It's fifteen minutes to the bottom leg of this trail. The fastest way down is in tandem. I've done it before — it's like a three-legged race."

"I — I don't think I can make it."

"Lady, even with a broken leg you can make it — we'll go slowly — but you must have the guts to try. We'll also flag the next skier who comes by and have him go for help. Meanwhile, my way is the fastest way down."

Without waiting for an answer, he moved behind her, grabbed her under the armpits, and helped her to her feet. Staying behind her, he kept his arms around her waist, gripping his poles so they extended like the hands of a clock at twenty past eight. He said, "Keep your skis together so my skis are outside yours. Then we'll ski down together slowly. Keep your weight off the injured leg."

The pain had wiped Kaluste from her mind. All she wanted was to survive the trip down. Jennifer hadn't gotten a good close look at rescuer but she was almost sure it was Wallack. Her one glimpse told her he was a tall American wearing a ski outfit that didn't match. He held on to her firmly as she leaned back against him, her right ski firmly on the ground while she dragged her left leg gingerly. Balanced now with her weight on the right ski, they pushed off and let gravity do the rest. His grip on her remained firm as he maneuvered down the trail. From time to time, he used a pole to maintain balance. Once he released one arm from her waist to use his pole to avoid a mogul. Slowly but surely, they began to descend.

They took two rest stops, but he remained behind her to help her stay upright. It was an effort for Jennifer. They each ate one of her chocolate bars. It took an hour to reach the plateau. There he located a rescue toboggan and put Jennifer on it. Then it was a milk run to the bottom. The skier whom they had asked for help had informed the infirmary. An intern with a medical crest on his parka, was waiting. He removed her boot. She moaned when he

tested her knee. He suggested she go by ambulance to the infirmary.

"Take me to my hotel," said Jennifer. "I'll call a doctor from
there."

Despite her mild protests, Wallack accompanied her in the
ambulance. Once in her room, he helped her onto the bed. "I'm
burning up," Jennifer said. "Will you help take off my ski clothes?"

With boots, ski pants, jacket, and sweater off, Jennifer was
clad only in her long silk ski underwear. He removed her socks
carefully and examined the knee which was swollen to twice its
normal size. "It look's like you've been kicked by a mule. Doctors
recommend ice compresses to reduce swelling." He phoned the
concierge and asked him to track down a doctor. He also ordered
ice. Only after she removed her dark goggles and he took his first
good look at her was there a sharp intake of his breath.

CHAPTER

TEN

"**M**Y NAME is Jennifer Joubert," she said holding out her hand. Peter shook it. Her face was pale and he knew she was in pain.

"You sound American, but your name is French. Is that your married name?"

"Yes, my husband was a race-car driver. He was killed at Le Mans two years ago."

There was an awkward silence that was broken by a knock at the door. As is customary in Europe, the waiter let himself into the room with a master key and brought in a bucket of ice. Peter tipped him and ordered a bottle of Napoleon brandy. He quickly dumped some ice cubes in a towel, folded it, and wrapped it around her knee. When the shock of the freezing ice penetrated to her knee, she shuddered.

He saw the anguish on her face, lifted the ice pack for temporary relief, then replaced it. He knew that soon numbness would set in and she would be able to tolerate the chill. To make her more comfortable he placed a pillow under her knee to keep bent slightly. When he looked up to see if she was comfortable, he got a full view of the shapely contours that filled out the silk underwear.

Jennifer grimaced, adjusted her position on the bed, and smiled with relief. "I'm fine now. I'm comfortable." She stretched out her hand and placed it on his. "You've been very kind to me, and I don't even know your name."

"Peter Wallack."

"Thanks for your help, Peter Wallack." Suddenly she groaned. "I have a cramp in my right calf."

Peter grabbed the calf in his right hand, dug his fingers into the muscle, and squeezed. "Try to relax," he said as he began to knead the muscle. "It must have tightened up on the way down."

As quickly as the cramp came on, it subsided. "Thanks, Peter, that's better."

His gentleness and genuine concern made her wish that it was a more honest encounter. She was a sucker for a tall, boyish-looking, brainy man with a gentle nature and a warm disposition.

He lifted the ice pack and looked at the knee. The swelling had started to subside. He placed the ice back on her knee. She seemed relaxed as she closed her eyes. Feeling awkward, with nothing more to do than stare at this beautiful invalid, Wallack ran his hands through his unkempt hair, took out his pipe, and wandered around the room. He looked out the window, then returned to Jennifer, who had been watching him. Spotting the MacDonald mystery, he said, "I never seem to have the time to read fiction — except for the Sunday comics. I wouldn't even admit that, but since Einstein confessed to being a fan of Sunday comics, I feel free to make the same admission."

To himself Peter wondered why he was making such a dumb comment. This exciting and intelligent woman was disturbing him. His quandary came from his loyalty and friendship with Sidney. Suddenly he felt guilty. Now he was wondering whether he could be mistaken about this reddish blonde with the lush body who seemed to be sending him intimate signals. Maybe he was misinterpreting gratitude as something else? Or maybe it was wishful thinking. Whatever it was, he couldn't take his eyes off her.

Jennifer, in turn, inspected the tall, shy man whose demeanor was reminiscent of the reluctant-hero roles played by Jimmy Stewart. He was dressed in ill-fitting old ski clothes. The contrived meeting on the mountain trail had worked all too well. She had actually pulled it off. If it weren't for her twisted knee, the

whole thing would be corny. Yet, if Peter Wallack hadn't brought
her down, she might possibly have remained frozen and forgotten
on the mountain.

There was a knock on he door as the waiter reentered,
placed a tray containing the brandy and four glasses on the table,
waited for his tip, and left. Peter opened the bottle and poured an
inch of brandy into each glass.

He sat down beside her, handed her a glass, and said,
"Guaranteed to ease the pain."

They sipped their brandies and Jennifer said, "I never
thanked you properly. I could have been stuck up there and frozen
to death." More by impulsive than contrivance,, she put down her
glass, put her hands behind his head, pulled him down, and
kissed him on the lips.

It was a friendly kiss, but she saw he was flustered. Impishly
she kept her hands laced behind his head. Peter wondered
whether it was an invitation. He saw that her eyes were moist and
thought it was because of the pain in her knee. His heart went out
to her. He put down his drink, leaned down so that their brandied
lips met. It was a long kiss. Her open mouth was open, and the
sensual thrill sent electricity through him. Being pressed against
her enticing body aroused him even more. When he raised his
head to look into her face, her hair was spread on the pillow and
she was crying. His right thumb wiped away her tears. Then he
noticed her earrings. He lifted one for a closer look, then turned
her head gently and saw the second one.

"Yours?"

"One is. The other is a gift from a friend."

"I never met a girl who's a Phi Beta Kappa I didn't like."
Before Jennifer could answer, there was a knock on the door. Peter
opened the door to admit the doctor, a medium-sized man in his

sixties with horn-rimmed glasses sporting a designer ski jacket.

An expert in ski injuries, his inspection was swift and precise. "There is no break. It appears you have twisted your knee or you have been hit on the knee — perhaps with your own ski? Continue with the ice to keep down the swelling. Stay in bed one day. I shall come tomorrow. Try to stand several minutes each hour for the circulation. Change body position in bed frequently. Here is a prescription for painkillers. I give you one now."

He went to the sink and returned with half a glass of water and a pill. "If the swelling is down by Wednesday I shall wrap it with elastic bandages for comfort. I shall send crutches, but practice carefully before you emerge from the room." The doctor bowed, put on his ski cap, and left without further ceremony.

"Will you help me stand on my feet?"

"Do you think it wise?"

"Yes."

Peter sighed, removed the ice pack, and helped Jennifer swing around so that her legs dangled just above the floor. She placed one arm around his waist and lowered her right foot onto the ground, keeping her left just off the floor.

"That doesn't look comfortable," Peter said. "Why not let me balance you?"

She shifted, placed her right arm on his shoulder, and leaned against him. Then he was forced to put his arm around her waist. It was quickly becoming a chess game with unexpected moves. She turned to face him, so he put both his arms around her waist. The embrace was so close that she could feel his heart beat.

They clung together on three legs, their hearts pounding against each other, his face resting against the top of her head. As they embraced, the intimacy excited her, too. "Peter," she said, "you're much too dangerous to have around."

She touched her left foot to the floor and tested it. It was painful, but now it could bear her weight. Out of relief, Jennifer laughed for the first time. "I can stand. I guess the doctor was right, it isn't broken." Then she sagged in his arms as he held her more tightly. "Peter, the pill is making me sleepy. Please help me back to bed."

Lifting her onto the bed, Peter set her down gently and raised her injured leg carefully. Then he repacked the ice around her knee. The top button of her underwear had come undone, revealing her cleavage. He breathed heavily, buttoned it, kissed her on the mouth, and left. He was so turned on that he felt he was in danger of losing his self-control. He wanted nothing to spoil the chance of a lasting relationship. Suddenly a lifetime with this woman was something he wanted more than anything else in the world.

By the time he reached his room, it was 1:30 P.M. He wasn't hungry, so he decided to skip lunch and do some thinking. While he couldn't get Jennifer out of his mind, he nevertheless forced himself to review the information on the two companies so eager to acquire his. There were typewritten notes covered with his notations strewn around the room.

Xynatron was offering $40,000,000 in a cash buyout — 10 times the company's $4,000,000 in earnings after taxes. Because of the tax ramificatons, the first payment would be an immediate 29 percent down. The remainder was to be made in equal payments over five years, with the unpaid balance drawing daily interest at the prime rate in New York. All officers of the company would get three-year contracts, with the exception of the chairman who would receive a five-year contract plus a sweetener: an annual 5% bonus on all gross business above current sales. Peter's accountants had suggested that he demand that enough money and/or securities be put in escrow to guarantee the unpaid balance. Xynatron agreed.

The Tompion offer was different: a merger with a tax-free exchange of stock. All of Med-Pharm/Rainbow stock for $22 million in Tompion common stock, using the closing stock price on the day of the merger. In additon, a special issue of convertible preferred stock with a value of $14 million would be created and placed in trust for Peter's brother's widow and children. The preferred stock, with higher dividends, would guarantee $440,000 a year to his sister-in-law and the children, while the stock had a chance to appreciate as Tompion grew.

Peter could not concentrate. His mind was wandering. The white-skinned beauty with the red-blond-hair and breathtaking body was making him tremble. Because he could not concentrate, he began to pace the room. It didn't help. He decided to cool off with a walk. He put on his walking boots and ski jacket and left the hotel, heading toward town. He tried to keep his mind blank and not think, but that proved impossible. Peter was not aware of the man in a gray parka following him. He was unaware of anything. The wind picked up, so he put the hood over his head.

He walked aimlessly for miles. When it was 3:00, he started back to the hotel. Along the way, he noticed a candy shop and he bought the largest box of chocolates available.

As Peter entered the hotel lobby, his four executives greeted him jovially. "This — ah, candy," said Peter. "It's for a — for a girl I met on the slopes."

"So soon?"

"That's quick work, Peter."

"She had a nasty fall. I helped her."

"How convenient," Sidney said.

"She wrenched her knee. I helped her down the mountain," he said, then added, "and she's beautiful."

"I want to meet her," said Warren Furillo, the executive vice president of Rainbow. They trooped up to Jennifer's room. Then Sidney Howe was paged to pick up a cablegram at the concierge's desk. Sidney got the message and hurried to join the group. Peter knocked on her door.

"It's open. Come in."

They marched in and Sidney noticed Jennifer's beauty immediately. She was dressed in Chinese silk pajamas. A pair of crutches lay on the bed. Peter noted that the pyjamas were not as sexy as her long underwear. Her left leg was propped on a pillow. The knee was wrapped in the towel, but the ice had melted. "Would you mind getting some ice, Peter? I'm not too good on crutches."

'Sure," he said. "Meanwhile, everybody, this is Jennifer Joubert of Dallas, Paris, and Chamonix. Introduce yourselves."

Max Butterworth, Warren Furillo, James Lester, and Sidney said hello. While the men stared at Jennifer, Sidney decided to look at the knee as Peter returned with the ice. Sidney saw the garish blue color where the blood vessels had broken and where it had swelled despite the ice. Any reservations Sidney had had disappeared.

Soon they were drinking brandy, munching chocolates, and bantering with Jennifer as though she were an old friend. It was plain that she had eyes only for Peter. She seemed wary of Sidney.

"Maybe," thought Sidney, "Peter has lucked into a good thing. She obviously adores him. But she's a bit young. Probably mid-twenties. Father fixation, perhaps? Might be good for him."

Then she opened the cablegram. As she read, her face turned pale. Her secretary had forwarded information that Graves Registration in Washington reported the site of a plane crash in Cambodia. The aircraft was the type her husband was on. Personal possessions, a watch and a silver cigarette lighter, had been recovered. The items were being flown into San Francisco, and her presence was requested immediately to help with the identification.

A serious Sidney said loudly, "May I have your attention, please. The Air Force may have found Harry's body, and I have to help with identification. I don't want to spoil your vacation, but I can't stay — I have to fly to San Francisco immediately."

Peter said, "We're sorry, Sid."

"Oh, Sidney!" said Jennifer. "My husband was killed two years ago. I'm so sorry for you. Would you mind leaving, everyone? I want to talk to Sidney alone."

When the men left, the two women looked searchingly at each other. They both burst into tears and held each other, the bond of death and tragedy bringing them close. Each comforted the other.

Jennifer asked, "Is Peter a special friend?"

"He is a bachelor. He is also my employer and my friend — a close personal friend — nothing more. His associates and I are all good friends. We care a lot about Peter. We don't want him to get hurt."

"I would never hurt him. He saved my life. I'd have frozen on that mountain. He reminds me of two people who had a great influence on me. My father — who died when I was ten — a kind, gentle, understanding, beautiful man — and Ira, a young man I knew at the University of Texas — I learned the meaning of honesty and humility from him. Strangely, we had only one date. But it was a wonderful evening. I've never forgotten it. Peter is a lot like Ira. Tall, gangly, his mind's in ten different places, none of which I can reach.

"Ira was like that. While we weren't in love, he brought out all my maternal instincts. He was so eager to give me a present. But he had no money, so he gave me the only thing of value he that he possessed: his Phi Bet key. He knew that with mine they would make unusual earrings."

For a while nothing was said. Sidney saw Jennifer as the ultimate female — Mother Earth — beautiful, warm, voluptuous, and vulnerable. She decided at that second that they could be friends for life. She would be wonderful for Peter — if he married her. The timing was perfect. Sidney bent over and kissed Jennifer's cheek. "Get well soon. As for Peter, I think you're a most unusual lady who arrived at the right time."

Tears were streaming down Jennifer's face after Sidney left. She felt strange because everything she had said to Peter and to Sidney was true. Yet she was doing Kaluste's work. It made her feel sick and cheap inside.

CHAPTER

ELEVEN

BY WEDNESDAY evening, Peter and Jennifer had become inseparable. He went to his room only to sleep, shower, and change clothes. Her room was now filled with flowers and any suitable gift he could find to cheer her up — from giant pandas to books on art and history. Each gift brought Peter the reward of a long kiss.

With Peter's help, Jennifer was walking well on her crutches. He took a proprietary interest in her sorties, escorting her to the local shops, or to the dining room for meals. Med-Pharm meetings were being conducted in Peter's suite, and Jennifer was a welcome addition. Gradually she became an astute participant in the discussions. Scrupulously objective she became the sounding board for anyone interested in scoring a point. Without any guidance on her part, all were leaning heavily in favor of Xynatron because, as Butterworth phrased, it, "Hard cash is better than paper stock. Now is the time for us to cash in."

To see if there was dissent, Peter asked for a vote. He was pleased that all his executives, including himself, were in favor of Xynatron, but it was Furillo who reminded him that Sidney had left her proxy and comments in an envelope. Peter tore it open and read the contents:

I vote for Tompion for the following reasons:

(a) It has shown excellent growth and stability since Admiral Dutton became chairman.

(b) The tax bite on a cash deal is too big even on an extended payout.

(c) We would also be at the mercy of Xynatron. At Tompion we're a major stockholder. Peter and two others will be on the board of Tompion. You would still run Med-Pharm.

(d) Xynatron, a major holding company, is an unknown quantity to me. Too many complex connections, despite excellent public relations and a good Wall Street reputation.

(e) I admire Admiral Dutton.

SIDNEY

Peter knew that Sidney, who was not an operations person, was astute in her evaluations of situations and people. She gave him something to think about. He would consider her comments very carefully in private, but out loud he said, "Looks like Xynatron."

The executives wanted get a good night's rest for an early start on the ski slopes. By 9;00 P.M. Butterworth pulled everyone out for one quick drink at the bar before going to bed, leaving Peter and Jennifer alone.

"I ordered a couple of bottles of Piper Heidsieck to celebrate your decision, Peter," Jennifer said. She pointed to the closet where she had hidden the ice bucket. They toasted Xynatron. Then they drank to each other. In fifteen minutes they had finished one bottle. Peter put down the glass.

"Jennifer. No more drinking for the moment," he said rather mysteriously. "I've considered everything over very carefully, and I've decided I cannot wait any longer. I must conclude my experiment."

"What experiment?"

"I'm a research scientist. I conduct experiments."

"Of course."

"I've been thinking about an article I read recently, and I want to test the idea. Are you game?"

"I don't know what you're talking about."

"Answer the question."

"Sure — but I'm getting a little giddy."

"Giddiness is no problem. I read in a scientific journal that seven is a magical number. My first experiment is to kiss you seven times."

Jennifer looked at him as though he were out of his mind. She considered it for a minute, smiled, then nodded to humor him.

He asked her to sit up on the bed with her back propped against the headboard and her injured left leg extended. She complied. Then he took her head in his hands and turned it and inserted his tongue gently into her left ear, licking it in a slow kiss. An electric shock went through her. She began to shiver.

"That's one," he said. Then he closed her eyes, turned her head, and did the same thing in her right ear. She could not control the sensations flashing through her body.

"Two," he said. Her eyes opened as he straightened her head and lowered his lips to hers gently and put his tongue into her mouth. She felt as though she were melting. Then suddenly her body seemed to have a life of its own. She began writhing in his arms. Jennifer was afire.

"Three."

By the time he released her she was limp. Peter removed Jennifer's sweater, unhooked her bra, and released her beautiful breasts. Jennifer was breathless in anticipation. As Peter lowered his head, she pleaded, "Gently — please."

He was so gentle that she barely knew when he began to breathe on her nipples, like a feather's touch. Jennifer began to shudder. He was kissing her right nipple playfully when he said "Four." Then he moved to her left nipple and said "Five." She was squirming now.

Peter's gentleness made her unable to control herself. Ever so slowly he descended and kissed her stomach.

"Six," he whispered hoarsely.

His tongue felt like ice and fire. She dug her nails into his back. Jennifer was aroused uncontrollably now. She wanted him desperately. With his fingertips, he touched her reddish pubic hair.

"Seven," he whispered as his tongue touched her vulva.

Jennifer screamed.

Time stood still. Jennifer was in a trance. She did not know how long she remained in the throes of ecstasy, her many orgasms bringing her to levels she did not know existed. No man had ever given her such exquisite pleasure.

By the time Peter was in bed beside her, she began living in another world. The nights with her husband and the sporadic and quick encounters with Kaluste were pale experiences. This was love. And this was the man she was to betray.

As time went on, they drank more champagne, bathed each other, and made love until the gray of morning. Half-asleep in her lover's embrace, Jennifer said, "Peter, I have a confession to make."

PART III

CHAPTER

TWELVE

April 1985, Carlyle, Georgia

The ordeal of reliving her dark secret caused Jennifer great pain. She sobbed in red-eyed anguish. Her sorrow deepened the lines on her face. Sidney embraced her and began to rock her back and forth. At the same moment, wild ideas caromed around in Sidney's head.

Aware now of Kaluste's involvement from the very beginning was the final piece of the puzzle that had been in the back of her mind for five years. It was now clear that a Kaluste lieutentant had sent a fake cable to Chamonix so Sidney would fly to San Francisco, only to learn that the Air Force plane mentioned in the wire was a fiction. A call to the Pentagon produced double-talk, so she considered it another military snafu. It never occurred to her to question why she had been tracked down by the U.S. Air Force.

With only a few vacation days left, she had rented a jeep, bought several pairs of shorts and T-shirts, Adidas, some camping equipment, and drove south along the coastal roads at a leisurely pace, camping along the way. She swam in the ocean, flirted with the surf bums, who invited her to fish fries and beer parties. By the following Monday, she had returned to the world of big business.

Now she wondered exactly why Kaluste had manipulated her.

As Jennifer's sobs abated, she sat up, her eyes still red-rimmed and swollen, her face puffy and white. While she wasn't a drinker, Sidney knew there was a time and place for alcohol. She poured a stiff drink for Jennifer and a diluted one for herself. They drank without another word being spoken. Slowly the liquor began to work. Jennifer fell slowly into a fog while Sidney started to think more clearly.

Sidney led Jennifer to the master bedroom and put her to bed. She picked up the clothes that had been thrown on the floor, hanging up Jennifer's dress, placing her shoes on a shelf in the closet, tossing underclothes into the hamper. She kissed Jennifer's cheek, switched off the lights, and left the door open so that the light from the hall shone faintly in the bedroom. Sidney went to the study, curled up her legs under her, her mind racing back to Chamonix and the single event that seemed to have taken control of their lives.

Sidney knew enough about Constantin Kaluste to recall that he had masterminded dozens of international business coups. She also knew that Peter Wallack's death might have been his biggest blunder. It was not disimilar to the events that led to Watergate. If Nixon and his cohorts had just concentrated on getting elected, he'd still be king of the hill.

In the same way Kaluste, unwilling to face defeat, had gone crazy. He had won the takeover battle to acquire Med-Pharm, but to insure against any slipup he maneuvered Jennifer into an affair with Peter Wallack. The one thing that could defeat Kaluste was Jennifer's confession to Peter. It was a surprise that Kaluste never considered.

Now Sidney knew Kaluste's fatal flaw. His ego.

Sidney reviewed the facts Jennifer had revealed. Peter had outlined a game plan which he and Jennifer agreed to. She would confirm to Kaluste that Xynatron had won Med-Pharm. Meanwhile, Peter would return to America and decide what action to take. One thing was certain: Xynatron would never get Med-Pharm/Rainbow. Peter had to devise a plan to deceive Kaluste and free Jennifer of her obligation to him. Peter and Jennifer were in love. She agreed to return to the States and marry him.

Peter's plan worked perfectly. Jennifer, on crutches, went to her new apartment in Paris. Sure that her telephone was tapped, she and Peter had lengthy transatlantic telephone conversations. Any listener would know they were in love. In the conversations about Med-Pharm, Peter would say that he was looking forward to working with Xynatron.

Then Peter introduced his concern about the Defense Department into the conversations, pointing out that the Pentagon would have to approve any merger involving a defense contractor. Not complying would risk the loss of all Med-Pharm's defense contracts.

Peter flew to New York secretly one weekend for a confidential talk with Admiral Dutton. Peter and the Tompion International chairman met for lunch at Lutece. They hit it off immediately. Peter was so excited that he was quite unaware he was dining in one of the finest restaurants in New York. Their second meeting took place Saturday evening at the admiral's town house. Roger Evans, head of Tompion Financial, was there. Peter took a liking to Roger, a man younger than himself, slim and lithe but not quite as tall as Peter.

Peter was waving his pipe around as he spoke, high on Tompion and its future. It was Roger who proposed to the board that Tompion acquire Med-Pharm. In his quiet, understated way, Roger outlined the terms of the acquisition that he and the admiral knew would fly with the board. That evening they made a handshake deal with Peter Wallack for the purchase of Med-Pharm/Rainbow.

Constantin Kaluste was the final order of business. Drawing on his years as director of the CIA, the admiral, with the precision of an old intelligence hand, prepared a scenario for Peter. To rescue Jennifer from Kaluste's clutches, Peter would agree tentatively to Xynatron's terms. He would sign a letter of agreement with Xynatron, issue press releases, and go through the motions of being acquired while the admiral started digging.

It didn't take Dutton's friends at the agency long to find tracks that led from Kaluste to perfectly legitimate but dummy American corporations which were major stockholders of Xynatron, a publicly traded American company. Several major brokerage houses owned Xynatron stock in street names, which was legitimate. Actually, they were fronting for clients: Swiss bank account numbers, ostensibly the accounts of companies in France and Germany. It was possible to trace a direct connection back to Paris, Geneva, and, finally, Kaluste.

When the admiral informed the Defense Department, officials were shocked to learn of the connection. There had never been a hint that Xynatron, traded on the New York Stock Exchange, had dubious foreign connections. The admiral arranged for a series of letters to be exchanged between Med-Pharm/Rainbow and the government. A final official letter was sent to Peter which stated unequivocally that Med-Pharm/Rainbow, a top-level defense-systems supplier, would lose it contracts automatically if it merged with foreign-controlled Xynatron.

At this point, Peter made his calls to Jennifer in Paris. Under the circumstances, Kaluste accepted defeat. For a man who planned his battles like a general, he failed to understand how the U.S. Government could become suspicious of Xynatron. He conducted a thorough investigation of his people, but found no leak in his security system.

At their last meeting at Jennifer's apartment, Kaluste said, "Someday I will own that company. We say *au revoir* for now, Janifer. I shall miss you. Perhaps you will marry a rich American?" He smiled.

Several months later, Jennifer sold her apartment and automobile. She planned to return Kaluste's money, but Peter advised her not to: it might make him suspicious. She kept her wardrobe, which she felt she had earned. She flew to New York and checked into the Plaza where she was married in view of Central Park. Sidney Howe was matron of honor.

CHAPTER

THIRTEEN

SIDNEY was uneasy. Roger Evans's gaze made her nervous. The company jet was on its way back to New York at 450 m.p.h. There were three passengers: Ronald Cohen, Tompion's executive vice president and chief house counsel, Roger Evans, president of Tompion Financial Services, and herself.

While it was company policy to permit no more than two senior executives to fly on the same plane, the admiral waived the rule after hearing Sidney's report. "I want your asses back here — fast!" His order came fifty seconds after Sidney told him that the cause of Peter's death was homicide, not suicide.

Steve Corcoran refused steadfastly to believe that Peter had killed himself. He convinced the sheriff, and then they both convinced the FBI investigators that suicide by nuclear isotopes was highly improbable. With the Nuclear Regulatory Agency's approval, Admiral Dutton assigned two Navy nuclear submarine captains, disciples of Admiral Rickover, for their expert opinions. An autopsy was scheduled on Peter Wallack's radioactive body.

Dr. Russell Sanger made his confidential report to the FBI. The pathologist, dressed in a protective suit, discovered that Peter had died of a brain injury. He had been stabbed by a long, sharp surgical instrument shaped like a steel knitting needle. It had been rammed up through his left nostril into his cerebral cortex, killing him instantly. Bruises on his upper arms indicated that he had been forcibly restrained.

The autopsy, performed under strict regulatory guidelines, was slow and arduous due to the difficult working conditions caused by the radiation. Dr. Sanger's report determined that the nuclear isotopes found in the body had been inserted past Peter's pharynx through his esophagus into his stomach *after* death had occurred. This was indicated by deep cuts and scrapes along the muscular tube that neither bled nor had become inflamed. The autopsy indicated that the isotopes were introduced by a metal or glass tube inserted in Peter's throat and forced into his upper intestines.

Sidney called the admiral immediately.

"Tell no one — including Jennifer," the admiral said.

"Jennifer is in Austin seeing her mother."

"Return with Ron and Roger on the company plane — immediately."

Sidney rounded them up at Med-Pharm headquarters, where they had been completing the official paper work. She relayed the admiral's orders. They gathered their papers and stuffed them into briefcases. All the legal work with the local attorneys had been completed by Ron. Roger had examined the company books and made a spot inspection as a safety precaution. Everything was clean.

Sidney considered Ron a much closer friend than Roger. When she first arrived at Tompion, she and Ron had gone out several times for dinner and theater. While they respected each other and were attracted sexually, Ron preferred the beautiful but empty-headed women who adored him. He had been divorced twice and he admitted openly, "After work, I'm lazy. I refuse to wear out my brain during leisure hours. Work hard, play hard. That's my style."

Once, when they were unusually candid, he caught Sidney off guard. "What do you look for in a man?"

She thought about it for a minute. Men came in assorted sizes and shapes and colors. She didn't think she could describe her ideal man. She thought of her husband who had faded into a memory dressed in Air Force blue. He seemed almost a figment of her imagination. She could hardly remember him. Then she began thinking about all the men she had ever cared about.

"I like a man with a strong character. He should be intelligent without being arrogant, who will love me in a gentle, honest way. He could be short or tall, fat or thin, bald or shaggy. It's his character that counts." They had laughed over her description of her perfect man. Right then they swore to be friends forever, and he promised to find her the perfect man. From time to time, they had dinner or lunch just for good, bright conversation. She never mentioned the fact that he once confessed to liking only empty-headed women.

Roger D. Evans was different. He was an enigma, totally different from any man she had ever known. In her five years at Tompion, they had had very little contact. He went out of his way to avoid speaking to her. He was six feet tall and slim, not as well built as Ron, who was an avid tennis player, pumped iron, and did laps in the swimming pool to keep in shape.

As a psychologist, Sidney still couldn't fathom the man. They had had many conversations, but they all concerned business. Roger Evans had no penchant for small talk. He never chatted with her, never made a single flattering remark about her hair or dress as the other men did. If anything, he was probably the only male executive at Tompion who never made a pass at her. Was that what irked her about him?

Think positively, she thought. In the isolation of the airplane, she found herself wondering why they never were comfortable in each other's company. Both sat on the board of directors. Roger seemed well liked by the other members of the board — all men, except for her. He was polite, rather shy and businesslike. She could not find a single negative characteristic to explain her uneasiness.

What did she know about Roger? He was forty-one years old. She assumed that he was married. He had joined Tompion in 1975, five years before she had. Admiral Dutton brought him in to take over a faltering financial division doing about $100 million in business and losing $1 million a year. Soon after joining Tompion, she heard stories about Roger Evans. The admiral had said to Roger, "Make or break Tompion Financial — I won't tolerate a one-percent loss in this division."

No one ever understood why Evans was selected for the job, but he built the division into a $2 billion business, and it became the most profitable subsidiary of the conglomerate. He ran a lean division.

Roger was a loner. His only close friends were the admiral, Ron, and Thomas Grosso, who ran the insurance and real estate division. Sidney came to this conclusion because they were the only people he saw frequently.

She watched Evans remove his horn rimmed glasses and tuck them into the breast pocket of his jacket. His right fingers rubbed his neck along the furrow of a deep scar. He stretched his legs, clasped his hands in front of him, closed his eyes, and went to sleep. A wisp of light brown hair fell over his face, and the lines on his forehead disappeared as sleep overtook him. Asleep, he appeared younger.

Sidney turned to look at Ron, only to find him watching her. She smiled and debated whether to go over and chat with him about the strange personality of Roger Evans, but he appeared to be distracted. She broke off eye contact and look at her watch, a beautiful gold Piaget with a dial and hands so small that they were difficult to read. They would arrive at La Guardia in forty-five minutes. Listening to to the hypnotic drone of the jet engines, her mind turned to Peter's murder and Jennifer's story about Kaluste.

She began to feel drowsy, closed her eyes, and drifted off.

Suddenly she was awaken by a scream. Roger was shriek-ing, straining against his seat belt, and Ron was slapping his face. Then Ron fell to his knees, trying to force Roger back against the seat. Uncertain what was going on, Sidney unfastened her seat belt and went forward to help. Just as she reached Roger, he let out another animal shriek that was so frightening it made her jump away. Ron, perspiring from the exertion of trying to restrain Roger, managed to pull out a small syringe from a pen holder and plunge it through Roger's jacket and into his arm. Roger's eyes were wild and confused, his face a sweaty mask of terror. He struggled madly against the restraint of the seat belt. Suddenly he slumped forward, unconscious and shivering.

"Get a blanket!" Ron ordered. Sidney searched the overhead compartments until she found one and then covered him up. She had never witnessed an episode of stress and trauma of such magnitude, including her clinical work at the hospital. Roger finally went into a deep sleep. Ron found a towel and began to wipe Roger's face gently. Sidney had never seen one man show so much affection for another. It did not strike her as effeminate in any way. Finally Ron sat down. His hands were shaking.

"What was that all about?" Sidney asked.

"I prefer not to talk about it."

Ron was embarrassed. He went forward to talk to the pilot. Sidney sat down, buckled her belt, and watched as Ron picked up a microphone. He talked by shortwave radio to someone on the ground. She looked back at the inert body of Roger Evans. He was breathing evenly. Ron returned to his seat but refused to catch Sidney's eye. He opened his briefcase and read some papers, but Sidney could see that he was not concentrating.

Sidney stood up and went to the lavatory to freshen up. Her

skirt was wrinkled, her hair was askew, and she had cramps. Her period was about to begin. She washed her face with a damp towel, applied fresh makeup, and brushed her hair. She looked better, but she felt rotten.

When she reached her seat, the seat-belt sign was on. Five minutes later, the plane landed at La Guardia Airport. The company limousine was there to meet them. Sidney watched as the stewardess, Ron, and the chauffeur maneuvered Roger out of the plane and into the car. Then he was buckled carefully into a sitting position.

"Sid," Ron said, "would you be upset if I asked you to catch a cab? I want to take Roger home."

"Yes, I would."

"I insist."

"And I insist you let me come with you. I want to be with you and Roger."

Ron sighed. "Okay, let's go. We're taking Mr. Evans home first."

It was 6:00 on Friday night. There was heavy traffic in both directions on Grand Central Parkway. To avoid it, the limousine cut over to Ditmars Avenue and cut back onto the Triboro Bridge. Roger Evans was still unconscious, sitting upright on the front seat, held in by a safety belt. Ron didn't speak to Sidney, he simply stared out the window. She was annoyed by his silence.

"Ron, talk to me." There was no reply. "Ron, I thought we were good friends. The president of Tompion Financial has just suffered an episode of violent hysteria. I have an idea that it didn't take you by surprise. You seemed prepared for it. Why is a man in his emotional condition permitted to run Tompion Financial? Have you told the admiral? Ron, what's going on?"

"I wish you wouldn't ask questions."

"Ron, answer me. Does the admiral know?"

Ron sighed and said, "Shit!"

Sidney sensed an inner struggle in Ron as he searched for words. Finally he turned to her and said, "Do you know what PTSD means?"

"Yes. Psychologists are starting to use it, but it's a term coined by the Vietnam Veterans Counseling Centers. I believe it means Post Traumatic Stress Disorder."

"That's what it is."

"I didn't know Roger was in Vietnam."

"There are a lot of things you're not aware of."

"What in hell is *that* supposed to mean?"

"Exactly what I said."

Sidney was furious with him. Her words were angry as she raised her voice and said, "Damn you, Ron, why in hell won't you tell me what's going on?" She was breathing fire. Ron glared right back at her and faced her down.

At last he seemed to come to a decision. He picked up the car phone and punched out a telephone number. There was an immediate response. "Admiral, this is Ron. Tom reach you? Good. He told you what happened? No, it wasn't as bad as the Thanksgiving episode. Sidney is with us. She's asking questions I can't answer."

His hand, gripping the phone tightly, showed white knuckles. Gradually he began to calm down. Then he said, "Yes, sir."

Ron put down the phone. He was suddenly hoarse. "Sidney, I know you're pissed off at me, and you have every right to be. You've been away for two weeks, but your day isn't over. We're dropping Roger off at the admiral's house. A doctor will be there by the time we arrive. And you're being dropped off there as well."

"I am?"

"You am?"

"I can't, Ron. I have a hectic day tomorrow — a million things to catch up on. I also need some time to straighten out my private life."

"Sidney," Ron said, "shut up!" He shouted the last two words.

She was silent. Ronald had never yelled at her — nor anyone else, so far as she knew.

Ron was agitated, but he was trying to bring his voice under control, "I've tried every way to keep you out of this. You want to know everything. Well, you're going to find out. If it were up to me, I wouldn't tell you a damn thing. But it's the admiral's ball game, and he owns the team. We're just a couple of the players. You're dining alone tonight with Admiral Orville Dutton. I refuse to be there."

* * *

Sidney was standing in front of the living room fireplace. The admiral appeared, dressed in khaki fatigue pants and shirt with his sleeves rolled up over powerful forearms. It was the first time she'd ever seen him not dressed in a navy blue suit, white silk shirt, and silk tie.

He held her by the shoulders, gazed down at her and kissed her cheek. "Sidney, you're a beautiful lady, indeed. If I were twenty years younger, I'd bed you and wed you so quickly you wouldn't know what hit you."

Without cracking a smile, Sidney batted her long eyelashes, looked at him coquettishly, and said, "Now you're making me wish you *were* twenty years younger. From what I hear, you can still charm the pants off a girl."

There was an pause, and then they both burst into laughter. When they were alone Sidney and the admiral always played a make-believe sexual game. He was at the age to be amused by it, while she was at the age to be flattered.

They sat down in the matched wing back chairs. "Do you want to discuss Peter's murder?" Sidney asked.

"I'm sick about it." There was deep anguish in the Admiral's voice. "I've called the director of the FBI. They're going to dig deeply into this one, but they're going to need all the help we can give them. They'll be talking to you, looking for background material.

"I want you to handle the press. Meanwhile, I created a damage committee today. You're on it. I know tomorrow's Saturday and I know you're beat, but the company's in real trouble. That means we're all in trouble. The first meeting will be here at 11:00 A.M. tomorrow. The single item on the agenda is how to stop the attack on Tompion, which includes Peter's murder."

"Then you think it's tied in?"

"Don't you?"

"Yes. And I've been thinking a lot about what has happened lately. I believe we've got to add another disaster to the list." He looked at her quizzically. "Aside from the Pigglies rumors and the murder, I think we have to include the *Charlemagne* movie fiasco. Think about it. The scandal caused a multimillion-dollar loss, and it set us up as a target for vicious world-wide publicity. It's puzzling to me that two otherwise responsible movie stars suddenly went public sexually and ruined their careers.

"They're Hollywood pros. They wouldn't lose their heads in a cheap scandal. It's too pat. That's why it still bothers me. The only answer that makes sense is that it was staged deliberately. Either they were drugged or somehow coerced into it."

"You could be right. Our problems actually began with *Charlemagne*. This should go on the FBI agenda."

Sidney opened her mouth to say something, but nothing came out.

He saw her hesitate and added, "What?"

"Kaluste."

"Ah, yes, Kaluste. So Jennifer told you."

"She's on a guilt trip right now, blaming herself for Peter's death. That's why she told me the whole story."

"I apologize for not confiding in you at the time it was happening, but you hadn't come aboard yet. The first I knew of your existence was through your memo listing the reasons why you were against Xynatron. Peter showed it to me. It was very astute. That's when I decided I could use you in New York. There seemed to be no need to tell you about Kaluste. Only Ron, Roger, and I knew the story."

"Admiral, my mind's been racing in a thousand directions. Maybe Kaluste wants revenge?"

"I had that suspicion the instant you told me that Peter had been murdered." There was a long silence. They looked at each other and Sidney shuddered. "We can't rule out the fact that someone inside Tompion has been in contact with Kaluste."

"Strange." Sidney then told him of the bogus Air Force wire that had sent her racing to San Francisco. "Kaluste could only have known about Peter and me and my husband's being MIA from someone inside the company." Her last word was underscored by thunder outside.

"A summer thunderstorm," said the admiral. He walked toward the windows that faced the East River. Sidney followed him. "The barometer has been falling for hours." Suddenly there was a crash accompanied by chain lightning that turned the East River into white fire.

Sidney shivered. "I feel like a character in a gothic novel."

She turned to him and said, "Admiral, with Peter murdered, then you, Ron, Roger, Jennifer, and Peter were the only ones who could possibly have been involved with Kaluste."

"Correct. That's what is eating me alive, and that's why I wanted you here tonight. I want you to conduct a thorough investigation to unmask the traitor who is ruining our company. You have carte blanche — money no object. And I want you to check me out as well."

"Why you, admiral?"

"We're a public company. A successful investigation will uncover the guilty and clear the innocent. I want to be cleared."

"That's a big responsibility, admiral. A probe like this is bound to raise a lot of heat."

"Remember what Truman said? If you can't stand the heat, get out of the kitchen. Now, how about a drink before dinner?"

"No, thanks. I'll have wine with dinner. I need a clear head. Anything else on tonight's agenda?"

"Your fight with Ron?"

"It wasn't a fight, it was a one-sided argument. He did all the screaming. It was strange because Ron has always been so level-headed. And why did Ron have to tell you? Are you guys starting to gang up on me?" She smiled so that he would know she was half-joking. "Is this all part of what you want me to investigate?"

"Yes, Sidney, my girl, and tonight I'm to tell you an unusual story. It may have nothing to do with Tompion, yet it may have everything to do with Tompion. It's going to be difficult for me to tell — because I don't know the whole story and because it tears my heart out. So sit back and let me tell it in my own way."

This man who had gone to Annapolis, grown to leadership and had commanded an aircraft carrier in wartime, was looking at her with eyes asking for understanding. He respected Sidney's intelligence and company loyalty, her coolness under fire, and her zest for difficult assignments. She was trustworthy and honest, but she was tough enough and adventurous enough to make a good CIA agent. Most of all, she was discreet. He was going to trust her as he had never trusted anyone in his whole life. Admiral Dutton's story would break one of his cardinal rules: betraying a confidence. This was the source of Ron's anger. But the threat to Tompion had an overriding importance.

As chairman of Tompion International, the admiral had to prevent the company from crumbling. He needed somione for the job. He wasn't young enough to do it. Sidney was. The only flaw in Sidney was that she was too involved with the company. He understood intuitively that she was lonely. He recognized that she was a one-man woman searching for a one-woman man. A corporate executive earning over $250,000 a year plus fringes and pension, stock options, and other executive perks would not endanger her lifestyle or her future. Yet with Sidney he was never quite sure. She might be outsmarting him by having several lovers, yet somehow he didn't believe that.

The admiral lived in a five story brownstone house on Sutton Place. Although a Chinese couple, a housekeeper-cook and her butler-handyman husband, looked after the house, it was Slade who announced that dinner was being served. They ate in the high-ceilinged, formal dining room which was 35 feet long and 25 feet wide. Two people in a large room sitting at a table which could seat twenty-four. Sidney faced the massive canvas depicting the Battle of Leyte Gulf painted by a U.S. Navy artist assigned to Admiral Halsey's Task Force 58 in 1944.

"Sidney, may I ask you a personal question?"

"If it's not *too* personal."

"You always look great. Your clothes are in style and in

excellent taste. But you never seem to rush off shopping for clothes like our other lady executives. What's your secret?"

"Admiral, how much is it worth if I tell you?"

"How about a second scoop of the chocolate ice cream we're having for dessert?"

"You're on." She picked up her glass of Chablis, twirled the stem in her long fingers, sipped it, smiled, and looked the admiral directly in the eye. "I hate shopping. At college I used to make my own clothes, thanks to my mom's good training with a sewing machine, an old Singer foot treadle I still use. With less time to spare at Carlyle, I hunted around until I found a great seamstress. I'd buy clothes off the rack, and she would restyle them for me.

"When I came to New York and saw the way the other women executives dressed, I was ready to pack it in and go home. They wore Diors and Balenciagas and Chanels. Great clothes but not my style. I had two choices: join them or leave town. All I had going for me was a size-eight figure and a weight that didn't fluctuate.

"I made a decision to be clothes conscious, but in my own way. I arranged to meet with the head of clothes design at the Fashion Institute. I told her I hated to go shopping, yet I had to look good at 9:00 A.M. meetings which could stretch into dinner — often with no time to change.

"The woman at the Fashion Institute told me, 'You want professional advice from a teacher who helps students make money designing clothes for women like you? It would be counterproductive. However, my students know about design and marketing but little about communications. How about teaching two semesters based on your book, *The Psychology of Print*, in exchange for whatever help I can give you?'

"I agreed. She made an appointment for us at a small

boutique on Madison Avenue. To make a long story short, the two women who run it are fabulous. In an hour we had a deal. They would select my clothes, mostly solid colors, lots of tailored suits, mostly jerseys and wools — everything practical and non-wrinklable and nothing extreme. Most sample dresses and suits are made up in size eight. They buy salesmen's samples for me, so I'm in style before the new trends hit the street.

"My new friend at F.I. also found a French hairdresser for me. He redesigned my hair. I used to spend hours getting my straight hair permanent-waved, but he said in his heavy accent, 'The wavy 'air want eet straight and zee straight 'air want eet wavy. Why not make believe you 'ave wavy hair and you want eet straight? *Bien.* Now we feex your 'air proper.' He did and still does. He cuts it in such a way that by running a comb through it, I'm kempt. *Voila!*"

"Very, clever, Sidney."

"Thanks."

They continued to exchange pleasantries as they ate their way through a black navy bean soup that was so thick the white shredded onions floated on it like a miniature armada.

When they finished the last course, including the promised extra helping of chocolate ice cream, the admiral said, "We'll have coffee in my study."

Sidney had been to the house many times for dinner, cocktail parties, and conferences, and she felt comfortable here. The admiral was either a widower or divorced (she never knew which), so occasionally he asked Sidney to be his hostess, particularly at a top-level dinner conference.

They entered a small elevator and it rose to the fifth floor, the only floor Sidney had never seen. When she stepped out, she was surprised. The admiral didn't strike her as being sentimental, but the room was a museum of memorabilia. There were photographs showing him with American presidents, secretaries of state, and King George and Queen Elizabeth, as well as award ceremonies showing the admiral being decorated for valor in service. There were scale models of Navy ships and souvenirs from ships and battles. Plaques and commendations were grouped together, while the shelves were crammed with books on World War II.

At the far end was a desk, a comfortable executive chair, and a black leather couch. In the corner, an end table supported an old, elegant bracket clock. It had an ebony case with a silver dial and ornate black hands which chimed the quarters on two bells with a delicate ting-tang. Without inspecting it, Sidney guessed it was a Tompion.

He pointed his finger at the small silver coffee urn on the desk, and said, "Pour the coffee."

She saluted.

The admiral was obviously tense. Though Sidney didn't feel any tension between them, she sensed that something dramatic was about to take place, and she worried about what he might say. It was her intuition. There was too much preamble to the discussion. The admiral was trying to make it look casual, but it was taking on the aspect of melodrama.

They sat at opposite ends of the couch to make use of the end tables for their coffee cups. Dramatically, the next question, when it came, caught her by surprise. "Sidney — why haven't you remarried?"

Sidney choked on her mouthful of hot coffee. It took several minutes of coughing before she could talk. Her emerald eyes were watery, and her voice hoarse. "What — brought — that up?"

"You're beautiful in so many ways. Don't blush, but you're

built for speed like cruiser, you're intelligent and — you not only have class, but you have street smarts. You're a fine lady and I care about you. You should be loved regularly — by the right man."

"Okay, admiral, find me the right man."

"I have."

"You *what?*"

"I have."

"I don't believe what I'm hearing."

"Listen, Sidney, I found the right man for you, in my opinion — perhaps not in yours. Maybe you're really not his kind of woman. But since I know he's already in love with you, that's fifty percent of the problem solved, right?"

"Admiral, aren't you being a little presumptuous?"

"Hold it a second, Sidney." Then he mimicked her, doing a fair imitation of her voice. "Two minutes ago, you said, 'Okay admiral, find me the right man.' And when I tell you I've found the right man, you accuse me of being presumptuous."

Sidney started to laugh, tears running down her face. She moved closer to him, leaned over, and kissed the admiral's cheek. He, in turn, patted her fanny. When she cocked an eyebrow, he said, "When you joined Tompion five — six years ago, I told myself, 'She's cute. When do I get pinching privileges?' When I asked you, you said, 'In six months,' quick as a flash. Therefore I have just enjoyed the privilege you bestowed upon me so graciously."

"Admiral, you're too much. If you had a son, I'd marry him sight unseen."

"Put it in writing?" he said pointing to his desk.

Sidney smiled, stood up, picked up a pen and paper and wrote it out, dated it, and signed her name.

"Admiral, enough of this kidding around. First you're interested in my clothes, then my love life, next you'll want to know the shade of my pantyhose. You ask me to do something extremely serious. Then you start scampering around the edges of something else in order to put off telling me about it. What's going on? And while you have the floor, tell me why Ron suddenly becomes emotionally upset and wants to bite my head off. I thought we were good friends. Ron knows Roger is unstable. Is he capable of running Tompion Financial?"

"Sidney, all your questions require answers. That's why I want you to dig into this mess. The admiral took a deep breath and squared his shoulders as though he were going into battle. Then his body slumped and he began to talk.

"I don't have the complete story — but I know enough to give you a picture and backgrounds of three young men. Tom Grosso, Roger Evans and Ronald Cohen.

"In the sixties you were a kid, so you might not remember. In early 1963, 200,000 people marched for civil rights in Washington. John F. Kennedy was assassinated in November 1963. The later assassinations of Bobby Kennedy and then Martin Luther King intensified the anti-Vietnam riots that rocked most colleges. It was a decade of turmoil in America.

"Since I was stationed on a ship in one battle zone or another, I escaped the horror and reality of it all. I was on the outside. To me, everthing that was going on was merely a series of newspaper stories."

"I was a teen-ager in the 1960s, admiral. I felt it."

"Tom and Ron and Roger were students at UCLA. They first met when they became involved in the civil rights and anti-Vietnam War movements during their sophomore year. The more they were abused by the authorities and public opinion, the more involved they became. By the time they were seniors, they had become fast friends. Their final protest was to burn their draft cards, grow beards, drop acid, and smoke pot. They considered moving to Canada.

"The only eighteen-or nineteen-year-olds I knew in the 1960s were on my ship. They were clean farm boys with crew cuts who dressed well. Looking back, I still find it difficult to understand the depths of hostility of the rebellious kids of that period.

"Tom, Ron, and Roger found a common purpose even though they all came from different backgounds. What they had in common was a sense of decency, dignity, and fair play. Tom's father drove a cement truck. He was a member of the Teamsters Union. He wanted Tom to join the union and forget about college. Tom wanted to be a lawyer and go into politics. His father thought he was crazy, so Tom worked at a variety of different jobs in the summer and saved money. In spite of his father, he won a scholarship and was able to pick up a couple of supplementary grants. I saw the records. He worked like hell to get a college education. Then, all of a sudden, in a surge of integrity, he abandoned it.

"Ron's father was a federal judge in New York, a domineering man who believed he was never wrong. Ron applied for and got into all the top schools — Harvard, Yale, UCLA, Michigan, and, I believe, Columbia. His father was a Columbia alumnus and insisted that Ron go there, but Ron didn't want to live near home. His father suggested Harvard, but New York is only one hour away on the shuttle. Ron selected UCLA, which was far enough away from his father to feel comfortable. Like Tom, he, too, was very bright and a fine athlete. At UCLA he made the debating team, the chess team and the tennis team.

"Roger's background is completely different, and, in a way, more complex. He's a brilliant mathematician. I think he's a genius. Brilliant young mathematicians are treated like academic royalty because they are so rare. Wherever they go to school, their performance is watched over by the scientific community.

"Roger was treated with respect from the time he was in the fifth grade when, at the age of ten, he explained solid geometry to his startled math teacher. He could do trig at eleven and at thirteen was already into the theory of numbers. Every university wanted him. His parents were divorced. His mother, an actress, was raising him alone because she wouldn't take alimony from her ex-husband, who was in the military. And she didn't want his advice, either.

"At home Roger became a mama's boy. He wasn't permitted to play baseball or football because of the risk of serious injury. So he played chess, read voraciously, and studied the piano. He had a mature brain in a scrawny, underdeveloped body and wore steel-rimmed glasses. He met Ron at the university chess club, and Ron became fascinated by this quiet, shy, skinny kid who could checkmate him with ease.

"When Ron learned that Roger was a math superstar, he didn't mind losing to him at chess. Of course they played often enough so that Ron was able to improve and occasionally win a game. But that's not the complete story. Roger saw his father regularly several times a year.

"After Roger became part of the antiwar movement, his father lost interest in his son.

"I'm his father."

CHAPTER

FOURTEEN

SIDNEY was so taken aback that she couldn't speak. The admiral stood up and began to pace the room. "If it hadn't been for the Tompion problems, this would never have come out. I'm baffled. I need someone objective and emotionally uninvolved to delve into this thing deeply."

He took out a stack of letters from his desk and dropped them on the couch. "Maybe you'd better start with these. I'll be back in an hour. That'll give you enough time to read them."

The admiral left and Sidney looked at the stack of blue APO letters sold at the Army PXs. interleaved with letters in white envelopes. Her mind was whirling. After a few minutes, she was composed enough to read. The postmarks started in July 1966 and went into 1967.

> Dear Dad:
>
> I don't know how to begin. I realize that we have not been in touch for years but it's Mom's wish that I write. Are you still mad at me? Past anger and resentments at this time are minor in light of my perilous future.
>
> I've been in Nam two months and I see the huge buildup of helipads and monster fuel depots and it looks like we'll be here forever. I despise war. It never solved anything. My friends Ron and Tom and I have managed to stay together in Delta Company.
>
> I have to tell you something I can't tell Mom. We've been on patrol one month and Delta Company has taken a beating: five dead by mortar fire and three WIA (wounded in action) by snipers.
>
> I Killed an NVA (North Vietnamese Army) regular and it frightened me so much that I became

violently ill. I shook for two days. I was so scared I wanted to desert. I didn't think I'd ever shoot anyone, but a sniper shot Tom in the thigh. When Tom screamed, I was so upset that I fired back by reflex action and got him in the chest.

The Lt. told Tom he won a Purple Heart and Tom told him to shove it up his ass. There are a lot of black GIs in Delta including Sergeant Joe Bascome. This morning Joe was hit by shrapnel. Ron saw blood spurting out of his groin. First he got sick, then he applied a tourniquet with his own belt. Under fire Ron carried him back to the a pad for a "dust off" (a med Evac chopper) and saved his life. Sgt.'s on his second tour. He told us we're in a big buildup. Last year U.S. casualties were running up to 400 a month. Now it's twice that.

If you're not still upset and angry at me, Dad, I need a favor. Bascome told us to get 12-gauge shotguns because it takes too long to aim an M-16. Charlie knows the jungle. You never see him. While we look for shit sticks and booby traps, suddenly bullets are coming at you.

We need three Remington 870s. They're five-shell pump guns for rapid fire. Have barrels cut to 18 inches.

Some bored grunts, here a long time, are lacing their cigarettes with heroin. It's stupid. But so is meaningless killing for a meaningless hill.

What are we doing here?

Your son
Roger

Dear Roger:

I was both happy and sad to get your letter. Happy that you wrote me and sad that you are in the worst kind of fighting — guerrilla action in a steaming jungle.

You and your friends are getting the packages. They will be flown in from an aircraft carrier.

Soldiers are not the ones who start wars, they only fight them. War is declared by politicians who are supposed to be wiser than we are. The angry protests prove it's not a popular war. The tragic part is that our young men have to leave home to fight and die in it. With all my heart I want you to survive.

I love you, son. I always have.

Dad

Dear Dad:

After one week in the hospital and one week R&R, Tom came back to Delta. The 870s came. Thanks.

Some areas of the jungle trees have no leaves. They're defoliated. It protects our defense perimeter.

Ron and I spent three days in Saigon. It's another world. The Viet language sounds like birds singing. I know the GI phrase book by heart but I will study the language. Ron dated a teacher. I won't date because I keep thinking of Lilly. She never wanted me to be part of this stupid war. She gave her life to stop it.

When I see kids in black pajamas throwing grenades at us to protect their villages, I know Lilly was right.

Rumor has it that Pvt. Carter, an 18-year old in

Baker Company, refused a direct order to shoot a boy carrying an AK47. He was up for a court-martial. Instead he put his M-16 in his mouth and pulled the trigger.

Get us home! Stop the war.

Love,
Roger

Dear Roger,

Ron and Tom's fathers and I met in New York for dinner at The Four Seasons. Did you know Ron suggested it? After a long talk, the three of us realized that this war is unlike any other war in American history.

The Vietnamese have fought each other for centuries and we fight on their terms. General Westmoreland says we're winning but the death toll rises. The President thinks more soldiers and modern weapons will turn the tide.

The judge showed me a letter Ron wrote. It said you and three members of Delta were caught by the VC. They shoved a piece of bamboo in your mouth, gagged you, blindfolded you, tied your arms behind your back until your shoulders were out of joint, and you didn't scream. After three days, you engineered an escape and led the men back to base using your watch as a compass.

I'm proud of you, son.

The fathers decided to meet regularly. Tom's father wonders if it's true you told the C.O. to shove the silver star up his ass and if the C.O. did it.

Love,
Dad

Dear Dad:

Medals are for heroes. I'm scared to death. All we're doing is trying to survive. I shoot at the enemy to keep him from killing me. I don't hate him any more than he hates me. I'm just a round-eye whom he believes came to steal his country. The French, with lots of experience fighting stupid wars, got out. Why can't we?

Yesterday, in the jungle we found two Marine 'copters that had been shot down. Mangled bodies were strewn over a quarter-mile area. We all got sick. Sgt. Aylsworth called in Graves Registration.

Ron and a buddy had bad luck. His buddy was ahead of him on patrol, stepped on a mine, and was killed instantly. Ron was hit by shrapnel and the blast kayoed him. He's OK, but his ears ache. He used the shotgun. It worked fine. He sends thanks again.

Love,
Roger

Dear Roger

Your tour is now half over. Ron's father called and told me Ron is back with the Company but still has a ringing in his ears. He said Ron and Tom saved your life in a rice paddy when you were shot in the neck. Tom kept off the attack with a Russian-made assault rifle he took off a dead VC while Ron held your artery with two hands to keep you from losing blood, shouting, "Dammit, Roger, don't you dare die till I beat you at chess."

Tom killed seven VC before the 'copters came. At the Evac hospital there was no plasma, so two black

GIs in your company, Smith and Maxwell, gave over a pint each to save you. Later Tom pinned his Silver Star on a dead soldier wrapped in a poncho. Ron exchanged his bronze star for a paperback on Justice Louis Brandeis.

I love you and pray for you.

Dad

Dear Dad:

I bought a paperback of the Naked And The Dead. I guess WWII was horrendous, too. Somehow that war had a purpose. It was good versus evil.

This war is dumb vs. stupid. If I survive I will do everything to stop war madness and war buildup.

Can you imagine that the big hero in Nam is John Wayne? I can't believe it. The real heroes here are GIs and the Marines who eat shit and get shot at. Yet they admire a pro-war movie star who's making a fortune imitating them.

Real life adulates fantasy while fantasy adulates real life. Does President Johnson really play poker with John Wayne? Maybe that's where the Commander-in-Chief gets his macho ideas?

My neck is healed but stiff. It's hard to move my head. The psychiatrist, Major Cripps, is a turd. He says I'm malingering so as not to go back to my outfit. Tom, Ron and I kidnapped the prick, shoved an M-16 in his hands and forced him to accompany us on patrol. When the shooting began he shit himself. We wouldn't let him wipe up till we got back. He was stinking mad and reported us. The company commander was upset and promised a speedy court-martial

Later, the C.O. gave us each a shot of Hennessy and we all laughed till we cried. I didn't know West Pointers had a sense of humor.

Love,
Roger

Dear Son:

I see that you carved your shotgun butts down like pistol grips. The leather bandoliers for the shells look good. Did Ron really learn to do leathercraft at a summer camp called Wa-Na-Sookie?

They say that the PX at Cholon near Saigon is bigger than Macy's and GIs going home buy cars there. I also understand that Wall Street brokers now fly to Saigon to sell stocks to servicemen.

What is the refugee situation like? I don't agree with the administration policy of "urbanization" — i.e., devastating villages so refugees flee to and choke the cities. Your mother and I spent a week in Virginia with some friends. I might be transferred to England shortly.

Love with prayers,

Dad

Dear Dad:

I am becoming more disillusioned than ever. Officers and diplomats keep elegant mistresses, but they issue orders preventing grunts from dating local girls. All that's left are hookers, massage parlors masseuses and bar girls.

Heroin, hash, opium and mescaline are all here for the asking. It's not usually the guys at the front who are on stuff, but the bored grunts in Saigon. Personally,

I suspect the VC sell dope in South Vietnam for two reasons: first, to raise money for Hanoi, and second, to demoralize GIs and Marines.

Our New Year's resolutions include:

Keep off the hash. If we lose our edge, we're dead.

Drink moderately (the French beer tastes like pee).

Hard liquor only on R&R.

I will teach Vietnamese and chess to Ron & Tom.

Tom will teach us Italian and how to sing operas.

Ron will teach us law and as many Yiddish words as he can remember.

If you ever heard a conversation of English, Italian, Yiddish and Vietnamese you'd burst out laughing.

Airlifted on patrol on Christmas and we caught a 2-hour barrage of mortar fire. It had us screaming to ourselves. The Sgt. was so PO'd, he circled around and shot the men with the mortar. We lost seven.

I don't understand this stupid patrol 20 miles from Saigon. Nobody can win a battle for a hill identified only by a number. Generals are public relations experts who only care about body counts. Opposing generals should have a fast draw contest. Loser goes home.

I'm having nightmares. I was surprised to find that other GIs in my company suffer from nightmares, too.

                                         Love,
                                         Roger

CHAPTER

FIFTEEN

SIDNEY was suspended in a half-world somewhere between sleep and consciousness, squirming to get more comfortable. She was breathing deeply. She struggled in an effort to plunge deeper into sleep, but something kept pushing her upward toward consciousness, like a swimmer coming up for air.

At first she seemed to be listening to music. She pulled the cover over her head, inhaled, then sank back into sleep. But the sound of music was too persistent. She became aware of it slowly. Suddenly she became disoriented and frightened. This was not in her bed! Where was she?

She threw off the covers and opened her eyes. A brass desk lamp illuminated the Navy photographs on the wall. After reading most of the letters she felt tired so she stopped and walked around the room, looking at photographs on the wall.

The last thing Sidney remembered was looking at a large color photograph of the three comrades in camouflage fatigues hugging each other and weeping in front of the Vietnam Veterans Memorial in Washington. She recognized the Tompion executives, and hot tears had come to her eyes. Part of it had been in memory of her missing husband. She must have cried herself to sleep.

Now she sat up found her shoes on the floor. Someone had put a blanket over her as she slept. That must have been hours ago. Her tongue was thick and her eyelids were coated with glue. Her jacket was folded neatly on the chair, but the skirt and blouse she slept in were as rumpled as a bag lady's wardrobe. Groggily, she got up, pressed the light switch, then moved unsteadily toward the bathroom for ablutions and repairs.

As she washed her face, the cold water brought her back to

life. After straightening and adjusting her clothes, she dreamed of a hot tub and a good night's sleep. She ran her purse comb through her hair, rinsed her mouth with Scope from the guest bottle, and applied a touch of lipstick. The dark circles under her eyes and her blanched face gave her a drawn look. She wasn't ready to meet the world. She was exhausted and knew she looked ghastly. Nevertheless, she felt passable enough to go home. The time hadn't registered clearly when she first looked at her watch, so she looked again. It was 5:00 A.M.

Sidney was nervous about her assignment. Thinking about it, she heard the music again. Walking back through the admiral's study, she thought the music came from a piano. The sound came from a distant room in the house, one or two floors away. Yet it was so faint it could have come from a child's music box. It was filtering in through the fireplace and was difficult to identify. Before moving back to the couch, she made the decision not to wait around until the house came awake. Someone must be up. She was determined to track the source of the music. She was also in great need of a cup of strong black coffee. It was a minimal requirement before finding a cab and going home.

Sidney picked up her jacket and carried it over her left shoulder as she pressed the elevator button. She went down one floor, but when the doors opened, she heard nothing. About to go down, she decided to check the music room. She opened the door cautiously and the music thundered out. She slipped in, closed the soundproof door, and glanced at the record player. It wasn't on. In the almost-darkened room, she edged toward the grand piano and was startled to see a pianist.

Roger Evans, in a tattered gray sweatsuit, a white towel wrapped around his head and horn-rimmed glasses slipping down his nose, was playing Beethoven's *Appassionata* Sonata. He was concentrating on reading the music while chewing his lips as though it was too difficult a piece. But even Sidney's untrained ear recognized that the texture of the sound and the dynamics were almost of concert caliber. He was totally unaware of her presence.

Sidney held her breath, found a chair, sat down, and listened. She had never been so close to a fine pianist at work, and her heart beat faster with the excitement of the music as it flowed out of the instrument. This was the very compositon that had influenced great composers like Mahler and Tchaikovsky yet had never been equaled. At 5:30 A.M. Roger stopped playing abruptly, looked at his watch, and stood up. Only then did he spot her.

"What are you doing here?"

"Sorry, I didn't mean to startle you. I heard the music upstairs and was curious. I like your playing."

He looked at her, gestured thanks with his hand, and took the towel off his head. Finally he grinned shyly. "Didn't mean to bark. Sorry. I'm going running. See you."

He started to walk by her and, without thinking or even wondering why she said it, she blurted out, "Want company?"

He stopped, looked at her, and shrugged. "Okay."

"My gear is in my luggage. Any idea where it might be?"

"Sure." He walked out of the room toward the elevator. She followed.

On the second floor where the guest rooms were located, he checked three rooms. Her bag was in the third one. He turned to leave. "Sit down, I won't bite you," she said.

She took out her running gear and stepped into the bathroom, emerging a few minutes later in beautifully designed red shorts and top, New Balance sneakers, and a matching sweatband. Though Sidney was aware that she had a good figure, she

never gave it much thought. But she saw the impression she was
making on Roger. He was inspecting her as though she were a
new Rolls Royce he wanted to own. It was so good for her morale
that it almost woke her up. Finally she picked up her wallet and
said, "I'm ready when you are."

They went to the kitchen, where Roger poured two glasses
of Gatorade. Wordlessly, he continued to stare at her with the
smoldering look that once had frightened her. When he looked
her directly in the eye, he didn't even blink.

Outside the light was grayish and the air damp and heavy. A
mist hung over the East River. He began his stretching exercises
and she followed suit. Then he looked at her, nodded, and began
to run. The pace was comfortable and she had no trouble keeping
up. They didn't speak as he led her north along Sutton Place
heading for Gracie Mansion, where Mayor Koch was probably
still asleep. In the first fifteen minutes, only one taxi went past
them. Instead of running side by side, he continued to keep two
paces ahead of Sidney, who was disappointed he didn't keep
looking at her. She didn't usually seek attention, yet somehow she
wanted it from this very unusual man.

Roger was deliberately keeping her out of his line of vision as
he suddenly turned west onto a cross street and then north on
First Avenue. At 96th Street, he turned west again past Second
and Third Avenues, then turned south on the east side of Third.
She almost certain that he could see her in the store windows in
order to gauge his pace ahead of her. Milkmen and food suppliers
were unloading their wares in front of the restaurants. When they
approached a diner near 55th Street, she ran up to him and
grabbed his arm. "I'm famished. I need a cup of black coffee and
something to eat."

He stopped running and walked beside her into the restaurant. As though a genie had answered her wish, sitting on a large tray was a heaping assortment of freshly baked pastries. She pointed to an exceptionally large lemon Danish. The portly counterman served them at a booth, promptly pouring two cups of steaming coffee.

"The admiral told me you're his son."

Roger stopped chewing. "It's not public knowledge. I guess he had his reasons."

"Yes."

"Know why?"

"I can guess. I saw you go through some kind of seizure or trauma on the plane. Ron had all the paraphernalia to help you. Obviously it had happened before. Then Ron and I had a terrible argument about it afterward for no reason — because until then we were good friends. It upset me. He told the admiral and the admiral invited me to dinner to tell me your story. He's worried about you. He knows I'm a psychologist. Perhaps he feels I can help you. I also have the suspicion he's playing matchmaker by throwing us together."

Roger smiled. "He sold me your promissory note for two cents."

"What promissory note?"

"That if he had a son you'd marry him."

"If you look at the note, it's signed Marie Antoinette."

"I didn't expect you to lose your head over it."

She laughed. He called the counterman over and ordered scrambled eggs with an English muffin. They said nothing until his eggs came. Then Sidney reached over and helped herself to half a muffin. He caught her wrist. "I didn't give you permission."

She giggled and said, "Order another and steal half." Inwardly she thought, *Why am I acting like a schoolgirl?*

After some deliberation, Roger said, "Sidney — this is confession time. If I appear nervous or upset near you, it's because women like you scare the hell out of me. No offense meant." He lowered his eyes. "Strong, positive, self-assertive, take-charge women both fascinate me and scare me. They tend to swallow me up and run my life. I don't want to be handled or controlled or bossed. I've had enough of it. I want to breathe. I need my freedom. So for me the best way to keep out of trouble is to avoid dominating women."

She licked some butter from her fingers. "That's one way of coping with the problem."

"It's only a problem if I recognize it as a problem."

"True. But the better way would be to understand yourself and try to overcome it."

"Sure, but why bother?"

Sidney said nothing. "Roger, aside from all our personal idiosyncrasies, we still have the Tompion problem. And that's serious. Our futures are at stake. Can we at least be friends — even if you think I'm a dominating woman?"

"Sure."

"I have learned from Ron that you suffer from Post Traumatic Stress Disorder. Unfortunately, it's common with Vietnam vets. I have a theory that the wives of veterans may suffer from it as well. After ten years my husband is still MIA. I have nightmares, too. Will you let me try to help you?"

"How?

"Any way I can. You see, until yesterday you frightened me. To be very honest, you scared the hell out of me. If we respect each other's problems and discuss them honestly, maybe we can help each other. It's worth a try."

Roger looked directly at her, pushing his glasses back onto the ridge of his nose. "Okay. In the new spirit of cooperation, but really because I have no money on me, your first gesture of friendship will be to pay for breakfast. Then I suggest we get back to the admiral's house so you can get more sleep. I'll change the meeting to one o'clock.

"Now, Sidney, dear friend, my gesture of friendship to you is truth. You're a devastatingly beautiful woman, but you look like hell."

CHAPTER

SIXTEEN

IT WAS was 4 P.M. The meeting had been going on for three hours. They were seated around the dining room table which was littered with crumpled balls of yellow legal paper. The Admiral at the head of the table, Ron Cohen and Roger Evans were on his left and Sidney, Steve Corcoran and F.D.R.Brown on his right. Roscoe Tompion Granby, the President, sat at the other end of the table.

Two startling pieces of new information were introduced at the meeting. First, Steve and F.D.R., together with the sheriff of Carlyle, had tracked down an accomplice to the murder of Peter Wallack. He was a local tough and small-time pusher with limited intelligence. He knew the territory. F.D.R. had a hunch that if anyone in Carlyle was involved, the chances were good that the murderer would flaunt his new-found wealth.

A local party girl had told a girlfriend, who told someone else. F.D.R. tracked down the man, one Johnny Briggs. He was known as "Gangrene" because in a fight he was pure poison. F.D.R. traced Briggs to a local black bar and invited him outside for a talk. At this point Briggs tried to maim him with a fist full of brass knuckles.

Unknown to F.D.R., Briggs had a following of sorts and "a talk outside" generally meant a bloody fight. But F.D.R. deflected Briggs' right cross and, though he was fifty pounds lighter, hit him three times in such rapid succession that a few boozy onlookers barely saw the right, left, right — the last punch to the Adam's apple. Briggs slipped to the sidewalk unconscious.

A white deputy sheriff, who was there and who enjoyed A bloody fight as much as anyone, was an onlooker. F.D.R. asked that "Gangrene" Briggs be taken to the sheriff's office. The skeptical deputy called in and was surprised that the request was granted. They hoisted Briggs into the deputy's car. With one hand on the butt of his .375 Magnum he invited F.D.R. to ride to the county jail with him. F.D.R.'s second request was for the sheriff and Steve Corcoran be present. The deputy radioed ahead.

Once Briggs was conscious, the Sheriff, Steve and F.D.R. went to work on him. He soon confessed his role in Peter's murder. Two white men, one named Smiley and the other Jack had approached Briggs through mutual underworld friends. They offered him $5,000 to drive them around town, get some information about Med-Pharm and then, after a brief look at the plant, drive them to the airport.

The information they wanted concerned Wallack's work habits. Briggs was asked to get duplicates of office keys from the night watchman. That was easy. He was was already in possession of a set, stolen when he worked briefly at Med-Pharm as a guard in 1981.

After calling Sidney's apartment to report the new evidence, her telephone answering service forwarded F.D.R.'s urgent call to Admiral Dutton's house. Since Sidney was still asleep he spoke to the Admiral. The chairman asked F.D.R. and Corcoran to fly back to New York to report the new evidence to the meeting

The second surprising piece of information had been picked up by Roscoe Granby. A two-handicap golfer he was often invited to play at member-guest tournaments and Pro-Ams. At a member-guest golf match at Wingfoot Country Club in Scarsdale, N.Y., his host's friends had tried to pump him for "insider" information about Tompion.

"Is Tompion selling out?"

"It what price should I buy in?"

"The story is that you're selling off several divisions. The separate parts are worth more than the conglomerate as a whole. Which company should I bid on?"

Granby, despite his deceptive look of incompetence, was an astute man. He was clever enough to write out the questions while pretending to fill out a duplicate scorecard. The friend was Cecil Beckworth a member of a small money management firm. But the other two players included a golf hustler named Gerald Parker and the international dealmaker, Tony Preston Ashbury, who had offices in London, Berlin and Paris. Granby suspected he was considered too ineffectual and too uninformed to recognize the name of Ashbury.

It wasn't the first time Granby had been underestimated. Granby, enjoying the game, had been able to read from the conversation that several brokers were actively buying Tompion International stock. No one had acquired more than five percent; over that amount they would have to declare it to the Securities and Exchange Commission. He learned that the buying had been going on quietly for months.

Then Sidney was asked to report on her talks with Ginger. Discreetly, she went into the Kaluste involvement of five years earlier. Though she had no proof, Ginger was almost certain he was involved in Peter's murder. She said, "If Kaluste is behind Peter's death, it could only be personal."

Then the Admiral asked for everyone's attention and remarked, "Obviously, we must fight back. We've being softened up for a take-over bid. We must work out quickly a sound plan and counter-attack. The point is how, where, and when? We must first identify the enemy, then select our target and hit back with everything we've got."

"We need confirmation of our suspicions in order to get a fix on the enemy," Ron said. "What do we do until then?"

"I'm for attacks on several fronts at the same time," Sidney said.

"I agree," said Roger. "In order to be effective, our task force needs specialized personnel and a big war chest."

"Right," said the Admiral. "I believe we already have the specialized personnel necessary to go with. Any assistance we need we'll hire as required. At this point nothing is more important to the company and our stockholders than resolving this battle.

Roger said, "Those of us involved must be relieved of day-to-day duties to work exclusively on the counterattack. As you said, Admiral, we must bring the stock back up, even though we have the financials to prove our claim of a best-ever quarter."

"What about raising the dividend, Admiral?" said Sidney. "I also suggest we go public with this fight. I'd like to hire an outside P.R. firm, the best in the country, to handle Tompion and counter the enemy's moves."

"Good idea, Sidney. The dividend is a Board matter. As for going public with high power P.R., unless someone objects, Sidney should proceed with it."

Roscoe Granby said, "I suggest that you, Admiral, man the command post. You could go to Washington and mobilize the CIA and the Department of Defense, persuading them to block the sale of a highly sensitive defense contractor to a foreign power."

"Mr. Granby," F.D.R. Brown said, "It may not be a foreign power buying us. It may be American."

"Yes, and if it is, it may be a front," Roger said. "The vital factor is what Sidney pointed out. We have to be prepared to counter their every move. As we push each chess piece across the board it's purpose is to stall each avenue of attack......"

"....while helping the stock," Ron said. "The higher we go the tougher it will be for any group to acquire Tompion. We also must consider poison-pill possibilities, making a hostile takeover unpalatable. Admiral, our legal department can manage the day-to-day problems without me. I'd like to hire a top Wall Street Merger and

Acquisition law firm as well as a major investment banker like Dillon Read or Lazard Frères to guide us through the critical days ahead."

The Admiral smiled and said, "Right! Will you contact the best available people over the weekend?"

Ron coughed and said, "I've already spoken to the people I have in mind. It's set, pending your okay." Everyone laughed nervously as Ron added, "And these people have enough clout in Washington to get the S.E.C. and the F.T.C. hopping."

Then Roger spoke, "I will use my computers to probe the dealings of all of Kaluste's operations, known or suspected, as well the identity of all purchasers of our stock. A pattern could emerge. I'll begin right after this meeting is over."

"Admiral," said Sidney, "Steve Corcoran will be our liaison with the F.B.I. He'll ensure that new leads will be followed up quickly. It might give us the connection with Kaluste we're looking for. I also suggest putting F.D.R. in charge of the Pigglies investigation. Give him a free hand so he can get all the help he needs to locate the source of the rumors.

"F.D.R. can you handle it?"

"Yes, Admiral."

Sidney spoke, "Meanwhile I will continue talking to Jennifer Wallack. Finally, I personally want to investigate the Charlemagne scandal. For everyone's information, the Admiral and I have discussed this at length and we agree it must have been manipulated."

"You left out an important item, Sidney," the Admiral said.

"I didn't forget it, Admiral. I thought it best if you brought it up."

"We think," the Admiral said, "That we have a traitor in our midst."

CHAPTER

SEVENTEEN

SIDNEY and Steve Corcoran were seated in a small conference room at the New York City headquarters of the FBI, at 26 Federal Plaza. At Sidney's request, Corcoran had arranged a meeting with the supervisor in charge of the Tompion investigation. Corcoran didn't know the purpose of the meeting, except that Sidney wanted him present.

The supervisor came in and showed his bureau credentials. James Orwell White was a tall, slim man with black hair and a lot of nervous energy. Neither Sidney nor Corcoran had met him before. "I understand you're a former member of the bureau," White said to Corcoran as he sat down. "Sorry, I don't have anything new to tell you on the Wallack case."

"We have other reasons to be here," Sidney said. "Some of them may be related to the case." White took out a pad and waited for Sidney. "Steve, what I'm about to say is privileged information at Tompion. The admiral and I have concluded that there's a traitor in the organization. It may be related to Peter Wallack's murder.

"Whoever the corporate raider is he has access to confidential corporate information. For this reason, the admiral wants several people checked out:

"Jennifer Ann Wallack, formerly Joubert, formerly Black.

"Roger D. Evans, president, Tompion Financial. Vietnam veteran, Antiwar activist. Detests the military. Our Rainbow division produces secret electronics equipment for the army.

"Evans is the son of Admiral Dutton, who was divorced years ago.

"Ronald Cohen, executive V.P., Tompion. Friend of Evans. Served with him in Vietnam. Antiwar activist.

"Thomas Grosso, president, Unicorn Life and Casualty. Friend

of Cohen and Evans. Served in Vietnam. Antiwar activist.
"Admiral Dutton wants his own name on the list of suspects — to
clear his name."

White asked, "Whom do you suspect and why?"

"Five years ago, Kaluste tried to acquire Med-Pharm/Rainbow. Jennifer was Kaluste's mistress. With help from Jennifer, Tompion got the company. The suspects and the victim were the only ones who knew of Jennifer's connection with Constantin Kaluste. Subsequently, she left Kaluste to marry Wallack.

"During the negotiations, Kaluste was remarkably well informed about the internal activities of both companies — information that had to come from an insider.

"As for Roger, Ron, and Tom, their reasons seem more cloudy. All three were in Vietnam after being strong antiwar activists. Tompion is a defense contractor. The motive could be revenge, a way to get even with the establishment.

"Because of his antiwar activities, Admiral Dutton severed relations with his son. At present, Roger Evans suffers from extreme emotional distress. Ron Cohen also seems to be under severe agitation."

"In other words, Miss Howe, the possibilities you *haven't* mentioned are: Hate. Evans may be trying to get even with his father, or, this is his way to bring down Tompion and his father. Or hunger for power, a way to oust the admiral and take over the company, or greed, a sellout for a big score.

"As for Jennifer Wallack, she may have wanted her husband dead because she may still be in love with Kaluste and was a plant inside Tompion. Or she may have been coerced or blackmailed into cooperating.

"Corcoran, what's your opinion?"

"I have none at this time. This is the first I've heard of the suspicions. But anything is possible, and all angles should be checked out."

"What do you think, Mrs. Howe?"

"I don't believe any of them are guilty, so they should be cleared. But I do feel that whoever murdered Peters is hammering away at Tompion. That kind of effort takes a lot of money and and a lot of manpower. The description fits Kaluste."

"We'll contact the Sûreté for a rundown on Kaluste and Jennifer Wallack's stay in France. The men must all have service records on file. I'll be in touch with Corcoran."

* * *

It took five days for the FBI to respond. Corcoran was called down to FBI headquarters in Washington for a briefing. He flew down in the company jet and didn't return to the office until the following afternoon. He had several reports in his briefcase but he wanted no interruptions so he asked for a 5:00 P.M. meeting.

When he walked into Sidney's office, the first thing she said was, "You look sick."

"I've got a cold and I'm running a temperature."

"Is there anything to explain, or do the reports have it all?"

"I've got reports on Kaluste from the Sûreté and the CIA. There's a report on Jennifer from the Sûreté. There's a report on the Three Musketeers and one on the admiral. I had a long talk with a retired agent, Jesse Carver, who handled draft evaders in the San Francisco office. He's the one who wrote the 1965 report on Roger, Ron, and Tom. The admiral is as clean as Ivory Snow."

"Thanks, Steve. Now go home and take care the cold. Try hot tea and rum."

"I think I will. If you have any questions, call." He waved and left.

Sidney locked her door and notified the switchboard to take no calls. She poured herself a cup of black coffee and began to read. The Kaluste file had been transferred to Washington by wire and was limited. There wasn't much in there that she didn't know, except for one word that jumped out at her; "Ruthless." His reputed wealth was approximately $3 billion.

Jennifer's file was also limited. There was nothing in it that Jennifer hadn't already confessed to Sidney. Kaluste, uncle of her late husband, had been her mentor. She lived in Kaluste's mansion and was seen around Paris escorted by Kaluste. The report ended with her skiing accident, when she had moved out of Kaluste's house.

The long report was on the three Tompion executives. They had been active in antiwar parades, the civil rights movement, and student protests at UCLA. They had dropped out of college in their senior year. They had been drafted, burned their draft cards in public, and disappeared. Their names were turned over to the Federal Bureau of Investigation as draft evaders. Carver had written his report in longhand:

"On a telephone tip from one Bruce Hally, a truck with California license plates was stopped by the California Highway Patrol north of San Francisco at 3:00 A.M. this morning. In the truck were five young men and a female. The female, Lilly Anne Butterfield of Savannah, Georgia, a dropout from UCLA, is the wife of Roger Evans. She is not wanted by authorities.

Grosso, the driver, had an expired New Jersey driver's license. The men were brought to jail on suspicion of failing to report to the draft board. All the young men had registered with the National Selective Service. I presented my credentials and identified them. Grosso,

Cohen, Evans, Harrington and Brezinski.

Based on Hally's tip, the CHP Commander accused them of hauling contraband grown on a commune farm where they resided. They refused to talk. The next morning the nude body of a young man was fished out of the Bay with a bullet hole though the back of his head, gangland style. The students identified the body as Bruce Hally. When told they could either cooperate with the authorities or be held as accomplices to murder, they cooperated.

With their help, the owner of a small restaurant on the Bay was apprehended for Hally's murder. I informed the students that they faced five years in prison for draft evásion and another five years for growing and transporting contraband. By reporting "voluntarily' to the draft board, I would recommend all charges be dropped. They agreed.

All five reported to Selective Service Headquarters and were inducted immediately. We accompanied them to Fort Baker and turned them over to the Military Police."

There was another report on Roger D. Evans by Steve Corcoran:

"In off-the-record discussion with agent Carver (retired) at his home in Norfolk, Virginia, he recalled Roger Evans clearly. Evans had been classified at UCLA as mathematics genius with a scholarship to Princeton Institute for Advanced Studies. Not included in report was a government request to red-flag Roger Evans. He was to be turned down by the draft board. Evans was upset and demanded the same treatment as his friends. Unofficially, I advised him to enlist using his father's name Dutton, then once in the army revert back to his mother's name, Evans. All this would get lost in Army records. I arranged for all five men to be together.

Carver told me there was a second tragedy to the affair. While on leave the young soldiers participated in anti-War demonstrations. At a rally prior to their embarkation to Vietnam, Roger's wife was killed. She was struck with a policeman's nightstick during a demonstration."

Sidney turned to the Department of the Army records. They were terse. Tom, Ron, and Roger remained together in one unit. Roger had been captured by the Vietcong and escaped. All three had been wounded. All three had been decorated for valor. In protest against the war, all three had refused their decorations.

After a traumatic experience (not specified) Evans had been returned to the United States for shock treatment and psychiatric care in veterans hospitals in San Francisco and New York. He was medically discharged in 1969.

Sidney put down the last page and turned to face the city. Lights were being turned on, and there was a quiet glow to the dusk. She just stared off into space trying to absorb everything she had just read.

CHAPTER

EIGHTEEN

SAMANTHA O'Hare was a striking-looking woman who seemed to have escaped the aging process. Her blonde hair had lightened naturally over the years, and made the graying process very difficult to detect. She was sixty but could pass for forty-five. At 5'10" she never bent down when confronted by short people because, as she often said, "I'm not intimidated by *your* height." It was her way of forestalling comments on her own height. Her face was a healthy pale pink, and, despite its angularity, she was very feminine. Her deep blue eyes helped.

A full-figured woman with an erect carriage, she was, as the admiral said, "a no-nonsense lady." Which is why, with the rank of warrant officer, she had been his secretary in the Navy, his executive assistant at the CIA, and continued in that function at Tompion. Her Irish ancestry gave her a devastating wit, complete with tongue to match. It was an amiable disguise that covered a quick mind graced with common sense. She was a devoted slave to the admiral, and she protected him with proprietary interest.

A formidable guardian of the admiral's domain, Samantha had two secretaries of her own who handled the interoffice correspondence, meetings, agenda, schedules, memos, and reminders. "Sam," as she was known, devoted herself to the admiral's personal and confidential correspondence. When Sidney knocked on her door at exactly 10:00 A.M. on Tuesday morning to say hello, Sam made her usual joke about their men's names. "As one man to another, it's good to see you, me girl." They were genuinely fond of each other.

Sidney smiled and said, "Hi, Sam. You look great." After an exchange of pleasantries, she added, "I need to steal your brain for a few hours on a special problem — any objection if I speak to the admiral about it?"

"How could he do without me?"

"Probably very well."

"Shame on you, you heathen." They both laughed. Sam gestured to the inner office with her thumb, indicating that the admiral was ready for her. As she entered, she saw that Roger and Granby were already seated and waiting. She sat down without further ado and the meeting started.

"It dawned on me," said Admiral Dutton, "that we may be outsmarting ourselves. But before I postulate any theories, is there any progress to report?

"We've been accumulating material from around the world on a twenty-four-hour basis," Roger said. "But we're far from a merge-purge. We need at least thirty-six to forty-eight hours for that."

The admiral turned to Roscoe Granby. The elegant, patrician man-about-town looked a bit sad. "I'm suddenly getting calls from people I haven't seen in ages. All of them claim to be stockholders in our company, and almost every one of them is asking me for inside information."

"Has this happened before?" asked the admiral.

"Well, I get the odd call now and then — but I always reminded them we're a public company and how strict the SEC is on the matter. I say I'm obliged by law not to divulge anything. So people stopped asking me questions years ago. But now it's starting up again. I sense something different. All the questions are alarmingly similar."

"As though they've been coached?" Roger asked.

"Yes," Granby said.

Roger leaned toward him and asked, "Roscoe — have you kept a log of the people who called and the nature of their questions?"

"Naturally."

"Good! Have your secretary identify, where possible, their business affiliations, board directorships, large stockholdings, and major stock positions in various corporations. When we mix and match it against our computerized information, we'll have new names to feed into the data bank."

The admiral asked, "Sidney, are you making progress cross-checking the personnel files?"

"I'm having slow going, largely because of our policy of excluding certain personnel information from the computer. The policy is to prevent confidential data from being readily available to people inside the company as well as outsiders who could crack our computer codes. The confidential files are kept by division personnel managers for our 18,000 employees."

"It's not hopeless, is it?" the admiral asked.

"Wee—eell, not exactly." Sidney tapped her gold Cross pen against her teeth. "I asked our chief financial officer to scan the master computer payroll records of all permanent and part-time employees to identify people who worked at Med-Pharm in Carlyle between 1979 and 1980 and who, for one reason or another, were transferred to the New York office, left Med-Pharm, or moved to New York and were rehired here by another division. I'm particularly interested in Empire Films and Pigglies. And, as an afterthought, we're running the same dates but in reverse order — just in case something unusual pops out.

"My next request was to ask for identification of all personnel in Carlyle who have relatives working in other divisions."

"Do we keep such records?" Granby asked.

"Yes. We found it was good for morale if company policy encouraged family members to join the Tompion organization.

This is particularly valuable in smaller towns, where opportunities are limited. My last request was for a list of all consultants who work or worked for more than one division from 1979 to 1985."

"Good," the admiral said.

"Thanks."

"Excellent, Sidney," Roger said. "However one thing keeps nagging at me — something that kept me up most of last night. What if the suspected leak is not one person, but two or more? You might never tie them together, especially if they were planted there for one purpose but are otherwise unconnected."

There was a sudden silence when Roger added, "All this stems from yet another thought I had. Suppose the opposition got Roscoe onto the golf course to plant information —"

"— or disinformation?" The Admiral said.

"Exactly."

The admiral made a face. "It's getting like the CIA versus the KGB."

Sidney picked up on it immediately and said, "If I read you correctly, Roger, you suggest that we look at them as brilliant, devious, and ruthless."

"Aggressors have the choice of weapons and can make the decision when to strike and how to knock us off balance. If we have a mole in Tompion, he or she knows where we are vulnerable. If we accept that premise, they obviously know that Roscoe Granby is a very astute man who would not suffer fools gladly, especially on a golf course."

There was a lull where nothing was said as everyone's mind turned over the new possibilities. Roger was looking at Sidney, but this time she didn't consider it a stare as he caught her eye and nodded slightly. She perked up, certain that her outfit met with his approval. For a few seconds, the distraction wiped out everything else from her mind except how she had planned her outfit for the meeting.

She wore a simple summer suit: a pale yellow skirt and jacket made of linen with enough polyester to resist wrinkling. Her blouse was emerald green, and she wore emerald drop earrings, inherited from a great-aunt, that matched her blouse. As usual, she wore little makeup other than eyeliner and pale lipstick. The ensemble enhanced the color of her emerald green eyes.

Sidney was looking at the admiral when he asked, "Did you give Steve and F.D.R. their new assignments?"

"Yes, admiral. F.D.R. is in St. Louis. Steve Corcoran is working with the FBI on tracking the suspects they believe killed Peter Wallack. The FBI doesn't talk much, but it's Steve's impression that the two are a professional hit team."

The admiral said, "I'm flying to Washington to see what help I can get from the old-boy network. And Roscoe's agreed to wear a wire. It should help our case if we bring charges of harassment against whoever proceeds with a hostile takeover."

Roscoe said half-aloud, "Dad would turn over in his grave at the thought of my spying on people."

"Roscoe," the admiral said in the stern voice of an older brother, "in the first place, you're only recording your own conversations. In the second place, the value of your Tompion stock has been cut nearly fifty percent. There's an old French expression that says, 'Defend me from my friends: I can defend myself from my enemies.'"

The group laughed. When the admiral stood up, it was a signal for everyone else to rise and depart. As Sidney rose, she raised a finger, got the admiral's attention, and said, "I'd like to borrow Sam for a couple of hours."

The admiral's face wrinkled.

"Okay, let me have her for a long lunch."

"Okay, okay. Have her back by two."

"One more thing. May I confide in her about our investigation?"

"Absolutely."

On the way out of the chairman's office, Sidney stopped at Sam's desk. "Are you available for a confidential business lunch?"

"Fine, but let's eat in so we won't waste time wandering around town. The admiral probably told you to have me back by two."

"Exactly his words."

"He likes to spoil me little pleasures in life. How about Chinese?" Then, without getting a confirmation, she added, "I'll order it up for noon. Sweet and sour pork, chicken and bean sprouts, fried rice, egg rolls. Your secretary can make us tea."

"Secretaries don't make tea these days"

"Don't tell the admiral — he won't believe it. Your secretary will make tea, all right?"

"Sam, the National Organization of Women may not approve your male chauvinist ways."

"You know what they say in the navy — fuck 'em."

Sidney didn't raise an eyebrow. Instead she winked at Sam and left. She liked Samantha and enjoyed her salty sense of humor and her intelligence. She was fun to talk to. Despite her position as the admiral's assistant, she was closer to the headquarters staff in the lower echelons than any of the corporate executives.

The network among Tompion secretaries was formidable. They were sergeants in the army. Nothing moved without their say-so. They were the people who got things done. And they were always privy to classified information even their immediate bosses weren't aware of.

Samantha O'Hare was the topkick among the sergeants at Tompion. Her powers were great, her anger fierce, her loyalty unswerving. Anyone who had Samantha for a friend didn't worry about enemies..

When noon arrived Sidney's secretary, Amanda Massey, buzzed that the food had been delivered. Sidney looked at her watch and saw it was precisely 12:00. When Samantha O'Hare ordered, the Chinese restaurant wouldn't dare send the order a minute early or a minute late. As the door opened, Amanda entered, carrying a tray, the food on white ironstone plates covered by food warmers. Samantha was marching right behind her. Amanda set the food on the small, round conference table.

When Amanda said, "Sam — you want tea — Sunburst Orange. Mrs. Howe, you want Cinnamon?" When Sidney nodded, she left on her errand.

"I don't know how you do it, Sam"

"Yes, you do, or you wouldn't be the top woman executive in this place. I don't have real power and you know it. It's always the image of the admiral behind me that gives me clout."

"That's true up to a point. But people want to help you because they really like you."

When they finished their meal they sipped tea and opened fortune cookies. Sam frowned and showed her maxim to Sidney, "Easy does it.' They must have known I'm A.A."

"The saying has become part of our language. I'll bet the Chinese people who put it in didn't know its origin."

"Ah, Sidney, enough of the old troubles. Let's start on new ones. I understand you have become part of the family."

Sidney was taken aback. "What do you mean by that?"

"Only that you now know about Tom and Ron and Roger

and the admiral and his ex-wife, Cassie. That tells me a lot, Sidney. Nobody but the family knows. It means the old man loves you and trusts you."

"The way you put it, I'm honored."

"You should be — they're some pieces of baggage, those three young men. Tompion began to fly when they came in. It was the admiral's planning that did it. You see, Tom and Ron had gone back to college when Roger was in the VA hospital with a nervous breakdown. When Roger was released, he wandered around the country to see old friends from the antiwar movement, but they didn't want to see him. He'd been in the army, you see. So for a while he tried to live with his mother in Hollywood, but they were different people. It didn't work.

"Meanwhile, Tompion was moving along slowly, doing fine but not great. The admiral desperately wanted his son with him, to make up for all the missing years. But at first Roger wouldn't join Tompion. Then the admiral asked him to do some consulting work which involved evaluating the financial division. Roger agreed. His report was brilliant. The admiral pressed him for some time to join the company. The years went by, and about ten years ago, Roger said he would work for Tompion under certain conditions.

"First the admiral had to hire all three. At the time, Ron was with a big law firm, and Tom was running a medium-sized real estate firm. The admiral hasn't regretted it once. I can tell you he worships the ground Roger walks on and he dotes on the other two. Roger made other conditions. Five percent of the company's annual income, which would be tax deductible for charitable contributions, goes to various Vietnam veterans' organizations. And the final condition was that, wherever possible, disabled vets get preference in being hired."

"I know about that company policy because the personnel directors report to me."

"Of course. But I thought you might be interested in how it started."

"I am, thank you, Sam, because it ties in with what we're up to: trying to save Tompion. Actually, it's the reason for this meeting. I'm investigating a hush-hush problem in the company." Sidney then went on to tell her what she was trying to uncover, her efforts to go through papers and computer records. "But I also need some human input. I wonder if you can think of any area I'm not getting at — gossip, rumors floating around that might shed some light."

"You remind me of the admiral's tenure at the CIA. They had a shibboleth there — off the record, of course — that whenever you encountered a breach-of-security problem, you asked two questions: 'Who's screwing whom?' and 'Who suddenly got rich?' When you uncovered the answers to those questions, you usually resolved the problem."

"That's what I had in mind. I thought you might ask your secretaries, off the record, for help in spotting anything odd."

"Have you considered, Sidney, me girl, that it may not be someone inside the company informing, except indirectly. In the State Department there was a case involving a secretary, a sort of mousy girl, shy, a little stout, who worked at a U.S. embassy in Europe. Who would ever suspect this mouse of being a Mata Hari? Well she was, and she wasn't.

"An alert head of station spotted that this shy secretary was suddenly dressing elegantly in the office. She now wore contact lenses. She tinted her hair, wore more makeup and sexier dresses. But, most of all, her ebullience gave her away. Sure as the gods look upon me, the little lamb had found a lover. A tall, young, handsome stud who drove a car for a foreign embassy and drove her into ecstasy each night. During the day she photocopied classified and secret documents."

"What happened?"

"They caught her, explaining what she had been doing. She was horrified to believe that her boyfriend was a spy. He only wanted to learn how the embassy operated. The head of station made a deal with her and, in espionage parlance, "turned" her. A confidential briefing on who the chauffeur was and how he was using her angered the mouse. This is what the head of station wanted. Now he could show her a way to get even with him. She began to feed disinformation, prepared by the CIA, to the lover. Meanwhile, as the agency pointed out to her, she would be serving her country and continue to entertain her lover.

"We could have a woman or man, one who is being pumped for information deviously by a clever lover. Or even someone who is being blackmailed into giving information because of a past indiscretion."

"Sam, now you know why I asked for your help."

"I'll get to work at once. Sex gossip around the office always makes me day. I can still remember the nights with me own sweet Timothy, may he rest in peace."

They spent fifteen minutes together chatting on general matters. "By the way," Sidney said, "I haven't seen Tom around anywhere."

"One of his kids is having a problem at St. Louis University. He's gone out there trying to straighten the boy out. Incidentally, are you aware that Tom is being groomed to take the admiral's place when he steps down?"

Sidney was surprised. "I didn't know that."

"Nobody knows yet, but it's obvious. Ron realizes that he is a corporate lawyer and a crackerjack. But he isn't an operations man or an administrator. He wants to stay where he is. Roger knows he isn't outgoing. He's too shy. Besides, most of the time, he is in another world. Roger and Ron were the ones who recommended Tom. It also helped that he got a Wharton School MBA when he came back from Nam. The old man approved that."

"So he got three dynamos instead of one."

"Something like that. You're family, so I can tell you that Tom is the most stable of the three. Ron and Roger are still suffering the aftereffects of Vietnam. Ron's been married twice and divorced twice. He can't handle a relationship, yet it doesn't affect his work. Roger seems to be looking for the perfect woman, but he won't find her because he isn't looking in your direction.

"Tom is short and cocky, just like a peacock. He likes people and people like him. He can make small talk, and he's quick and glib on his feet. When he puts his foot in his mouth, Roger or Ron are there to yank it out. They fight and argue all the time, but they're like brothers.

"And did you know Tom's married to Ron's younger sister?"

"No. I've talked to Gail at company functions, but I didn't know the connection."

"Gail was in high school when she started corresponding with Tom. It was a class assignment. Write a friendly letter to a young GI in Vietnam. She picked one her brother's best friends. She was also involved in the civil rights movement as a kid and she admired her brother deeply. She ended up marrying Tom.

"Gail may only be a slip of a girl, five feet tall and ninety-eight pounds soaking wet, but she's a pistol at the PTA meetings and in politics. She's a lawyer, like Ron, and graduated from Yale Law School. They have two boys. It's a real stable marriage. Gail tries hard to make the marriage work and even harder to understand the effects of the war on Tom. Because of Gail, Tom has few problems."

CHAPTER

NINETEEN

THE next afternoon Sidney was involved studying the reports spread out on her conference table. She was baffled as she reread the accumulated information. Nothing went into neat slots, as she had anticipated. Even Sam's report concerning the assistant marketing manager at Granby Development seen coming to work in a new fire-engine red 450 Mercedes, turned out to be purchased with money he inherited.

As for the dozen people who had made intercorporate job changes within the conglomerate, four had been in accounting. It struck Sidney that the only job that enabled someone to wander about the conglomerate unquestioned was in the accounting department. She decided to put these four dossiers aside for microscopic examination. A check on the remainder revealed that they were in low positions in their departments, primarily in sales. Upon closer investigation, they all had legitimate reasons for changing jobs.

Sidney went to the trouble of screening her own staff. She was satisfied, but she was still uneasy about explaining her actions in detail. She called a staff meeting in her office. Behind closed doors, she confided she was working on a special project. Then she asked for their indulgence. She said she was not at liberty to reveal the nature of the project at this time, but expected complete cooperation and confidentiality. They all agreed.

Sidney was reviewing the accumulated files and reports prepared by her staff for the umpteenth time. Her discouragement was strictly the end-of-the-day blues. At this juncture, her secretary buzzed her on the intercom.

"Mrs. Howe, Roger Evans of Financial Services is on the phone."

"Thanks, Amanda." She pressed the blinking telephone

button and said, "Hello, Roger."

"Sidney, I've come up empty. How about you?"

"Zilch. Zero. For a moment I thought I was onto something this afternoon, but couldn't put my finger on it. So I guess I have nothing."

"You thought you had a clue?"

"No, just a will-o'-the-wisp that won't go away."

There was a pause. Then Roger said, "Two heads are better than one."

"Supposed to be."

"The car will pick you up downstairs in twenty minutes." The phone clicked off, and Sidney was left holding the receiver.

The jewel in the Tompion crown was located on Broad Street in the financial district in downtown Manhattan. She had been to offices of Tompion Financial Services twice in her five years with the company. The last time was more than two years ago. It was a boring meeting. She remembered looking out of Roger's window and seeing the bronze statue of George Washington at Federal Hall, marking the spot where he had given his Farewell Address to his troops. She had lost interest in the meeting and remembered begging off so she could read the inscription on the statue.

Current rumor had it that the New York Stock Exchange was threatening to move out of New York. Yet, after looking at the statue, Sidney knew that most of the wheelers and dealers had too great a sense of history to move to New Jersey. The daily financial transactions in a few blocks in lower Manhattan made the world turn.

Sidney pulled herself out of her daydream, gathered her papers, and stuffed them into a briefcase. Then she buzzed Amanda to hold her calls. She went to her clothes closet and selected a new bright blue dress with shoes to match and carried them into her private bathroom. Removing her beige skirt and blouse, she washed and then slipped into her dress. As she applied new makeup and brushed her hair, she knew she looked tired. She thought, *If he tells me again that I look like hell, I'll punch him out.*

When she was ready, Sidney asked Amanda to bring in her messages. There were a half-dozen, but none of them pertained to the task force. She instructed Amanda how to handle them. "I'll be at Mr. Evans's office. I don't know for how long, but you know the people to tell. You can reach me after five on the pager. When you're ready to leave the office, please advise my service."

A little after 4:00 P.M., Gates picked her up in the Lincoln. A month ago, she would have wondered how, with a fleet of company cars available, Roger Evans used the admiral's big Lincoln. Gates pulled away from Tompion Towers and moved eastward, slipping onto the East River Drive.

When the car left the drive at 23rd Street, she said, "Gates, you're supposed to take me to Financial Services."

"Miss Sidney, Mr. Evans requested that I take you to his house."

"Oh."

The car continued west on 23rd Street until it reached Lexington. Then it turned left for two blocks and turned right at the Gramercy Park Hotel. Gates drove left around the park enclosed in metal grillework. Sidney knew that only residents had keys to the park. Gates stopped in front of an elegant, old-fashioned six-story apartment house. As she climbed the half-dozen steps to the front door, the Lincoln pulled away. Sidney entered the hall and looked at the listing of residents, there were only three. She pressed *Evans.*

"Sidney?" a hollow voice asked on the intercom.

"Roger, Roger." Then she started laughing, her first good

laugh of the day. There was a buzzing, and the front door clicked open. Roger had No. 3, the top apartment. He met her at the elevator dressed in sneakers, chinos, and a fancy green-and-white tennis shirt. His hair was combed carelessly and his glasses were sliding down his nose.

"I thought we were going to work."

"We are, and who said you couldn't be comfortable at work? You look lovely. Blue brings out the green in your eyes." He led her into the flat, which turned out to be a duplex apartment, and, she learned later, had a garden on the top floor. She had no time to notice the decor as she followed him into a large, spacious office.

He motioned her to sit at the library table. "I thought we could use a war office for the duration, where there would be little interference and complete security. I have a sophisticated IBM computer, which is already connected to the office and research files. If we have a spy, he or she could be anywhere — even on my staff."

Besides the large computer, there was a personal IBM computer on a desk next to a NEC printer on a stand, a modem connecting the computers to the telephone, several filing cabinets, bookcases with dozens of reference books, Value Line reports, and commodity statistics. On the wall was a current map of the world.

Sidney stood up, opened her briefcase on the library table, and said a little icily, "I think what you're implying, Roger, is that it could even be someone on my staff."

"Exactly."

She felt a twinge of resentment and commented, "Well, for your information, I've already screened my staff and they're clean."

His voice sounded deliberately patient as he replied, "Sid-

ney, if someone is planning to take us over after sabotaging us —
someone with lots of brains and money — wouldn't he be clever
enough to hide an employee who would escape detection?"

"Aren't you exaggerating, Roger?"

"Perhaps, but if I am, I prefer to err on our side. It all came
together for me the minute the admiral said it was war. Then I
began to think of it in terms of a chess game, which is really
another form of war. The enemy makes the first move. This
enables me to put myself in my opponent's shoes."

Sidney sat down and put her chin on her hand, a dejected
look on her face. Roger leaned on the table and brought his face
closer to hers. "Either you're tense or I'm boring you. Maybe it's
just that you've been cooped up in a stuffy office all day. Let's take
a walk in Gramercy Park before we start work.

"If you'd like to get into something more comfortable,
Mother keeps some clothes here. You look about the same size."
She sighed and nodded her head.

He led her to the guest room on the same floor, told her to
help herself, and left. Everything in the room was antique white,
from the queen-size bed to the twin chests of drawers, the vanity,
and the chairs. Even the TV set was white and sat on a white
stand. Rummaging through the closet, she found several pairs of
dungarees, khaki chinos, and cotton tennis shirts. She found a
striped tennis shirt that matched Roger's exactly and she selected
it, along with a pair of men's chinos about her size. Impishly, she
took off her bra before putting on the shirt. She inhaled and
smiled. She zipped up the pants, pulled down the snug shirt, and
decided the clothes fit remarkably well — even the old running
shoes.

When Roger saw her, he looked surprised. "Jesus, you look
just like my mother. She doesn't wear a bra either."

Sidney laughed. "Some compliment!"

"It is. She's the movie star, Cassie Evans. You know you actually resemble her — the way she looked when she was younger. She's been going to NYU for three years to get the education she couldn't afford as a kid. Sometimes she comes here for weekends. She likes to wander around the area incognito. Casual clothes helps. On Mother's Day I bought matching shirts at Bloomingdale's. So she wears what I wear and passes herself off as my sister."

Sidney inflated her shirt with a deep breath and said, "I'm not keen on passing myself off as your sister."

When they reached the street, the sun was still out but the buildings on the west side cast long shadows across the park. Roger opened the gate and they went in. At first they just strolled slowly around the park in the vivid greenery of the trees and grass. In a corner of the park, two maids in uniform were watching three four-year-olds playing with a white plastic ball and an oversized red plastic bat.

Roger pointed out where Eleanor Roosevelt had lived, where the movie actor John Garfield had died making love to his girlfriend, told stories about some of the big houses which had been the homes of famous writers and artists. "That's the Players Club over there, where famous stage actors used to meet. It's fading now."

Then they sat down on a park bench just watching the birds, the squirrels and the children. At 5:30 they went back to the apartment. Sidney felt more relaxed. "I'd like to see the rest of your apartment, Roger."

"Work now. Tour later."

"Yes, sir."

Roger frowned and pushed his glasses back up to the bridge

of his nose. She sat down and extracted the papers from her briefcase. She reviewed her findings. After a few minutes, he interrupted her and said, "Would it disturb you if I walked around while you talked?"

"Of course not."

He began to pace around the room moving with a slow elegant grace that reminded suddenly her of a panther she'd once seen at the Bronx Zoo. The similarity just stuck in her mind. It became difficult for her to concentrate on what she was reading. "So far I've abandoned all except these four, which involve the accounting departments. They seem so unlikely."

"Why?"

"Well, each would not only have access to financial information, but could wander around unnoticed. We publish quarterly reports for stockholders. We also file annual 10-K and quarterly 10-Q statements with the Securities and Exchange Commission, and they become a matter of public record. But there are also detailed 8-K reports to the SEC that involve important material changes that can't wait for the next quarterly due date."

Roger stopped walking. "I sense that your will-o'-the-wisp comment on the phone may contain the germ of an idea that is still unformed. I know you're a psychologist, but things close to us are often invisible. I respect your brain and trust your instincts. I'd like to explore this avenue of inquiry further. Suppose I question you from several viewpoints."

Flattered at his respect, she said, "Okay."

"Let's make the assumption the person *is* in accounting and follow it to the end." She kept her eyes on him as he began pacing again. "I don't know if you remember the play *Jacobowsky and the Colonel* — it doesn't really matter what the play was about — but Jacobowsky had a way of using logic that was astounding. He said that every problem had two possible solutions. If you could eliminate the wrong one, you were left with the right one.

"So, if the person is indeed an accountant, there are two possibilities. Either an accountant-spy was recruited for some specific job, or our enemy had no choice but to use a mole who just happened to be an accountant.

"The latter would be impossible to uncover. Yet the very nature of the work implies unquestioned access to other departments. Yet, if it is the first possibility, the spy would have access to financials long before they were made public."

Sidney said, "And could doctor figures, bury reports, cause delays — and make it appear that someone else was responsible."

"Accounting can't be ruled out. Now let's examine your suspicious accountants."

"There are four."

"Where do they work and what are their backgrounds?"

"Well, Sylvia Hargrove, forty-seven, works at Empire Films Studios in Los Angeles, and has been there five years. Prior to that, she worked at Unicorn Life and Casualty in Denver. She's a bookkeeper in accounts receivable. Health was her reason for moving. Allergies."

"On a scale of one-to-ten let's give her a low three." Roger said. "Who's next?"

"Dominic Capriccio, thirty-four, employed at Pigglies in St. Louis for three years. Prior to that worked in production at Empire Films. He was in France during the sex scandal. He worked in payroll. His superiors give him high ratings. Reason for the move, he claims he wanted to stay in one place."

"He has possibilities. Let's give him a seven."

"Rita Honeycut, thirty-one, employed at Empire Films in Los Angeles as a controller one year. Prior to that worked at

Tompion Financial Services five years. She is a CPA and worked in the Adirondack Commodities Division. Her job was to review and recalculate all computations on commodity purchases and sales. Do you remember her? Was she beautiful?"

"Yes. An attractive redhead with a sharp mind. She wanted to go to Hollywood to marry a rich man."

"How did she get to Empire?"

"Her work was excellent and she wanted to move west. One day she came to see me in person and explained why. I laughed at her and she became very angry. But what the hell, she was honest, so I put in a good word for her and she was hired. The feedback is that she's doing well."

"Maybe she had designs on you?"

"She did. Who's the fourth?"

Sidney had expected more of an explanation. She was startled when Roger switched the subject. She took a deep breath and read, "Tanya Kensington, twenty-eight, bookkeeper, Purchasing Department, Tompion International HQ, New York, five years, Med-Pharm in Carlyle one year, purchasing department. Began when she was twenty-two. A bit young."

"Do you have photographs of our four candidates?"

"There's a head shot of each one."

Roger looked at Sidney and frowned. "If you have a photo of each one, why did you ask me if Rita Honeycutt was beautiful?"

"Female bitchiness."

"You're not the type, Sidney."

"You're right, I'm not. Frankly, I don't know why I said that."

"And you have a doctorate in psychology?"

Sidney took a very deep breath. "She's very beautiful even in that poor Polaroid shot." Her voice became almost inaudible. "I guess I was jealous."

"Why, for heaven's sake?"

Sidney looked at him and debated whether she was being silly or he was being naive. When she didn't see the light go on in his eyes, she concluded he was naive. Maybe the redhead wasn't his type.

"Sylvia, Dominic, Rita, and Tanya — are they all American-born?" Roger asked.

"Yes."

"Their jobs are as follows: accounts receivable, payroll, controller, and purchasing department. Let me make a statement and you try to break it down."

"Shoot!"

"All four are involved in sabotaging our company. All started working for the firm at approximately the same time."

"No, they started working at different periods of time. No two are even close."

"So it suggests just one. Do you think it's worth a phone call to see if any documents are missing in the accounting departments of the various divisions?"

Sidney picked up the phone and called Sam, whom she knew would still be at the office. When Sidney found her in, she asked her to reach Aaron Godinski, the chief financial officer of Tompion, and have him call her back. She read off Roger's phone number.

"Uh-oh, you're at Roger's apartment. Have fun."

By the time she could say, "We're working," Sam hung up. Roger looked at her quizzically and she said, "Sam will track him down wherever he is. We may have to wait a while for his call."

"Let's keep going. If you were a spy and wanted to sabotage Tompion, which one of these four jobs would you prefer to have?"

"The purchasing department."

"Why?" Roger began to pace around the room again.

"I can foul up orders. Order the wrong sizes for things, order too much or too little, or not order certain key items."

"Okay, now let's move laterally. Other than buying supplies, what other functions does the purchasing department perform?"

"If you wanted to order a computer, for example, it would go through purchasing."

"What else?"

"A fleet of cars for our salesmen. Purchasing would buy the fleet at wholesale."

"Okay, let's look at services."

"I can't think of any."

"Who hires janitorial services?"

"Head of maintenance."

"Could it be someone in maintenance?"

"Yes, but they aren't on the payroll. We contract for the service. They hire the people to do the work."

"We may be on to something. Let's keep that one in mind as a possibility. How about security?"

"Steve is in overall charge. He either hires the services of a local security company, or he okays a security company after it's been selected locally. Usually he flies to the division to assess what security is needed and the proposal for handling it. Then he decides what should be done."

"Okay, outside of maintenance and security, what other services do we use?"

"TV monitors for security control."

"Does one outfit handle all our companies?"

"I'm not sure. I'll have to check." Sidney made notes to herself on a yellow legal pad. "I'm starved. I haven't eaten since breakfast."

"Work first. Eat later. Copy machines?

"I don't know. It was decided that every company buy its own, depending upon requirements."

"What other services do the divisions buy in common?"

Just then the telephone rang. Roger picked it up, listened, exchanged a few words, then handed it to Sidney. It was Godinski. Sidney peppered him with questions about trouble in the various accounting departments. He replied that there wasn't anything abnormal that he had heard of, but he would report back in the morning.

She said, "Thanks, Aaron." As she was about to put down the receiver, she looked at it and shouted *"The telephone!"*

CHAPTER

TWENTY

SIDNEY began to speak rapidly. "The phone service. I remember now. We were installing a new phone service in Carlyle just before Xynatron made their offer. It was installed by a major firm and it was so inexpensive that we couldn't turn it down. About a year after I'd come to New York, the same company installed a system throughout Tompion."

"Who recommended it? Do you know the company's name, or who recommended it?"

"No. But do you think that he is in the purchasing department?" She paused to collect her thoughts and added, "If it's true that all the company's telephones could be wired directly to an outside extension, it would far simpler than having our phones tapped. And impossible to trace."

Roger added, "They wouldn't have to do it with every phone — just the telephones of key executives. It would also explain why no listening devices were ever found by security people when they checked the offices. The admiral is very meticulous about bugs. Sidney, can you recall the name of that telephone company?"

"I've been racking my brain and I can't remember. Sam's in her office — why don't I call her?"

"All right, but be careful what you say."

Sidney nodded as she dialed the office. "Sam, me again. I had trouble with my phone today — some static — whom do we call for repairs?"

Sam answered, "I'll do it now. We get excellent service. I'll have a repairman there first thing in the morning." Sidney gestured to Roger that she was unsuccessful. Roger pointed to himself.

"Thanks, Sam. Roger would like to talk with you." She handed the phone to him.

"Sam, I'd like a tricky phone installation in my home and would like to discuss it with the company. What's their phone number?" Roger listened, thanked her and hung up.

Then he dialed the number. When the switchboard operator said, "WT&T, how may I help you?" he hung up slowly.

"WT&T — they're a listed company on the New York Stock Exchange," he said. He walked over to his reference books and pulled out Value Line and located the page that described the company. He sat down and placed the book on the table as Sidney sat down beside him, leaning on his shoulder as they both read through the report. WT&T was a multibillion dollar telephone/communications organization with offices in London, Paris, Geneva, Berlin, and Tokyo. It was IT&T's chief competitor in worldwide telecommunications.

The New York stock markets were closed, as were their research libraries but it was only 3:00 P.M. in San Francisco. Roger seated himself in front of his large computer and switched it on. Using his modem, he typed out his identification number and several questions and directed it to a West Coast investment banker with whom Tompion did business. They hardly spoke for the next five minutes as the tension began to mount. Sidney was leaning against his back, looking over his shoulder at the monitor. Suddenly there was a flash on the monitor as the requested responses came though. There — in front of them — was the information. Three large companies were the majority stock holders, one American, one English, and one French. The name that jumped out at Roger was the gigantic Salumbe Teletronics of France.

"That company is controlled by Constantin Kaluste!" Roger said excitedly. "I ran across it just yesterday in my own research."

"Bingo!" Sidney shouted.

Roger stood up and they hugged each other. Suddenly embarrassed, he backed away apologetically. They looked at each other until Sidney moved toward him, her arms around his waist, holding on for dear life. He kissed the top of her head, tilted it, and kissed her softly on the lips. He saw tears streaming down her face. "Why are you crying?" he asked.

"I don't know. I've been hoping you'd kiss me."

He put his mouth to her lips, squeezing her cheeks between his left thumb and forefinger until her lips parted. He put his tongue in her mouth and she was overcome by a surge of uncontrollable passion. Her whole body seemed to come alive and vibrate in his arms. She felt his hands massage the bare skin of her back. It was electric. As they continued their long, erotic kiss, his left hand moved from her back to her breast and began to fondle it. His right hand unzipped her pants and began massaging her belly. By the time it reached her silky pubis, she was experiencing an orgasm. Her body trembled. Her arms were wrapped around him so tightly that she was crushing the air out of her own body. Suddenly she felt drained and exhausted.

"What will happen when we have sex?"

"Don't talk," she whispered.

Roger picked her up in his arms and carried her toward the stairs, kissing her eyes, her nose, and lips as he went along. Her body was warm and her eyes were closed. He carried her upstairs easily. In his bedroom, he put her gently on the bed which had already been turned down for the evening. He raised the tennis shirt over her chest, flicked his tongue like a feather's kiss over her body, and licked her erect nipples. Her sexual smell acted on Roger like an aphrodisiac.

" Rest for a few minutes. I'm going to take a shower."

Through half-closed eyes, she watched him strip. He had a

swimmer's body: wide shoulders and a narrow waist, and well-developed arm muscles that rippled as he pulled the tennis shirt over his head. When his pants and shorts came off, his penis was erect. It seemed enormous.

Sidney closed her eyes when the shower started. She must have slept because it seemed only an instant later that he was straddling her, his hair damp. He removed her shirt, then her pants and pink silk panties. She stretched under him like a cat, putting her arms above her head to flex her body muscles and stretch her breasts taut as she gazed up at him. He leaned down and licked the dark nipples until they popped up again.

Then he moved down her body, opened her legs, and placed his tongue lightly on her clitoris. He was gentle but firm as he began to excite her, but she could not contain herself and once more she began to writhe and struggle. He held her down until finally she let out a piercing scream of ecstasy. But Roger didn't stop. She lost all count of time or where she was.

Finally, when she was exhausted, she began to coax him to lie down beside her. When he moved beside her and faced her, she could smell his masculine scent mixed with the unmistakable aroma of soap. She kissed him and entangled her legs in his.

They stayed this way for a long time. Then she blew into his ear and began to kiss his face, then his chest, while her fingertips found his genitals. His penis was erect again and seemed to strain at the skin as she bent down and flicked her tongue on the head of it. Then she moistened it with her mouth, feeling it growing even larger. She rolled him onto his back, straddled him, and slowly inserted him into her body. Slowly, rhythmically, she began to move up and down, moaning, "Oh, God! Oh!"

As they began to accelerate their rhythm, Sidney sensed that he was deliberately holding back in order to please her. She loved him for it. She had a film of fine perspiration over her body now, and was surprised that she could have multiple orgasms. It took him a long time to come, and the explosion inside her lifted her into a new uncharted ecstasy. Finally they were exhausted. She stretched out beside him, and they fell asleep together.

They were startled hours later by the harsh jangle of the telephone. It was 9:30 P.M. Roger answered, his voice not at all sleepy. Once his eyes were open he was instantly awake. It was Steve Corcoran asking to speak to Sidney. He told him to hold, put his hand over the phone, and told her who it was. She nodded, sat up, and took the receiver.

"Steve?"

"Boss, I've got some bad news. Our suspects are dead."

"What happened?"

"It took us a long time, but we traced their flights through the airlines, first to Newark Airport, then Chicago, then on to the Kansas City Airport. When they started their Mustang in the parking lot, it exploded. The trail stopped there."

"Where are you?"

"At FBI headquarters in Washington. The J. Edgar Hoover Building."

"Steve, the admiral's in Washington at some navy function. You should have no trouble finding him — especially with FBI help. Reach him pronto and tell him we need him back in New York immediately."

"What's up?" Roger had his ear to the phone and he took it from Sidney.

"Steve, this is Roger Evans. Sidney hit the mother lode but it's not for discussion on the telephone."

"Understood."

"Oblique speak?"

There was a pause until Steve caught his drift and said, "Naturally."

"Remember Saturday 1:00 P.M?"

Another pause. "Yep!"

"It's roundup time."

"Read you four-by-four."

"I'm told you're an old movie buff."

"Correct."

"You arrange it on the Ameche your end?"

"The bells are ringing."

When Roger hung up, Sidney was standing in front of him, hands on her hips, legs apart, totally naked. She was looking at him strangely. "What was that all about?"

"I didn't want him calling the office. I didn't want to phone from here. The "Ameche" stands for Don Ameche, the movie actor who starred in the movie about Alexander Graham Bell. He'll contact the admiral, as you requested. But he'll also phone the rest of our task force to meet here as quickly as they can make it."

"When do you think that will be?"

"At best two hours, at worst, around midnight."

"Can we shower and then eat? I'm starved."

Roger smiled and led her into the large bathroom, which was tiled in pale green, switched on the light in the shower, and turned on the water. She tested it, stepped in, and he moved in beside her. She picked up the soap and began to soap him down, noticing, for the first time, the long, deep scar with a bluish tinge that went from the base of his neck and continued partway down his chest. She washed it, then his back and buttocks and his legs, and then she turned him around and began to soap him from his waist downward. By the time she reached his sex organs, her ministrations had brought him to a full erection. She soaped it slowly and carefully with her hands, and he began fondling her breasts while the water cascaded over them. He reached over and kissed her nipples.

He put his hands under her armpits, lifting her as he bent slightly at the knees. She sensed his intentions and opened her legs and wrapped them around his waist as he went into her. She remembered screaming but vaguely wondered why. When it was over, her knees were so weak that she couldn't stand. Roger propped her up against the wall with one hand as he soaped her body with the other. Finally, as they let the water cleanse them, he kept running his hands over her beautiful breasts, narrow waist, and flaring hips. Her legs were long and tapered like a dancer's, and when the water washed away the soap, a tired Sidney was clinging to him for dear life, not wanting to breathe or move. Roger picked her up and wrapped her in a large green towel, covering her completely.

She continued to hold his head and half-whisper into his ear, not wishing to look him in the eye. "It's been a long, long time since I've had a man — and longer than I can remember that I felt free to let myself go."

"I understand."

"I don't know what got into me."

"I did."

"I meant —"

"I know what you meant." And then they went into the kitchen and ate three tunafish sandwiches apiece. At 11:00 P.M. sharp, Roger's houseman, entered and Sidney saw a medium-sized Oriental man, slim, in black coolie trousers and shirt. He smiled as Roger introduced him, but it was apparent that his English was limited. Roger spoke to him in a foreign, singsong language she guessed was Vietnamese. He left quietly.

"I call Chi Loi 'Chili.' He is my teacher."

"What does he teach?"

"Among other things, he teaches me Oriental wisdom, patience, and aiki, a form of unarmed combat."

"Like karate?"

"More or less."

"Roger, I'd like to learn a few moves to protect myself from muggers when I run in Central Park. Would you teach me?"

"It'll be my pleasure."

The door chimes sounded. The first one to arrive was Roscoe Granby. Chili showed him straight into the war room.

CHAPTER

TWENTY
ONE

ROSCOE Granby was seated at the table holding a sheaf of papers when Sidney and Roger entered. "I hope you have good news," Granby said.

"Yes. We nailed Kaluste," Roger said.

"That's wonderful. Are these useless now?" Granby asked as he handed over the list of names, business associations, and stock holdings of his inquiring friends.

"No. We'll check them out and confirm our findings." Using his computer, modem, and his worldwide contacts, Roger started to track the web of connections. They all led directly to the Kaluste empire.

"Bingo!" Sidney said.

"Once you know where to look, the rest is easy," Roger said with a smile.

Ron arrived together with Tom. As they were filled in, they began to brim with excitement. By the time the admiral and Steve Corcoran arrived, there were empty coffee cups all over. Everyone was smiling.

"Admiral, the pieces all fit together," Roger said. "It's a Kaluste operation."

"Certain?"

"Positive."

"Do you have proof?"

This time it was Ron who answered. "It's all circumstantial."

The admiral said, "All right. What have you got and how did you get it?"

Roger replied, "Sidney gets the credit. She figured out —"

Sidney stopped him. "….I got to a point and could go no further. Roger was able to put it all together with inexorable logic. The answer is WT&T. It's Kaluste-owned. WT&T installed telephones at Med-Pharm before the merger. Later they installed telephones in New York. Admiral, they've been listening in on all our telephone conversations."

The admiral cleared his throat. When everyone was silent, he said, "Great work, you two. But before we start congratulating ourselves, I learned in Washington this evening that three different corporations, each owners of record of slightly less than five percent of Tompion common stock, are applying to the SEC to acquire more. They appear to be acting separately. From what you've uncovered, they're probably acting in concert. Our job now is to see whether we can link them to Kaluste."

Roger sat down at the computer and once more tried to track the companies. This time he drew a blank. There were no connections to Kaluste.

Tom said, "Is it possible these companies are simply acting on their own? Vultures out for a killing on the market?"

"Or greenmail?" Granby said.

"No," replied the admiral. "This operation has cost Kaluste a fortune. He would not allow anyone to interfere."

"He might welcome it, admiral, if he thought it would throw us and the SEC off the track," said Roger.

But the brilliance of the Kaluste pattern was all too clear to the Tompion executives. Finally, it was Ron who tried to put it together. "Admiral, how much stock do you consider friendly — that is, the Granby family, yourself, the executives here, the Wallacks, et cetera?"

"I keep an accurate count of it at all times, Ron." He took a notebook from his pocket and said, "About 23 percent. If all our executives exercised their stock options it would be 27 percent."

Tom said, "I suggest that we join the fight and exercise our stock options at once. I also suggest that the company lend money for this purpose to those who need it."

"That's perfectly legal, Tom, with board approval. Now admiral, I'd like your permission to check our list of major shareholders. Then our investment banker can identify the institutions and trusts holdings of large blocks of stock. It's a long shot, but according to our bylaws, we can block a takeover if we can get over 50 percent of the stockholders to side with us."

"With our stock sitting just above 50," the admiral said, "we won't have many friends among the institutional investors."

Tom who spoke up next. "The Pigglies rumor will be hard to stop, just as Procter & Gamble couldn't stop the Satan rumor. The *Charlemagne* affair is too far gone to investigate. The Peter Wallack murder case is stopped cold. That bastard Kaluste will tie us up in court. We'll be stopped from trying to change our bylaws and setting up a poison pill. The media will start carrying unconfirmed rumors. There will be speculation about our demise. Then Wall Street will start to hammer away at us."

Roger asked, "What are you getting at, Tom?"

"The way this Machiavelli works, every tentacle you cut off will grow back. The only chance we have is to strike back at Kaluste."

Suddenly interested, Sidney asked, "How do you do that?"

"I don't know," he said quietly, "but there has to be a way."

The consensus was that Ron be authorized go to any legal lengths to stop the takeover. Tom was assigned to work with Roscoe and the admiral in pushing the SEC and the Department of Defense to find provable links to a foreign government.

Roger said, "Tompion has large cash reserves. If we buy back a large number of our own shares, we shrink the number of shares and increase our percentage."

"It's a thought," the admiral said, "but we'll be competing for

Tompion shares with at least three other bidders."

Ron said, "They may already own more shares than we do. Remember, Kaluste has unlimited capital resources, while we have a fiduciary responsibility to our shareholders. We must be careful how we use the Tompion cash reserves."

Granby said, "To control 50 percent of Tompion stock we need thirty million more shares. The street value is about a billion and half. We'd use up our resources and go heavily into debt."

"It's another alternative, admiral," Tom said. "To get it in motion will require a board meeting and a public offering. That takes three months. Do we have time?"

Ron said, "Until we make a final determination, why don't we use it as a public relations bluff."

The admiral said, "Okay. We'll call a special board meeting and bring everyone up to date. Then we'll see what our outside directors have to say."

"One other suggestion," Roger said. His voice sounded so strange that even Steve, who was out of his element in this kind of meeting, looked at him. "Does it make sense to have a face-to-face confrontation with Mr. Kaluste? Perhaps there's a way to negotiate with him without killing Tompion."

That comment led to more discussion, more coffee, and more brandy. It was resolved at 3:30 A.M., when Roger volunteered to go and the task force agreed.

At 3:35 A.M. Sidney offered to fly to Austin to talk with Jennifer. It was important to get as much information as possible on Kaluste.

"You're right, Sidney," the admiral said. "It's as Henry Wadsworth Longfellow pointed out, 'If we could but read the secret history of our enemies.' Do what you can."

Then it was over. They separated and went home, the

admiral dropping Sidney at her apartment. She thought that she was too excited to fall asleep, but when her head hit the pillow, it was all over.

CHAPTER

TWENTY TWO

WHEN Sidney walked off the plane and entered the terminal, she looked at the dozens of people at the arrival gate. She didn't see Jennifer until a fat, sloppily dressed, oversized woman embraced her. When Sidney stepped back, she was shocked. She didn't recognize Jennifer. The 115-pound beauty had been transformed into a 200-pound slob in less than eight weeks. She wore no makeup, her hair was unkempt, and her off-the-rack clothing was too large and billowed around her body. The beautiful reddish hair that inspired her nickname — Ginger — was straggly; the once proud model's face with its high cheekbones was as round as a pumpkin. Her skin had an unhealthy pallor and there was a smell of liquor on her breath. Sidney felt sick.

"I know what you're thinking, Sidney. I'm a fat pig. I can't stop eating or drinking. All I do is think of Peter. I loved him so."

"You're killing yourself, Jennifer."

"I can't forget what I did to him."

They started walking to her car. "Jennifer, I came to see how you were doing. I also need your help."

Jennifer stopped, caught her breath, and asked, "What kind of help?"

"We think that Kaluste is trying to take over Tompion."

"I already told you that."

"I know. But we can't prove it. We have some suspicious connections, but not the kind of proof that will stand up in court. He's brilliant, all right. He's working through American corporations as respectable fronts. At the same time, he's sabotaging Tompion. Peter's murder, the rumors about Pigglies — and tampering with *Charlemagne* which almost resulted in a $50 millon loss."

They walked to a blue Ford station wagon. Once they were seated, Jennifer said, "Take my word for it. If Kaluste made up his mind to get Tompion, nothing can stop him. I know. I've seen him and Viktor work."

"That's why I'm here. I need your help. I want to get as much information as I can on Kaluste and his companies and the people he deals with. I especially want to know how he behaves with women — his preferences — blondes, brunettes, redheads — how he treats them — what turns him on — and how he acts in bed before, during, and after sex."

"We've gone over all this, Sidney."

"When we talked, you were depressed, in the middle of a tragedy. Everything was foggy. I want to go over everything again. From the information you gave me came the germ of an idea. This time I have a specific plan of action. I want to be fully prepared, and you're the only one in the world who can help me. And you'll be helping yourself. You're a big stockholder in Tompion, along with your sister-in-law and her children. If you're interested in preserving what you have and avenging Peter's death, help me strike back."

Jennifer stared ahead, started the car, buckled her seat belt, then turned to Sidney. With uncharacteristic venom she said, "I'll do anything to pay him back for Peter's murder. If I ever see him again, I'll kill him."

Tears were streaming down her face. Sidney pulled out a tissue and handed it to her friend. Jennifer wiped her eyes, blew her nose, and dropped the tissue into the plastic trash bag. Immersed in anguish and guilt, the red-eyed young widow released the brake, put the car in gear, and accelerated out of the parking lot.

* * *

Sidney stayed with Jennifer at her parents' house. It was an eight-room, split-level, frame house on two acres on Lake Travis, just outside Austin. She assumed that Peter and Jennifer had bought it for them. The two women shared the twin beds in Jennifer's room and talked each night until early morning. Sidney did most of the listening, probing for facts about Kaluste. At the same time, she began to delve into her friend's past, trying to get to the poison eating at her. She recognized that Jennifer was an emotional mess and needed professional help. But Sidney felt that it was worthwhile trying to find the key to motivate Jennifer back to normal. She needed a purpose in life, and Sidney hoped to help her find it.

One day when Jennifer was shopping for groceries, Sidney spoke to her mother, an attractive, well-groomed lady. She had no ideas on how to cope with Jennifer and was of no help. Sidney realized that if Jennifer remained in Austin with her mother she would continue to vegetate. Sidney became convinced that Jennifer needed a reason for living, something that would turn her away from self-pity.

A few nights later, while they were sitting in the bedroom, Sidney divulged her scheme. Jennifer suddenly became animated. "It's a desperate plan, but brilliant. It may not work, but I see what you're trying to do. Are you positive that Tompion can't stop him?"

"It's just a feeling. The people at Tompion are sharp, but suppose they're too late? The key isn't always how smart you are, it's how you're perceived by outside investors. The institutions which buy most of the stock on Wall Street are fainthearted. They'll desert you at any sign of trouble, and they'll back anyone who can show them a profit. Kaluste and the companies fronting for him know this. They started collecting voting rights to Tompion stock held by institutions before we even thought of doing it.

"They will hamstring the courts with charges and counter-charges. But look what it will do to Tompion. It will bog down into a stalemate. More likely Tompion will go to whoever will pay the highest price. By the time foreign manipulation is proved in court, Tompion will have been acquired and dismantled — impossible to put together again. Kaluste has a cruel, devious mind and a well-organized plan of attack. His billions give him a power that's impossible to stop in any normal way."

"But you think you can stop him."

"With your help and a little luck."

"And you want to make your own luck."

"Exactly."

"Let me get this straight. Your plan is to make yourself so appealing to Kaluste, that when he meets you he'll chase after you. That's why you want a picture of the type of woman who appeals to him. You also want to know his sexual preferences and what turns him on. Sidney, do you intend to seduce him?"

"Yes."

"It won't work."

"Why?"

"It might be possible, except for Viktor. He's more than Kaluste's bodyguard, he's his protector. He's the one who injured my knee. Viktor is a killer. He's killed people to set up oil deals for Kaluste. I know he was behind Peter's death. You must get past Viktor for your plan to work." Suddenly Jennifer's face lit up. "This is Texas, Sidney. I own several guns, including a small two-shot derringer. Once you get him into bed, you'll kill the bastard, right?"

Sidney smiled.

"I'll help, but I want to be part of it. I've got every reason to.

What you're planning costs money. You can't use corporate funds, so you must be using your own money. Don't. I'm worth millions, and I'm willing to spend every fucking nickel to nail him."

Sidney began to think. Her mind gradually revised her original plan to give it a better chance to succeed. With Jennifer's eyes following her she began to pace the floor. Her new plan might just help her friend's mental condition.

Sidney said, "I'll let you finance it under certain conditions. First, you have to pull yourself together. Start by losing weight and looking after yourself. If we pull this off successfully and you get back to normal, I want you to move to New York. Work with me at Tompion. It's time we had another woman on the board of directors."

Jennifer jumped up and began hugging Sidney.

Sidney hugged her back with genuine affection. "All right, here's what we have to do. First, deposit half a million dollars in a numbered Swiss bank account for a war chest. Second, I want you to show me how to load and shoot the derringer. If it's an antique, you can get it through customs. If not, the studio can say it's for a spaghetti western.

"Third, you're going to a beauty parlor. Fourth, we go shopping for some decent clothes in your size. Five, we have to type a list of things to do. Six, you're flying to Paris as my advance man. Thank heavens you speak perfect French. Do you still have close friends there?"

"Of course. Occasionally they'd fly in to visit en route to New York or Hollywood. They're mostly artists and actors. Peter called our home 'The International Watering Hole,' but he loved it."

"Now I want you to find a small hotel where I can register under my own name which I use as my base of operations. Luckily, your present condition will serve as your disguise. Still, you might be spotted. If word gets back to Kaluste that his niece was seen in Paris, it means trouble. Use a pseudonym and stay at a different hotel close by."

"A small *pension* might be better."

"Great! You'll leave as soon as possible and find out if Kaluste is in Paris. Call me if he isn't. Next, try to remember at which elegant restaurant Kaluste is most likely to have dinner, which is also frequented by film stars.

"When you get there, rent the most fabulous, the most luxurious mansion available for a month. Our Empire Film office may help, but use them only as a last resort.

"How about a bank? Do you have one in Paris?"

Jennifer thought for a moment and said, "You know something strange? I refused to take money from Kaluste to get at Peter, but he deposited a good chunk of money in my name. The proceeds from the sale of the car and the apartment went into that bank account. I didn't spend a penny of it, so it's still there. Wouldn't it be great if we could zap the bastard with his own money!"

"It would indeed."

CHAPTER

TWENTY
THREE

TWO WOMEN were sitting naked on the wooden benches in the sauna, one of the many services provided by Club Helene, an expensive health club in the East Sixties. Samantha O'Hare sat ramrod straight, the results of her years in the navy. For a tall woman, her breasts were small and they remained firm. Without her makeup, Sam was covered with freckles, not only on her face but on her chest and back. She was a striking-looking woman for her age; firm flesh, flat tummy, and narrow hips.

"All right, darling," Sam said, "I figure you're not gay, so what are we doing here?"

"Sam, in the ten days since I returned from Austin, Tompion has been in quiet chaos. Even though the stock has risen to 58, people in middle management are scared. Some are resigning. Now that the hostile takeover is out in the open, our lawyers are locked in a death struggle to prevent it. The admiral is on the front lines in Washington with Ron and the investment bankers. Tom is the acting deputy chairman of Tompion, trying to hold things together. Roger's meetings with Kaluste have turned out to be *merde,* as the French say, but he's sticking to it.

"Jennifer, who knows Kaluste, says he will do anyything to mislead Roger. So, at the admiral's suggestion, Roger has hired two ex-CIA agents to investigate Kaluste's past and try to uncover direct links to the sabotage or the acquisition. But let's face it; France is Kaluste's power base."

"The admiral says we're going to win."

"Perhaps. Maybe it's his way of telling us to keep a stiff upper lip."

"I think you have the old man figgered out. Darling, this place is getting very hot. Do we have to stay in here?"

"The answer is yes. Here's a pail of water to pour over your head. Sam, our phones are tapped — probably our home phones, too. We're leaving them as is to keep from tipping off Kaluste. We don't know how many of our people are on his payroll. Incidentally, no one knows we're here. Samantha, I'm about to try something crazy — something that could save Tompion."

"Tell me."

"It may not work, so don't get your hopes up just yet. But I need someone I trust to be aware of what I'm doing. I have typed out a long memorandum that I placed in a safety-deposit box at the Chemical Bank on Fifth Avenue. It's in both our names. Go to the bank in the next day or so and sign the signature card.

"When I get to Paris, if all goes well, I will mail you a package care of the American Express office on Park Avenue. Deposit it in the vault immediately. Jennifer is assisting me and knows most of what I'm doing — but not everything. Only the two of us will know the complete story. Tomorrow, I want you to call The Union Bank of Zurich, I'll give you the number. Call from a public phone in a restaurant. Order a numbered account and a special vault in my name. Then wire the number to me. I'll give you a personal check for $50,000 to transfer to Union. The money is to establish my bona fides. Tell them to expect a special package for safekeeping."

"You sound very CIA."

"I wish I had their expertise!"

"Why don't you speak to the admiral?"

"I can't. My plan involves seducing Constantin Kaluste."

"Holy Mother of God —"

"If I discuss this with the admiral or Ron or Roger or our other male executives, do you think any one of them would let me go through with it? Never! A gentleman tries to protect a woman against every man but himself. And what will they think if they know what I'm doing? But you know I'm doing it for them and the survival of Tompion International. It's something only a woman can do. Besides, men will never understand that sometimes the female of the species is stronger than the male."

"And smarter. I see your point. Protect the female and all that."

"I sometimes think that women are smarter as well as different. Being a woman can come in handy sometimes."

"All right, girl, I'll do what you say because in my heart I believe you know what you're doing. But for the life of me, I don't know why you'd risk your life."

"Yes, you do."

Sam looked at her for a long time and said, "Yes, I do. Now can we get the hell out of here? Steam heat is fit only for Satan."

A stack of white sheets was piled up outside the sauna. They each wrapped themselves in one, toga style. Then they walked over to the swimming pool. They sat in lounge chairs, each with her own thoughts. Then a young woman attendant in a red tank suit brought them iced tea. "Sidney, is there any way I can help?"

"Are you with me all the way?"

"I am that, girl. Now what in blazes are you up to?"

"Before I go into it, I have a list of jobs for you. You'll find it in an envelope with the $50,000 check. But let me run through the list now. I arrive in Paris on Sunday, July fourteenth, Bastille Day. Jennifer has already learned from actresses who go out with Kaluste that he will be spending two weeks in Paris. Most of the time he'll be entertaining Arab sheiks. I'll be staying at the Plaza Athenee but Jennifer has a small flat at a *pension*. I want Arko Puchakis, president of Empire, to get me the best makeup person in Europe and a genius with wigs.

"I need a French public relations person, someone unconnected with Empire, to start placing stories in the French press. I suggest a planted story about a new American Broadway actress in Paris to buy designer originals for her first film. It must be the name of a legitimate film about to start production in Europe soon. I'll be using my maiden name. Make certain that the film company promotes me as the star.

"Stewart McLean, head of security of our European division of Rainbow Electronics in England, is to receive instructions to meet me in Paris and that he is to cooperate with me totally, no questions asked. I need him for only one day. I pray he's not a Kaluste man, but with luck it won't matter.

"One more thing for Arko. I need to be escorted on just one evening by a world famous star. Clint Eastwood, Paul Newman or Robert Redford — whoever is in Europe at the time. If none of them are in Europe, have him select one of the top French stars. But he must not be too young."

"Is that it?"

"Actually, no. I want you to arrange private showings for me at Courreges, Gres, and Yves St. Laurent. Just say you're head of the Empire studio costume department."

"Okay, Sidney, but before I split me gut for you, will you tell me what's going on?"

"I've told you. I'm going to seduce Monsieur Constantin Kaluste."

"Oh, girl, you have the look of a saint and the body of an angel. Should you be messing with the devil?"

"Sam, *now* I'm going to tell you exactly what I'm up to." Sidney outlined each step of her plan in precise detail, but it wasn't until she finished Sam showed distress.

"Will it work?"

"I'll know when I try it."

"You're a brave girl, but I agree with Jennifer. Why don't you just shoot the bastard."

"She would prefer to cut off his joint."

"Now, that's an idea. I can let you have me late husband's straight razor, God bless his immortal soul. And if you have no use for the Frenchman's tool yourself, Sidney, would you send it back to this lonely old woman?" They both laughed. "Sidney, I love you like me daughter. When your husband was lost, I know you suffered many heartaches and sad times. Since you came to Tompion, I've grown to love you. I've been puzzled why you didn't find another man and have children, a fulfilled life."

"Eleven years have gone by since Harry was first listed as missing. A third of my life. Each year it got harder and harder to handle as hope became more forlorn. I had to construct a life for myself."

"Independence doesn't keep you warm at night."

"Sometimes I cry during the night, worrying that I've insulated myself against the world to prevent being hurt again."

"You're another victim of the Vietnam War. I hope life will have better days in store for you."

"At my age, most of the good men are taken. What's left? I either don't meet the right men, or I attract weak men looking for a strong woman, or men who want a mother, or men with emotional problems." Then she paused. "Or men who've been overmothered and want a woman who is submissive or unsophisticated, grateful to keep house."

"It's the way of the world, Sidney."

"I guess."

"There are other men who could get married, but don't want to. People who live in constant terror of the past."

"I don't follow."

"Well, Roger."

"Roger?" Sidney sat up and looked her.

Sam sipped the dregs of her iced tea and then fixed Sidney in her gaze. "I told you Roger had a nervous breakdown. Did I tell you why?"

Sidney shook her head.

"When he was on a search-and-destroy mission in Vietnam — Tom and Ron weren't with him that day — his platoon searched a small village in Quang Tri. They found just women and children and a few dozen old men. Perhaps two hundred all told. As the platoon was moving out, the GIs heard an airplane approaching and they scattered, taking cover in the jungle. The plane was ours. It dropped napalm on the village, setting the inhabitants on fire. Most of them were roasted alive. Roger and his platoon watched in horror.

"A young, inexperienced pilot on his first mission had made a ghastly mistake, but it didn't lessen the agony of the villagers. Some of the GIs went berserk. Roger went into catatonic shock. He froze. The Air Evac medics found him mute. At the hospital, he neither moved nor spoke. He wouldn't eat. He lost weight. He was out of control."

"It took him a very long, long time to heal. He was in General Hospital in San Francisco, but the admiral had him moved to a VA hospital in New York. He hired the best psychiatrists available. Tom and Ron returned to the States when their time was up. Married, but they saw Roger often. They soon decided on colleges. Ron went to Columbia to be near Roger. Tom went to the Wharton School of Finance at the University of Pennsylvania in Philadelphia, only two hours from New York, so he, too, could be near Roger and his family.

"Cassie flew in once month to visit him and stay a week. Then she gave up Hollywood for Broadway and moved to New York. She decided to get a high school equivalency diploma and then go to college.

"It took the psychiatrists and a great deal of love, faith, and understanding by his family and friends to help Roger pull through."

"Sam, you never get over that kind of trauma."

"No. He still has terrible nightmares. The admiral says he's afraid to sleep just to avoid having them."

"I saw him have one on the company plane."

"Some of his good friends and his parents carry around tranquilizer needles to knock him out. They know he's only a danger to himself."

"I don't believe that Roger is suicidal."

"That's exactly what the doctors say."

They stopped talking. Sam was thinking about Sidney's dedication to Tompion, a loyalty so strong that she would embark on a mad scheme to save it. Sidney was thinking about Roger and her sexual encounter with the strange, brilliant, gentle man; the pacifist who'd gone to war, seen it at its worst, and suffered nightmares that nothing on earth could erase.

CHAPTER

TWENTY
FOUR

SIDNEY was waiting to board the Air France Concorde for its 1:00 P.M. flight. It was 85 degrees and muggy in New York. A few more degrees and it would rain, she thought.

She was following a French conversation lesson on her Walkman, regretting that the second language for her Ph.D. had been German. She'd read Freud, Jung, and their successors in German. Now she wished they'd written in French. But, thanks to an excellent memory, she was able summon up her high school French with a blitz brushup at Berlitz. She was able to carry on a rudimentary conversation with a terrible accent. There was a Petit Larousse French-English dictionary in her purse. In her carry-on case were a book by Sartre and current copies of *Paris Match* and *Elle*.

They left Kennedy on time. The Concorde was cramped, but the food was superb. She spoke to the stewardesses in French. They were most helpful in correcting her pronunciation. She felt a shot of adrenaline as they neared Paris. Her heart was pounding. Yet, instead of being apprehensive, she was looking forward to her audacious gamble. The stakes were enormous. A bright future, stock options, a high salary, and the perks to come were reason enough. But there were also the careers of the admiral and her friends, not to mention Roger.

If she failed, maybe she'd resign her job and teach or become a suburban housewife in Connecticut. The thought didn't frighten her because she was thinking of Roger. Perhaps she shouldn't think of Roger.

Sidney would have to tell him she was in Paris and give him a plausible excuse. The flight to Paris took just over three-and-a-half hours. As she buckled her seat belt for a landing at Charles de

Gaulle, she began to get stage fright.

She was on the ground by 10:45 P.M. Customs and noise at the terminal were a blur of confusion. Sidney took a wide-brimmed straw hat out of her hatbox and put it on. The surprise came when a handsome Frenchman in a smart black uniform holding up a card with HOWE on it walked by. She identified herself and the chauffeur took charge, whisking her through everything, then ushering her into a vintage Cadillac limousine that still retained a touch of class. This was traveling in style. With her luggage in the trunk they headed towards Paris only 17 miles away.

* * *

The Plaza Athénée was more beautiful and luxurious than Jennifer's description. Her suite was beautiful, magnificent even for a four-star hotel. Two large doors led into a hallway dominated by a Baccarat glass chandelier. The large living room had a fireplace. French doors opened to a balcony overlooking the street. The bedroom was immense, decorated with antique furniture and a dressing room. All this for 1,750 francs a day, $200.

The bathroom had a bidet, a large tub, a large sink, and huge bath towels. There were call buttons to summon the floor maid, the waiter, and the valet. The suite was everything Jennifer said it would be but bigger and better.

Sidney unpacked and hung up her dresses and bathrobe, thankful that she didn't have to wear suits for a week or ten days. She traveled light — as she expected to buy a new wardrobe. She unpacked her underthings, pantyhose, shoes, jewelry and sweaters. The last item was the straight razor that Sam insisted she take along. She hadn't been able to refuse her, and now it somehow seemed comforting. She took another look at her sweatsuit and running shoes, wondering whether she'd have time to run.

Sidney went into the bathroom and removed her makeup. Then she took off her traveling dress, a nonwrinkling jersey the color of a pomegranate, kicked off her shoes, undressed, and put on a lace nightgown. For few minutes she exercised, getting out the airplane kinks before slipping into bed. She had found that the only way to overcome west-east jet lag was to observe the new time. She would read until 2:00 A.M., take a Valium to relax, and sleep six or seven hours.

Her morning schedule included breakfast with Jennifer. Her first assignment was makeup at 10:00 A.M. Sidney had the kind of face that always reflected strain or fatigue. Rest was vital to her. Except for emergencies, Jennifer and Sidney agreed not to use use the telephone.

Sidney awoke at 7:00 A.M., bathed, and put on her robe. She called room service and ordered coffee in French. The waiter was courteous and served her coffee on a silver tray. It was excellent.

Putting on an apple-green jersey dress, and comfortable walking shoes, Sidney left the hotel before 8:00.

Paris in the rush hour had the same sort of excitement she found in New York, but for some reason the pace seemed less frantic. Perhaps it was the people or the aura Paris generated. It was a five-minute walk from the Athénée to Jennifer's *pension*. Jennifer greeted her warmly, reminiscent of the happy enthusiasm she had displayed prior to Peter's death. Her two-room suite turned out to be small but homey, with a bowl of fresh fruit on the table. Jennifer phoned the *patronne* and was informed that breakfast was ready. Jennifer said she was reducing, but trying not to starve herself until "Operation Kaluste" was over.

The *patronne* and Jennifer spoke French so rapidly that Sidney caught only an occasional word. The woman did not speak

English. Nevertheless Jennifer did not translate what she said until the woman hurried out to buy bread, fresh fish, meat and vegetables at the local market. Their breakfast included a fruit salad, coffee, and brioche.

As they ate, Jennifer reported on her progress. "I rented a fabulous house on the Ile St. Louis. It's on the Place Dauphin below Notre Dame Cathedral and the Palace of Justice.

"After thinking about it, I decided to make the deal with the broker myself. I know enough about makeup to make myself look older, and being fat and speaking French like a native, it's highly unlikely that I would ever be recognized. The house cost a small fortune. I also posted bond and paid a high premium for insurance on the contents. Wait till you see it. Now, for the tenth time — I want to move in with you as your maid."

"Absolutely no! It's going to be hard enough for me to get away with it, but if Kaluste or Viktor recognizes you, the whole plan is compromised."

"Okay, Sidney, just a thought. Now, I've taken care of everything on your list. The money is in the Union Bank. I closed my personal bank account. The money is half in American Express travelers checks and half in cash. I redeposited the travelers checks in two separate banks in differing amounts. That's in case Kaluste ordered my bank to alert him when the account was activated. Knowing him, he would have the power to check banks looking for identical deposits.

"Jennifer, you ought to be a spy."

Her eyes flashed with anger when she spat out, "I'd rather use the guillotine just once."

Sidney said she would call from a telephone kiosk when everything was ready — in any event, not later than twenty-four hours. Jennifer gave her two sets of keys to the house and receipts for the rental and the bond. Meanwhile, five friends, none living currently in Paris, were going help: as a butler, a chauffeur whom she'd already met, a personal maid, a housekeeper, and a chef on vacation from a cruise ship. Everything was going smoothly.

Jennifer handed her a Paris bankbook showing a deposit in excess of 1,150,000 francs — roughly $100,000. The account was in the name of Cindy Farrell, Sidney's maiden name. Jennifer also gave her the transfer slip from the Swiss bank, a sheaf of francs in large denominations, and $15,000 in new $100 bills. Then Jennifer tied a scarf around her head to hide her hair. They waited for the studio makeup people.

Promptly at 10:00 P.M. there was a knock on the door. Jennifer admitted two gay Frenchmen dressed in apache outfits; skintight pants, patent-leather shoes, striped T-shirts, and pomaded hair. They spoke only a smattering of English, so Jennifer filled them in.

Jennifer told them Sidney wanted a lustrous rich auburn wig with lots of hair done in the latest vogue. They had brought an assortment of wigs with them, and the hairstylist fitted them. They finally agreed on curly shoulder-length hair, but the wig needed adjustment.

Jennifer was insistent that Sidney enhance her cleavage to create a more voluptuous figure. The Frenchmen asked Sidney to remove her bra. Her first impulse was to refuse, but it was a necessary part of her disguise. She removed her dress and bra.

The makeup men didn't think her breasts needed a buildup. Jennifer told them it was for role in a film. Now they understood. She did the math conversion from inches to millimeters. By adding four inches, Sidney would have a lush, well-defined cleavage. One of them described an hourglass figure with his hands, exactly what Jennifer wanted. She told them to pad one inch at each hip, creating a proportionate curvature.

Finally, Jennifer told them to alter Sidney's face with makeup so she wouldn't be recognized. They asked Sidney to sit down as they opened layered cases of cosmetics and began experimenting. They turned out to be two geniuses. Wearing the wig, they used a special shade of rouge to heighten her cheekbones, applied mascara and eye shadow and extra-long eyelashes to enhance her deep green eyes. Then a beauty spot was added to her cheek that instantly transformed her appearance. When she looked in a mirror thirty minutes later, she did not recognize herself. She was now the seductive, sensual Broadway star, Cindy Farrell.

"Magnifique!" Jennifer said. The two men stood there beaming. Then Sidney told Jennifer what she wanted and Jennifer gave the men instructions in rapid French. For next two hours, one artist remained behind to teach Sidney how to apply makeups for day and evening. Starting the following day, the makeup experts were to be on call between 9:00 A.M. and 11:00, and 4:00 and 6:00 P.M. should they be needed.

When the men left, they promised to deliver the wig, plus a spare wig with a highly styled, piled up hairdo. Fascinated by the magic of makeup, Sidney practiced applying and removing it as Jennifer issued instructions.

"With larger breasts and hips, you'll have to get bras and panties to fit. Remember: black lace panties and bras for evening wear, black garters — he's a sucker for those — and very high-heeled shoes.

"Sidney, go to the Galerie Lafayette and buy some stopgap clothes until your designer clothes are ready. Remember to have them delivered by morning. Tailoring is slow, but for some extra francs, a seamstress will work all night. With a bit of luck, you should be ready for your first appointment at the couturiers in the morning.

"And don't forget to register your signature at the bank so you can write checks."

* * *

Just before noon the next day, Sidney made arrangements with the hotel manager to keep her suite even though she might be absent for several days, perhaps as long as a week. Sidney opened her purse and proffered 20,000 francs in advance. Without batting an eye, he took out his book and wrote out a receipt. She advised him that she was going to the country and would leave most of her luggage at the hotel, taking just an overnight case.

A bellman brought it to the street where Louis, the chauffeur, and the Cadillac awaited. He drove around the city for about thirty minutes at a leisurely pace. There was no reason to suspect they were even noticed. The car dropped her a block away from the *pension*. She walked the rest of the way and went into the house with the overnight case. It contained only one change of clothing. Now, in Ginger's room, she began to transform her appearance.

It took about forty minutes to adjust the padded bra, panties, and the dress. She carried her wig in a box. She wore a light raincoat in case the *patronne* noticed. Then she left and began to walk along the Right Bank of the Seine. In twenty minutes, a vintage white Rolls Royce pulled up beside her and stopped. She got in beside Jennifer who was grinning from ear to ear. It was the same chauffeur, Louis.

It was a short drive to the Place Dauphin house. When Sidney got out of the Rolls wearing her wig, she made an electrifying appearance as the Grande Dame. The house looked like a picture postcard. A butler opened the door while the chauffeur brought in the bags. It was a stunning house decorated with authentic Louis Quinze furniture. The paintings were mostly French impressionists. There were two sculptures by Rodin and, unexpectedly, a large painting of a nude, curvaceous, redheaded woman who could have been a *Playboy* model. Her proportions were larger then normal and guaranteed to make any man go weak at the knees. It could have been a painted photograph of Cindy Farrell.

"Jennifer, I don't believe it."

"Great, eh? There was an Aubusson rug tapestry there. Two days ago I was walking through the flea market and I spotted the painting — it must be four feet by six feet. The date is on the back. I suspect it's a copy of a *Playboy* centerfold and was painted about 12 years ago. I bought it for 5,000 francs and took it to the *pension*. I didn't want to let my art training go to waste, so I bought some oils and brushes and painted the blonde hair and the pubic hair auburn, did some shading on the face, flattened the tummy and painted the fingernails red.

"Your wig is redder, but I don't think it matters. I must remember to add the beauty mark. It will impress the hell out of Constantin Kaluste. It's close enough to pass as a portrait of you. It's insurance. If he thinks it's you, it's guaranteed to turn him on."

Jennifer had a plan of the house and they went from room to room until they reached the master bedroom on the second floor. She watched as Sidney made a careful inspection of the mirrored wall, the closets, and the heavy drapes. There was a new 25-inch TV set and a videocassette recorder. There were four speakers in four corners of the room for a quadraphonic stereo and hi-fi set, tape deck and tuner, as specified by Mr. McLean in their phone conversation. Sidney pointed to her watch and Jennifer agreed. It was time to go shopping.

CHAPTER

TWENTY
FIVE

SINCE her return to Paris, Jennifer had become more daring and resourceful. She knew there was only one person on Kaluste's house staff she could trust, and she intended to make use of Gaston. Actually, it wasn't so much a matter of trust as blackmail. Gaston, Kaluste's Corsican chauffeur, was too enamored of his job and big shiny Mercedes to want to be fired as a Peeping Tom. He was in his early fifties and his ambition was to make enough money to return home and open up a cafe. She did not want to face him in person because of her embarrassing girth but her voice hadn't changed. When she ran the household she knew all his haunts and Gaston was a creature of habit. She would contact him by phone.

She located him on Wednesday evening at a Left Bank tavern he habituated which catered to old soldiers. He was somewhat surprised to hear her voice and he immediately acknowledged his great debt to her and told her a Corsican never forgets a debt of honor.

Jennifer said perhaps someday she would ask him for a favor, but right now she had returned from America and wished to surprise his patron with a chance encounter at a restaurant. She was Constantin's niece so Gaston thought nothing of telling her that Kaluste was entertaining Arab guests Friday evening at La Tour d'Argent. She thanked him and phoned Sidney immediately.

"Does he always sit at the same table?"

"Always — he's Constantin Kaluste."

"Does he usually sit in the same chair?"

"Most of the time."

"Can you figure out a particular table, not too far from his, that he must pass me when he enters?"

"Yes."

"Great! The studio arranged for France's musical star, Pierre Danton, to be my dinner companion any evening this week. I'll give you a number to call — it's his secretary — have him make the reservation for 8:30 P.M."

"Oui, madame," said Jennifer and they both guffawed. Then she added, "Just a little background. Danton is a famous singer in Europe. He also famous for his social movies for the pseudo-intellectuals. Very handsome, about fifty, tall and thin with fantastic charisma. He and Kaluste know each other — a sort of friendly competition, or an exchange of lies. I wouldn't be surprised if they kept score or exchanged intimate information. When do we discuss the final details?"

"I have an all-day conference tomorrow with an Englishman. How about dinner here at eight?"

"See y'all," said Jennifer, exaggerating her Texas drawl.

* * *

"How do I look?" Sidney asked as she swirled around on spike heels in her new $17,500 blue-green chiffon gown.

"Perfect, just perfect!" As Sidney modeled the dress and herself, Jennifer was amazed at the extraordinary results. "His mouth will water when he sees you, and if he doesn't get a crack at you — he'll have a stroke."

"Did we forget anything?"

"No, but I think I should give you a few modeling tips. You have trouble walking on those stilts — just try putting one foot in front of the other as though you're walking a straight line. You'll not only have balance, but your derriere will undulate provocatively. You'll swivel at the waist and your breasts will swing from side to side enough and jiggle the merchandise."

"Like this?"

"Yes, but practice a bit till you get it down pat."

Sidney walked around the bedroom and Jennifer handed her a telephone book to balance on her head. The mirror reflected a moving picture of a lush redhead with all the accoutrements of a courtesan. Finally she removed the dress and shoes and put on a robe.

"Sidney. One last thing."

"Yes?"

"Here's the derringer." Jennifer handed the small two-barrel gun to Sidney.

"No, Jennifer. I don't intend to shoot him."

"But I thought —" Her voice trailed off.

"I never said I'd kill him. I have something else in mind."

Jennifer's face became a mass of rage. "I see what you want, Sidney. This whole seduction bit is simply a ruse — you really want to seduce him — you want to be sure of keeping your job."

"Jennifer — darling — that's not true. You're upset." Jennifer pulled back the gun angrily and stalked out of the room with Sidney following. "Jennifer — Jennifer — give me a chance to explain."

The door slammed. Jennifer was gone.

CHAPTER

TWENTY SIX

ENTERING the restaurant at 15 Quai de la Tournelle on the arm of the dashing French screen star turned everyone's head. But Sidney could have done it had she been alone. The dress looked as though she'd been poured into it, the $17,500 blue-green silk chiffon dress caught the light and sparkled off her seductive body. Her hair was a mass of red curls, and the makeup had transformed her into a fantastic beauty. Everything enhanced the cleavage which was displayed prominently. She wore no jewelry. Luckily, the eye shadow covered the dark worry lines from lack of sleep over Jennifer's irrational behavior.

Pierre Danton, her escort, arrived at her house by taxi. He was so astounded by his astonishingly beautiful escort that he hovered over her as they entered the Rolls and didn't stop talking until they reached the restaurant. Danton had been expecting a brassy American blonde. Instead she had turned out to be a Venus. His vanity had been such that he hadn't bothered putting on his best evening wear and had chosen, instead, a dated dinner jacket. Now he was in anguish. She outshone him, and he was trying to make it up to her by being overly attentive.

They were greeted at the entranceway by a charming woman who turned out to be a member of the family. She took Sidney's wrap and they were led to a downstairs lounge area decorated with old letters from Churchill and Mitterrand and other leaders going back centuries. Pierre turned on his charm and went all out by ordering Chateau Lafite-Rothschild. Sidney winced, knowing she was picking up the tab. When they were served he gave her a history of the famous Tour d'Argent.

"It has been in the Terrail family for centuries. Kings and world leaders eat here. You can go back to King Henry V of

England. The knife and fork were first used in this restaurant."

When their table was ready, a tuxedoed waiter appeared and led them to an ancient, ornately decorated elevator that should have been preserved in a museum. They were deposited on the second-floor dining area where they were warmly greeted by the owner, Paul Terrail. When introduced by Pierre, Sidney commented that she had a greeting for Terrail from his nephew Patrick, who owned Ma Maison in Los Angeles. She said she hoped the cuisine would be equally fine here. He was pleased. They were seated next to a window with an expansive view of the Seine.

In a setting of elegance where many of the personalities try to outdo each other, Sidney shone like the North Star. Her watch read 9:10 P.M. when the Maitre d' hovered over them. Sidney's uplift bra was too tight and much as she would have liked to loosen it, she didn't deem it wise. They drank more wine and she leaned forward, offering Pierre a full view of her breasts, and asked him to order for her. He did — the most elegant and expensive meal offered by the restaurant: pheasant.

There were murmurs of recognition when Kaluste entered with three tall men in flowing gowns. As they walked by, Kaluste caught sight of her, caught his breath and hesitated. Then he noticed the movie actor and beamed. He stopped at the table, staring at her. *"Pierre, mon ami,"* he said and began to chat rapidly in French. She didn't comprehend the French, but she understood the intent.

Sidney was not introduced to Kaluste, and she didn't know whether it was rudeness or pride of possession. Refusing to be ignored, she rose, said *"Pardon,"* and left for the powder room. She was nervous and wanted to double-check her dress. It was also probable that a resourceful man like Kaluste would figure out a way of contacting her.

When she emerged, a tall, dark man in a smart tuxedo draped to his athletic build was waiting for her. "Madame," he said and handed her a small envelope.

Without looking at it, she tore it up and handed it back to him, her eyes piercing his like laser beams. Then, with a haughty look of disdain, she departed.

At the table, Pierre rose and the waiter seated her. "That man is Constantin Kaluste."

"So?"

"He is the world's richest man."

"He's only a man. Where I come from, we say, 'He puts his pants on one leg at a time, like the rest of us.' "

"He has a lot of power."

"Good for him."

"He is attracted to you."

"That's nice. Pierre, you sound frightened."

"I am. We have a sort of friendly rivalry. He asked who you were and I did not wish tell him — he got angry and said very calmly, that he would not only ruin my career, he would cut off my genitals and stuff them in my mouth."

Sidney felt a shiver down her back. This man was terrified and looked as if he were about to run away and hide. "We wouldn't want that to happen, Pierre. What do you propose?"

"That you meet with him."

"May we eat first?"

"But of course." He was breathing slowly and deeply now, his charming manner gone and chameleonlike he began to act more like a business associate. They ate leisurely. Without looking directly at Kaluste, she could see him staring at her, as were the three sheiks and the dark-haired man who had approached her.

Another bottle of Lafite was brought to their table with a note. Pierre read it and handed it to her. It read, "Stop by at my home after dinner."

Pierre simply wrote *"Oui"* at the bottom, asking the waiter to return it to Kaluste. He remained nervous through dessert and coffee, and while he began to help himself to the wine, she had nothing more to drink. She looked down and she wasn't sure whether it was her imagination, but she could see her pounding heart make her gown flutter.

Because of another appointment or because Arabs do not drink, the Kaluste party left early. Fifteen minutes later, Pierre and Sidney got up and walked through the room. They were again greeted by Paul Terrail. Pierre forced a grin as they said goodbye.

Pierre had the shakes so badly in the car that Sidney thought they should stop the Rolls before he took sick. It was a short ride to the Kaluste mansion. She closed her eyes and told herself to calm down before the chauffeur opened the door. She took a deep breath and held it.

The Kaluste mansion was as Jennifer had described it. They were ushered into the study, and Pierre Danton introduced Sidney to Constantin Kaluste and his dark companion in the restaurant, Viktor Kryszkowski. They talked for a while. Then Pierre suddenly took ill.

"Let me drive you home," Sidney said as she took him under the arm.

"I'll be happy to do it, madame," said Viktor. Without another word he gripped Pierre under the arm and trotted him away.

They were alone. Kaluste, his voice rich, his manner suave and powerful, began to patronize her, as expected, with vulgar comments about her breasts.

She lashed back at him. The first words out of her mouth were harsh. "Monsieur, you are rude. I do not wish to be talked about like a piece of meat."

There was instant anger in his eyes, replaced suddenly with respect. *A worthy adversary,* he thought. "You misconstrue, my dear. I see you wear no jewelry. I own an emerald mine, and your green eyes, white skin, and red hair — and magnificent chest — they cry out for an emerald."

"Kaluste," she said, deliberately using his second name as a pejorative. "Do I understand you correctly? You wish to buy me for a bauble?"

He was offbalance, but beginning to enjoy the pain of her tongue-lashing. This was a worthy opponent. He was less sure of himself, but he managed a smile as she cocked an eyebrow. They were playing the oldest game in the world. He walked over to a Matisse painting, moved it aside, and exposed a wall safe. Opening it, he pulled out a small tray. He looked over several jewels and then took one, a pear-shaped emerald of some 20 carats on a heavy gold chain. It was the rarest gem in his collection.

Sidney had to admit that Kaluste was a handsome man. His moustache was neat and he was as immaculate a human being as she had ever seen. His tuxedo was made of midnight-blue silk, his shirt pale blue. The stone he carried with such affection sparkled as its facets caught the light. He carried it to her, unfastened the catch, and let the stone fall just above the crevice of her breasts.

"Formidable!" he said. He put it around her neck and fastened it. It fell appropriately like an arrow on its appointed target.

"It's beautiful, but I cannot accept so valuable a gift from a stranger."

"After this evening we will no longer be strangers."

There was fear in her heart when she said, "I am not a run-of-the-mill harlot."

"One can tell."

"I do not like aggressive men."

"What kind of men do you prefer?

"For a man to know me — he must — shall we say — be submissive."

"How delightful! Shall we visit my chamber?"

"No, Kaluste." Sidney thought everything was moving too fast. She needed more time to get used to him and her plan.

There was a puzzled look on his face, his mouth open. The man who could have almost any woman in the world was being turned down and toyed with. He reached over and grasped her arm, hurting her. "You fool with me?"

Sidney looked him in the eye and tore her arm away from his grasp. "No. It's not you who should hurt me, it's I who should hurt you." Then she slapped him as hard as she could. He gasped either in pleasure or in pain. When he leaned over to kiss the top of her breasts, she bit his ear. Despite it all, Sidney was finding the encounter exciting, though it looked as if it were happening to someone else on a movie screen.

She patted him on the cheek and kissed him with closed lips. "You are a naughty little boy and you should come home with Mama."

"It is more secure here."

"What are you afraid of?"

"Constantin Kaluste is afraid of nothing."

"We go to my home. I can assure you that much pleasure awaits you there."

His composure broke as a film of sweat formed across his forehead. He seemed unsure what he should do. She began to walk out and he followed her into the foyer, where the butler was holding her wrap. Kaluste asked the whereabouts of Viktor and was reminded that Pierre Danton was ill and Viktor was taking him home. He asked for Gaston and his car and again he was told it was being used to transport Viktor and the movie star.

"We'll wait," Kaluste said.

She grabbed him under his arm making sure the mounds of her breasts were pressed against him. "We can use my car."

He was struggling between his own security and his sexual anxiety. She turned to the butler and asked him to fetch her chauffeur. When the white Rolls pulled up out front, Kaluste decided to chance it. Sidney didn't realize it, but as they walked to the car, Kaluste was hunched over, hiding behind her until they were in the rear seat of the car.

Then the beautiful redhead said, "Home, Louis."

* * *

Unknowingly, Kaluste's fear of assassination saved his life. Jennifer had been hiding outside his house waiting for a chance to shoot him. If Sidney wouldn't do it, she would. The desire for revenge was burning red-hot inside her. She clasped the cocked derringer in her hand, which, in turn, was enclosed in a large leather purse. Seeing Kaluste, she drew out the small pistol, but he was concealed by Sidney. To be effective she had to be less than twenty feet from her target. The car pulled away, but Jennifer knew where it was heading. She smiled now, for she had plenty of time. She decided to wait outside the rented house and shoot him as he departed. Yes — then the angry devils would leave her mind.

CHAPTER

TWENTY SEVEN

AFTER Sidney and Kaluste
entered the house, Louis, the chauffeur, parked the Rolls Royce
in the garage and walked into the house through the garage-door
entrance. The young provincial actress playing the role of the
waitress, would not come across unless he provided her with some
hash. He'd picked up some sticks from a young street dealer while
waiting outside the restaurant. While the money he'd get for his
role as a chauffeur was great, he had other urgent needs, and one
of them was waiting for him in his room.

If Madame wanted him, she would ring. Until then he was
free, and he didn't expect a call until morning. Not the way the
guy in the tuxedo had been tonguing her tits. Boy, she was a
fantastically sexy woman — but her mammaries were too big for
his taste. One didn't have to drown in them to appreciate a
woman.

He entered his room and switched on the nightstand lamp.
The maid was resting on his bed, the skirt of her maid's costume
above her waist and her tiny white briefs, straight out of St.
Tropez, looking like a string bikini. He made a grab at her with
one hand. All she did was smile and say *"Fumez."*

He lit hers, then his and as they smoked, his hand moved
expertly inside her panties. She didn't react or wiggle, remaining
as immobile as a statue. It took several minutes for the hash to hit,
and suddenly she went into a St. Vitus dance as she tore at his
clothes.

* * *

When Jennifer arrived at Sidney's house, she considered
entering and confronting Kaluste directly. But the Rolls wasn't
out front. Maybe they had gone elsewhere? With her set of keys,
she checked the garage. The Rolls was there, so Kaluste must be

inside. But besides Kaluste and Sidney, five of her friends were there, and they might try to stop her. Reluctantly, she decided it would be best to hide behind the rose bushes close to the front doors. She walked up the driveway and moved through the bushes and crouched down, oblivious of the thorns tearing at her flesh. It was a warm, clear night and she found it difficult to crouch, so she decided to sit on the grass and wait, the light from the hall windows allowing her to see around her. She opened her purse to check the gun, which she uncocked, and spent some time inspecting her purse. Aside from some tissues, there were cosmetics, a bankbook and a stack of U.S. $100 bills held together with a rubber band — $15,000 worth, the other half of Kaluste's cash that she had given Sidney.

The solitude was helping think more clearly. She inspected her bulging waist, heavy arms, and large thighs, and wondered what had happened to her. Her thighs were chafing and by tomorrow might develop a rash. She longed for some talcum. For the first time, she regretted her harsh words with Sidney. But other than personal gain, what reason could Sidney have for wanting to take him to bed? Comparing him sexually to her husband, Peter, Kaluste was a mama's boy.

* * *

Sidney was seated in a leather wing back chair holding a tall, thin crystal glass of champagne. Her legs were crossed, and she canted slightly to the right to increase the curvature of her body. For the first time in her life, she felt cheap — like a tart. It was important that she concentrate with a singleness of purpose; discard everything from her mind but the project at hand. After each sip of champagne, she would lower the glass and run her tongue slowly around her mouth, wetting her lips. She was taunting him, and it was having the desired effect.

Kaluste, the man who had dominated a thousand women and a thousand boardrooms, whose every action sent chills through financial markets around the world, was off balance. He decided every action and was always in control of every situation. Now he was being mastered by someone else. He was puzzled and ambivalent because he was sexually charged on an emotional level, furious on a cerebral level. He was well aware that once he dominated this woman sexually, she could no longer control him. But until that happened, she seemed able to pluck every string in his emotional makeup and manipulate his psyche.

He had never met such a woman. And her body was magnificent. More than magnificent — it was heavenly. He had an insane desire not to play her game, take her forcibly. Somehow she reminded him of Jennifer, but this woman had much more fight in her. She looked the way he remembered his mother. Gazing at Sidney, he remembered his mother clearly, watching her through a knothole, how she made love with different men. Many times he wanted to kill the lover and take his place naked beside her, caressing her huge breasts and making love to her. Instead, as he became of age, he would masturbate as his beautiful mother writhed and groaned and bit and slapped each lover.

Kaluste was fourteen when he watched his mother die, beaten after she had cruelly taunted her current lover, a merchant sailor. All this suddenly flashed back through his mind as he wandered around the room inspecting the sculptures and oils, taking quick glances at the redhead as she reminded him what was in store for him as her tongue circled the champagne glass. Bitch!

He was so unsure of himself that he dared not make the first move, even though she had reluctantly let him taste the top of her breasts in the Rolls. No, he must show patience — show that he was master of his emotions. But inside he could not contain himself. The desire, the anguish, and the thrilling youthful memories were fanning the flames of his passion. If she wished to be dominant — he must wait for her to make the first move.

At 12:30 A.M. Sidney rang for the butler and told him to inform the staff that they could retire. Despite this, she was stalling and she knew it. She was getting cold feet, and she was frightened. It was happening too quickly. She had expected several harmless encounters with Kaluste long before reaching this stage, but the first encounter at the restaurant had worked too well.

She had expected Kaluste to take the bait, then meet for lunch or dinner, then maybe a party, and finally the boudoir scene. All the information Jennifer had given her about Kaluste pointed to a set psychological pattern of behavior under the right circumstances. He enjoyed variety in his women, but with certain kinds of women, herself now included, Kaluste behaved almost uncontrollably, as though an unconscious self were taking over. Her analysis was correct: she had struck a nerve. Now she must follow through.

"Mon cher," Sidney said softly, "the hour is late. Would you care to visit my apartment upstairs, or would you prefer to go home to bed?"

To himself he said, *bitch — bitch — bitch.* To her he said with a smile, "A tour of your apartment might be pleasant. I trust the personal objets d'art in your apartment are interesting."

"I expect my private objets d'art to overwhelm you."

Gallantly, he said, "I expect them to be nothing short of spectacular."

"We'll make certain they are."

Sidney put down her glass and raised her arm for him to help her rise and escort her to the staircase. She walked ahead of him so that he could get a full view of the rear body action, and when she reached the fourth step of the curved mahogany staircase, she paused. He stopped and looked up at her. She raised his hand and licked his palm, turned it over, and nipped the back of his hand with her sharp teeth until he was in pain. Then she smiled devilishly and led him up to her room. Before shutting the door, she switched on the lights, released his hand, walked to the drapes, covering first one, then the second set of windows. The drapes were already drawn across the french doors leading to the balcony.

She was deliberately walking slowly, in the way Jennifer had shown her, and she sensed that Kaluste's sexual steam engine was ready to explode. Finally she led him to the center of the room, had him stand in a certain position as she turned and asked him to unzip the back of her dress. He fumbled as though he were a sixteen-year-old boy, but managed the task. She walked away from him, going through, from memory, the motions of a strip-tease she had once seen in Las Vegas.

First she raised one arm and pulled off a glove. Then she repeated the motion with the other arm. She shimmied out of her dress, keeping it over her body as though hiding shyly from him. Then she "accidentally" let it drop to the floor. When she faced him, she could see him staring at her black lace panties and bulging black bra. She knew the padding was sewn in cleverly, but she was still nervous. She stared at him, her nostrils flaring in anticipation.

Diverting his attention, she slipped her fingers under her long black silk stockings and released them from the fancy black garter belt so popular in Europe. She sat down facing him, legs apart, and removed her shoes. Then, standing up, she unfastened the garter belt and let it drop to the floor. She raised her left leg, and her foot settled on the slipper chair. His eyes were riveted to the inside of her thighs as she slowly rolled down one stocking, just the way she had seen Marlene Dietrich do it in a movie. She did the same with her other stocking.

Putting her spiked heels back on, she ambled toward him as he stared, mesmerized. She held a finger to her lips for him to keep silent. She helped him off with his dinner jacket, which she folded and placed on a chair. Then she removed his black bow tie. Next she removed the emerald studs from his silk dress shirt and the matching cufflinks. Sidney put them in his pants pocket, squeezing his hardness playfully on the way out.

Kaluste reached to her and buried his face between her breasts, but Sidney thrust him away and lashed out with a fierce slap. Then, gently, with her fingertips, she started massaging his reddened face, pursing her lips and murmuring as though to a child, "My poor little baby, my poor little baby."

The anguish was excruciating and humiliating, and he loved it. It was a long, long time since his mother had disciplined him like this. Yet anger was also rising within him. He wanted to hurt her. But he was not in his own home, in his own bedroom. Thus he would have to bide his time. Each new affair was a experience: some better, some worse. But this bitch was reaching into his guts and twisting them. When the proper time arrived, she would get hers.

She removed his white silk shirt, tickling his muscled body with her fingers. Again she held up a finger up to her lips, gesturing for continued silence. He wore no undershirt. She unzipped his fly and let his trousers drop to the floor. Like an orchestra conductor, she directed him to step out of his pants and with both hands she pushed him back so that he fell into a velvet armchair. Next she helped him off with his shoes and socks. He had nothing on but polka dot boxer shorts.

Sidney wondered by she was afraid of this man. He was neither more nor less than any other man.

She pointed to a small tattoo on his shoulder — crossed rifles, just where Jennifer said they would be. By now Kaluste was so close to his prize that he couldn't help himself and reached out for a breast. It was not unexpected — as she had teased him into doing it — but she backed away. He followed her, and she swung around suddenly. As his head was tilting toward her breasts, the large emerald pendant scratched his face drawing a line of blood along his cheek. It didn't prevent her from lashing out again, slapping the other side of his face.

Just as quickly, her mercurial mood changed as she cradled his face in both her hands and cooed, "No, baby, do not do that. You do not fondle mama."

He sat down, his face smarting, his body shaking as he was losing control of his actions more and more. She had contemplated removing her bra, but she simply couldn't. She faced him, arms akimbo in black lace bra and panties. For Kaluste it was a moment of heightened excitement.

Sidney motioned for him to stand up and again he tried to grab her but she gestured no with one finger. She had planned to remove his shorts but she could see he was erect; she motioned him to drop them. He did. She led him to the bed, and he followed like a grinning adolescent. She gestured him to rest on his back. He reached for her with outstretched arms, and again she slapped him hard across the face. She climbed onto the bed near his head, crossed her legs, then cradled his face against her breasts and said, "Eat, my darling baby, eat."

Her breasts, uplifted by the padding, overflowed the bra

with the nipples peeking through. His eyes closed as he suckled, and she steeled herself from feeling any emotion.

There were tears running down Kaluste's eyes when he cried out, *"Maman, Maman."*

"Yes darling, hush, be a good little boy."

He put a hand on her breast and the other around her waist. Suddenly Sidney was frightened. She thought of running out of the room, but forced herself to continue. Finally he reached for her crotch.

She released him and jumped off the bed. She shook her finger at him and in an angry voice admonished him, "Naughty boy, naughty boy. You don't do naughty things like that with your mama. No, no, no."

Suddenly Kaluste was before her on his knees in supplication, his penis limp and he was crying almost hysterically. "Non, Maman, non, Maman."

She began to strut around the room, picking up her robe and putting it on. He followed her on his knees crying, *"Non, Maman, non, Maman. Voici, voici,"* pointing to his limp penis."

For the next fifteen minutes, she forced him to act out every love-hate Oedipal scene she could think of between a boy and his mother. Jennifer had described completely his every reaction, and now he was repeating them. He was anxious to do anything to appease his mother, yet he was making his sexual desire for her apparent over and over again. Obviously his trancelike behavior was brought on by deep, unconscious guilt and self-induced hypnosis.

Finally Kaluste sat down facing the corner of the room, as though in punishment, and cried. Sidney shut off a switch on the wall, walked to her closet, and put on a street dress. At a VHS camera peeking through one of the quadraphonic speakers, she pulled out the videocassette and placed it in the recorder.

Then she approached the humiliated man and said in his ear, "Constantin, baby, let's see how you looking starring in a movie." As though deaf, he didn't budge. She slapped him, and this time she meant it. He looked up at her, surprised at her change of clothes, and startled by her manner. "*Mister* Kaluste, please sit down and look at this movie."

Suddenly he realized that something was amiss. His vicious temper flared and he charged her. She sidestepped him, not yet revealing the open straight razor in her right hand while she switched on the videocassette recorder with the other. And there it was in living color; every detail, every nuance, the images sharp and clear and self-explanatory — the complete strip scene and his final degradation. It was apparent that he himself had never realized the extent of what he went through.

When it was over, his face was chalk white. He spat out, "I am going to kill you."

This time Sidney shivered. It was becoming a frightening ordeal, but it was too late to do anything but play out the game. "You will not kill me, Kaluste. Tapes from the other two cameras are already on their way, one to a Swiss vault, and another to a New York vault. If I die, they will be delivered to the news media. No, Kaluste, I am here to transact a business deal."

That he could understand. "What do you wish?"

"You will stop your takeover bid of Tompion."

"Who are you?"

"That does not matter."

"How do you know I am after Tompion?"

"We have enough proof. Make an announcement in the morning that you have backed out of supporting the bids by your three American partners for Tompion."

"And if I do not?"

There was anger in her voice. "Look at you, you murdering creep. I will make you a laughingstock — laughed out of the salons of Paris and the world."

Kaluste grabbed his pants and dressed hastily, fumbling with his clothes because he was so choked with anger. He took one long last look at her standing there, her eyes flashing defiance. He hurried out of the room and scurried down the stairs to the front door as Sidney watched from the landing. She pressed the butler's call button three times, the signal that they were to leave.

What she had said was only part true. There were two other cameras filming the episode from different angles. She had prepared two addressed mailing cartons for them; now she sealed them. Sidney began packing her clothes, and the three cameras, each weighing two pounds. Then she hurried down the stairs.

CHAPTER

TWENTY EIGHT

WHEN Viktor returned to the mansion, he was at first surprised — then disturbed — that Kaluste would leave the house in someone else's car. It was unlike him. He went to great lengths to use only his armored car. When Viktor asked the butler where Kaluste had gone, the butler said he knew nothing other than that he had gone off with the red-haired woman. By nature, Viktor was a very suspicious man, but now the hairs in the back of his neck were standing up. Kaluste was his responsibility. Should anything have happened to him it would be a disaster.

The only person who knew the buxom redhead was Pierre Danton, and Viktor had just deposited the actor in his apartment. He picked up the telephone and dialed him, but after a dozen rings there was no response. Damn! Something was wrong, but he didn't know what.

He pulled out his new small-frame, pocket-sized Walther PPK/S automatic, now made in France by Manurhin. It was a .380 ACP caliber with a NiVel weatherproof finish. He had test-fired the handgun with 500 rounds in three days, and he liked its feel and accuracy. It hardly made a bulge in his dinner jacket. The chamber was full, with one round in the barrel and the safety on the left side of the barrel was on. He returned it to the chamois holster under his armpit.

He raced to the front door and down the steps. Gaston, who had not been dismissed, was smoking one of his stinking Gaulois cigarettes. Viktor ordered him into the car in rapid French with one of his usual insults, "Come on, you Corsican turd, return to Danton's apartment." After they took off, he shouted, "Faster, faster, you ignorant ass. Forget the gendarmes."

The long Mercedes, heavy with armorplate, screeched

around the corners at 50 mph. Luckily there was little traffic at two in the morning. Viktor dashed into the apartment house and waved to the doorman whom he'd seen fifteen minutes earlier. The ride up the elevator was interminable. At Danton's door, he pressed the bell, but there was no answer. He began banging on the door, and finally a stricken-looking Danton opened to see who it was. Viktor kicked in the door, breaking the chain.

With one huge hand, he lifted the hapless actor off the floor and slapped his face one, twice, three times. Danton paled. Viktor shouted, "Where does that bitch live?"

"What — what bitch? What are you talking about?"

"The one at Kaluste's house. Cindy Farrell." Pierre rattled off her address on Ile St. Louis. Viktor brought his face to within inches of Danton's and hissed, "Do you know her to be a movie star?"

"I don't know. She was getting some notice in the papers. Then the casting director of Empire Films said I must take her out for publicity. I expected a pig, but she was beautiful."

"Empire Films?"

"Oui!"

Viktor dropped the frightened man and sped out of the apartment. Back in the car, he picked up the telephone and dialed the number of the detective agency that worked exclusively for Kaluste's enterprises. "Emergency," he said. "It is extremely urgent — contact someone in Hollywood — it is still five o'clock there — a studio — an agent — a directory service — a reporter on *Variety* — anyone. Find out if there is an actress named Cindy Farrell. I want an answer immediately!"

Viktor ordered Gaston to drive swiftly to Ile St. Louis and find the house of Madame Farrell. They found it without trouble; a large house with a driveway. They parked across the street.

There were several lighted windows in the house, and as Viktor had to await the phone call, he ordered Gaston to check out the house. Gaston picked up a flashlight and slipped his old Luger into his jacket pocket and left. He returned fifteen minutes later and reported that he saw no one guarding the grounds, but he had looked into the window of the servants' quarters and watched the butler and maid going at it. He also reported that he shined his flashlight through the garage window and saw the white Rolls Royce there.

Viktor was torn between waiting for the phone to ring and dashing into the house to make certain that Kaluste was not in danger. His inner warning system was clanging away. He understood Kaluste's penchant for a certain type of woman — and how it sent him into another world. It might harm their close relationship if he spoiled his sex without a valid reason.

He decided to charge the house and placed one hand on the door handle when the phone rang. It was the senior detective. No Hollywood or Broadway directory listed a Cindy Farrell, and she was not a member of any professional acting union like SAG, AFTRA or Equity. Outside of Empire Films, no one in Hollywood knew her.

Viktor did not believe in coincidences. He was sure it was a trap of some sort because Tompion owned Empire. He motioned Gaston to drive up to the front door. He was going in, gun in hand with the safety off.

CHAPTER

TWENTY NINE

WHEN the big Mercedes pulled up in front of Sidney's house, Jennifer peeked through the bushes. at the sight of Viktor stepping out of the car she found herself unable to control herself. Like a bad dream, her knee seemed to flare up in pain in memory of their last encounter on the mountain. If there was one thing she wanted almost as badly as killing Kaluste, it was avenging Peter's death and this was the man responsible. She came crashing through the bushes, hand on the gun hidden in her purse.

The noise startled Viktor, and he looked at the heavyset woman bearing down on him. This was not something threatening him, so he holstered his automatic. Gaston remained behind the wheel, a casual observer.

When she was within a few feet, Jennifer shouted, "Murderer — you killed my husband."

"You are crazy, madame. I do not even know you."

Ginger pulled the bandana off her head as she drew closer. When she was no more than a foot away, he stared intently at her. On closer scrutiny, the hair was familiar and soon it dawned on him. "Jennifer," he said, "Constantin's niece."

"Yes. And the wife of Peter Wallack the man you killed."

"My, how the mighty have fallen, fat one. Your husband's death was no great loss to the world. Both of you deceived Kaluste. I should have killed you, too." Jennifer lunged at him, but with his greater strength, he shoved her aside roughly, muttering, "Go bother someone else, ugly one. You are interfering in my business."

But Jennifer was not finished. She had the demonic strength of someone possessed, and she charged Viktor as he started climbing the stairs. She was on top of him as they began to struggle. Gaston watched. He had no great love for Viktor, and, in truth, despised his demeaning ways. His sole responsibility was the safety and well-being of Kaluste when the master was in or near the car. It was not his affair if Viktor beat up some fat old woman. He did not hear the conversation — the car was virtually soundproof.

Viktor was having difficulty with Jennifer. She was now standing over him, groping inside her purse. He brought out his gun, not so much to shoot her, as to threaten her with it. Unafraid, she leaned forward and bit his gun wrist. Ambidextrous, he moved the Carl Walther pistol to his left hand, aimed it at her, and was about to pull the trigger.

She fell on him deliberately, pulling the trigger of her derringer by shooting him through the purse. There was a muffled report and a look of surprise on Viktor's face, his bright white teeth clenched as he grimaced in pain. As he raised his gun to kill her, she leaned over his face, spit in his eye, and fired the second shot through his heart.

When she stood up and saw what she had done, she began to shiver. The small gun was in her hand, and through his car window Gaston realized something was wrong when Viktor remained stretched out on the steps. Luger in hand, he opened the door to inspect the situation, walked over to Viktor, and saw the death look on his face. He had seen death all too often as a Legionnaire in Africa and at Dienbienphu. He saw the derringer in the fat woman's hand and took it from her. It was empty.

Keeping his gun down beside his leg, cocked and ready, he said, "Who are you, madame?"

"Gaston," she said, "you do not recognize me?"

The voice clicked. "Madame Jennifer."

He turned her so that she faced the lights from the house and could see the reddish blonde color of the hair and the resemblance when he looked hard. His voice lowered. "Why?"

"He killed my husband."

"Aaah!" That was something he could understand. He also knew that he would catch hell or worse if he did not take some kind of action against Viktor's killer. For the first time in his life, the man of action was hesitant. He was beholden to her, and a Corsican guards a blood promise with his own life. He was accustomed to underworld murder and double-cross and his view of life was simple. He opened up the trunk of the Mercedes, picked up the dead body, and placed it in the spacious trunk. He wiped the derringer clean and threw it and the Walther in after Viktor and shut the trunk.

"Madame Jennifer," he said, coming up to her, "it is time to run."

She looked as though she was about to be ill. He escorted her to the side of the house near the garage while keeping an eye on the front door. She got sick and threw up onto a flower bed. When it was over, she put her hand in her purse to take out tissues to wipe her mouth and touched the money.

"Gaston," she said, "you have more than repaid your debt. I know how you always wished to own a café. Here!" she thrust the money at him, "Take it, it would please me greatly."

Never one to refuse money, he pocketed the bills and watched her open the garage door. She was now out of sight of the front doors and said she was fine. Gaston was walking toward the car after secreting the money in various pockets, his mind racing as to which part of the Seine to drop poor Viktor, when the front door opened angrily as Kaluste raced down the steps.

Gaston ran along the driveway toward the car and opened the back door. "Home!" shouted Kaluste without questioning where Gaston had been.

The chauffeur started the car and moved out of the driveway. Kaluste had never involved Gaston in his private business dealings, and it might be too dangerous to do so now. He pushed the button to raise the glass partition, then picked up the phone and began to search for Viktor, but without luck.

He must burn down that house with everyone in it — get rid of all the evidence of his humiliation. It was too soon for the films to have been sent out, as she had said. When he reached his home, he asked Gaston to follow him. Sensing something terribly wrong, he did as he was told with his gun at his side.

Kaluste summoned the butler and asked for Viktor. The butler said he didn't know where he was. The last time he had seen Viktor was with Gaston. Kaluste glared furiously at Gaston.

With typical Gallic misdirection Gaston said, "He was looking for you. First I took him to the home of the movie star Danton. He came down fifteen minutes later and asked me to drive to the house where you were. When we got there, he went into the house and ordered me to wait. I opened the front door to have a smoke and I heard two shots. They came from outside the house. I went to inspect to make sure it was not you. I found nothing. As I was returning, I saw you come down the stairs."

"That's true, Gaston, I recall." Kaluste then dismissed everyone but Gaston. "I need some help at once, and I cannot wait for Viktor. There will be a big bonus for your silence if you do this well."

Gaston waited as Kaluste thought through his plans. He beckoned Gaston to follow, and he led him into the garage. "You have several cans of petrol?" he asked. Gaston nodded. I want you to return to that house and burn it down. If anyone tries to escape, shoot them."

Gaston felt a chill come over him. "I cannot, Monsieur Kaluste. I am a soldier — and at one time a smuggler — but I do not kill for money."

Suddenly all the pent-up fury and frustration exploded as Kaluste lashed out at Gaston's face, but the chauffeur merely raised his pistol and the backhand slap caught the gun and broke three knuckles in Kaluste's hand.

"You damned Corsican — you are discharged."

Gaston saluted with his pistol, threw the car keys on the table, and walked away. He did not smile until he was several blocks from the house.

Meanwhile, Kaluste could wait no longer. He soaked his hand with tapwater in the garage sink, wrapped a handkerchief around it, and tied a knot using his teeth. He found a five-gallon can of gasoline in the newly designed NATO container with a spout. He opened the garage with the electronic door opener and carried the can to the trunk with his good hand.

He inserted the key into the trunk and raised it. As though he had jumped into a vat of icewater he suddenly went cold. There were two guns beside the body. He checked the nickeled Walther. It was loaded and cocked, but unfired. The double-barreled derringer smelled of gunpowder. It had been fired. Both barrels were empty.

Kaluste turned deadly calm. There was no question that Viktor was dead, blood congealed around two wounds. Gaston had claimed he had heard two shots, and the chauffeur had never lied to him. In his mind the answer was obvious. The admiral had decided to play rough — as the Americans said — hardball. Unable to beat him in the world of high finance, Tompion had figured out how to trick him. Putting the body of Viktor in the back of the car was a signal that they would beat him at his own game.

Merde, he had lost the match.

CHAPTER

THIRTY

MINUTES after Kaluste left, Sidney had gathered her makeshift staff in the study. To each one she gave an envelope stuffed with francs. They were to leave immediately and travel back to their various jobs. The butler and maid look spaced out. She handed the chef an extra thousand francs. "Cart them away from the house and put them on a train for anywhere."

The chef smiled. He was off to Marseilles to wait for a ship, and he would take them along. The girl looked as though she was serviceable for another day or two.

Sidney asked the handyman to stay behind and drive the Rolls for her. He was delighted, as he had lost out on the job as chauffeur. With the lights out and the house shut down and locked, they got into the car and drove away. Sidney asked him to stop by the main post office at 52 rue du Louvre which is open twenty-four hours a day. She had two packages to mail.

When Sidney arrived afterward at the *pension* she bade the handyman goodbye, and he thanked her for letting him drive the beautiful English car. She gave him an extra 1,000 francs and asked him to return it to Empire Studios in the morning. He was free to drive it until then.

She carried her own suitcase up to Jennifer's room, only to find her friend curled up in the corner screaming at her, "I killed Viktor, I killed Viktor."

Sidney went over and began to shake her. "Stop the hysterics and tell me what happened."

"I wanted to kill Kaluste — but when I saw Viktor, I shot him. Now Kaluste is unpunished."

"No, my dear, not unpunished. I have something I wish to show you, after which I will burn it. Then we will both forget what has happened."

Jennifer look at her uncomprehendingly. Sidney slipped the third cartridge into the recorder and watched her friend's face.

* * *

When Sidney changed back into her normal clothes, she left the sleeping Jennifer on the bed. She was sure that when she awoke sometime the next day, the catharsis would have worked and it would all seem like a bad dream. Jennifer had purged herself of her demons, and in time would surely be free to return to her normal self.

Sidney called a taxi and rode back to her hotel. She took a hot bath and tried but could not fall asleep. The evening had unnerved her, and she needed comforting. She knew where Roger was staying, but she had not contacted him. Her mixed emotions about her seduction role with Kaluste still churned within her, and she realized that despite his deviant behavior she had not been insensitive to the sexual charms of the handsome Frenchman.

Roger kept popping into her mind as she gazed at the ceiling. What the hell, he wasn't the kind of man who refused a woman's charms even at 5:00 A.M. She picked up the phone and asked for the Bristol Hotel.

It rang once and Roger's voice said, "Hello."

"You caught the phone on the first ring — aren't you asleep?"

"Why? Are you trying to find me asleep so you can wake me up?"

"Of course not."

"And there was no operator, so you're in Paris. What are you doing here?"

"Can't you guess?"

There was a pause. "Men are supposed to do the chasing."

"Do you want company?"

"Yes." There was another long pause. "Look, Sidney, let's get something straight. I've thought about you a lot since that night. I like you, but if you're here in Paris, it's probably to start a relationship — it's fine with me. I feel the same way. But like I told you, if we're going to dance, then from now on I do the leading."

"Yes, darling."

"Now where the hell are you? I'm coming over."

With her voice soft and seductive, Sidney told where she was staying and the room number, while in her mind she was thinking she had enough time to put on the transparent peignoir that had set her back $500. It was time to cleanse her body and her soul.